Nat the Naturalist

George Manville Fenn

Chapter One.

Why I went to my Uncle's.

"I don't know what to do with him. I never saw such a boy—a miserable little coward, always in mischief and doing things he ought not to do, and running about the place with his whims and fads. I wish you'd send him right away, I do."

My aunt went out of the room, and I can't say she banged the door, but she shut it very hard, leaving me and my uncle face to face staring one at the other.

My uncle did not speak for some minutes, but sat poking at his hair with the waxy end of his pipe, for he was a man who smoked a great deal after dinner; the mornings he spent in his garden, being out there as early as five o'clock in the summer and paying very little attention to the rain.

He was a very amiable, mild-tempered man, who had never had any children, in fact he did not marry till quite late in life; when I remember my poor father saying that it was my aunt married my uncle, for uncle would never have had the courage to ask her.

I say "my poor father", for a couple of years after that marriage, the news came home that he had been lost at sea with the whole of the crew of the great vessel of which he was the surgeon.

I remember it all so well; the terrible blank and trouble that seemed to have come upon our house, with my mother's illness that followed, and that dreadful day when Uncle Joseph came downstairs to me in the dining-room, and seating himself by the fire filled and lit his pipe, took two or three puffs, and then threw the pipe under the grate, let his head go down upon his hands, and cried like a child.

A minute or two later, when I went up to him in great trouble and laid my hand upon his shoulder, saying, "Don't cry, uncle; she'll be better soon," he caught me in his arms and held me to his breast.

"Nat, my boy," he said, "I've promised her that I'll be like a father to you now, and I will."

I knew only too soon why he said those words, for a week later I was an orphan boy indeed; and I was at Uncle Joseph's house, feeling very miserable and unhappy in spite of his kind ways and the pains he took to make me comfortable.

I was not so wretched when I was alone with uncle in the garden, where he would talk to me about his peas and potatoes and the fruit-trees, show me how to find the snails and slugs, and encourage me to shoot at the thieving birds with a crossbow and arrow; but I was miserable indeed when I went in, for my aunt was a very sharp, acid sort of woman, who seemed to have but one idea, and that was to keep the house so terribly tidy that it was always uncomfortable to the people who were in it.

It used to be, "Nat, have you wiped your shoes?"

"Let me look, sir. Ah! I thought so. Not half wiped. Go and take them off directly, and put on your slippers. You're as bad as your uncle, sir."

I used to think I should like to be as good.

"I declare," said my aunt, "I haven't a bit of peace of my life with the dirt and dust. The water-cart never comes round here as it does in the other roads, and the house gets filthy. Moil and toil, moil and toil, from morning to night, and no thanks whatever."

When my aunt talked like this she used to screw up her face and seem as if she were going to cry, and she spoke in a whining, unpleasant tone of voice; but I never remember seeing her cry, and I used to wonder why she would trouble herself about dusting with a

2

cloth and feather brush from morning to night, when there were three servants to do all the work.

I have heard the cook tell Jane the housemaid that Mrs Pilgarlic was never satisfied; but it was some time before I knew whom she meant; and to this day I don't know why she gave my aunt such a name.

Whenever aunt used to be more than usually fretful, as time went on my uncle would get up softly, give me a peculiar look, and go out into the garden, where, if I could, I followed, and we used to talk, and weed, and train the flowers; but very often my aunt would pounce upon me and order me to sit still and keep out of mischief if I could.

I was very glad when my uncle decided to send me to school, and I used to go to one in our neighbourhood, so that I was a good deal away from home, as uncle said I was to call his house now; and school and the garden were the places where I was happiest in those days.

"Yes, my boy," said my uncle, "I should like you to call this home, for though your aunt pretends she doesn't like it, she does, you know, Nat; and you mustn't mind her being a bit cross, Nat. It isn't temper, you know, it's weakness. It's her digestion's bad, and she's a sufferer, that's what she is. She's wonderfully fond of you, Nat."

I remember thinking that she did not show it.

"And you must try and get on, Nat, and get lots of learning," he would often say when we were out in the garden. "You won't be poor when you grow up, for your poor mother has left you a nice bit of money, but you might lose that, Nat, my boy; nobody could steal your knowledge, and—ah, you rascal, got you, have I?"

This last was to a great snail which he raked out from among some tender plants that had been half eaten away.

"Yes, Nat, get all the knowledge you can and work hard at your books."

But somehow I didn't get on well with the other boys, for I cared so little for their rough games. I was strong enough of my age, but I preferred getting out on to Clapham Common on half-holidays, to look for lizards in the furze, or to catch the bright-coloured sticklebacks in the ponds, or else to lie down on the bank under one of the trees, and watch the efts coming up to the top to make a little bubble and then go down again, waving their bodies of purple and orange and the gay crests that they sometimes had all along their backs in the spring.

When I used to lie there thinking, I did not seem to be on Clapham Common, but far away on the banks of some huge lake in a foreign land with the efts and lizards, crocodiles; and the big worms that I sometimes found away from their holes in wet weather became serpents in a moist jungle.

Of course I got all these ideas from books, and great trouble I found myself in one day for playing at tiger-hunting in the garden at home with Buzzy, my aunt's great tabby tom-cat; and for pretending that Nap was a lion in the African desert. But I'll tell you that in a chapter to itself, for these matters had a good deal to do with the alteration in my mode of life.

Chapter Two.

First Thoughts of Hunting.

As I told you, my uncle had no children, and the great house at Streatham was always very quiet. In fact one of my aunt's strict injunctions was that she should not be disturbed by any noise of mine. But aunt had her pets—Buzzy, and Nap.

Buzzy was the largest striped tom-cat, I think, that I ever saw, and very much to my aunt's annoyance he became very fond of me, so much so that if he saw me going out in the garden he would leap off my aunt's lap, where she was very fond of nursing him, stroking his back, beginning with his head and ending by drawing his tail right through her hand; all of which Buzzy did not like, but he would lie there and swear, trying every now and then to get free, but only to be held down and softly whipped into submission.

Buzzy decidedly objected to being nursed, and as soon as he could get free he would rush after me down the garden, where he would go bounding along, arching his back, and setting up the fur upon his tail. Every now and then he would hide in some clump, and from thence charge out at me, and if I ran after him, away he would rush up a tree trunk, and then crouch on a branch with glowing eyes, tearing the while with his claws at the bark as if in a tremendous state of excitement, ready to bound down again, and race about till he was tired, after which I had only to stoop down and say, "Come on," when he would leap on to my back and perch himself upon my shoulder, purring softly as I carried him round the grounds.

I used to have some good fun, too, with Nap, when my aunt was out; but she was so jealous of her favourite's liking for me that at last I never used to have a game with Nap when she was at home.

Buzzy could come out and play quietly, but Nap always got to be so excited, lolling out his tongue and yelping and barking with delight as he tore round after me, pretending to bite and worry me, and rolling over and over, and tumbling head over heels as he capered and bounded about.

I think Nap was the ugliest dog I ever saw, for he was one of those dirty white French poodles, and my aunt used to have him clipped, to look like a lion, as she said, and have him washed with hot soap and water every week.

Nothing pleased Nap better than to go out in the garden with me, but I got into sad trouble about it more than once.

"Look at him, Joseph," my aunt would say, "it's just as if it was done on purpose to annoy me. Beautifully washed as he was yesterday, and now look at him with his curly mane all over earth, and with bits of straw and dead leaves sticking in it. If you don't send that boy away to a boarding-school I won't stay in the house."

Then my uncle would look troubled, and take me into his own room, where he kept his books and garden seeds.

"You mustn't do it, Nat, my boy, indeed you mustn't. You see how it annoys your aunt."

"I didn't think I was doing any harm, uncle," I protested. "Nap jumped out of the window, and leaped up at me as if he wanted a game, and I only raced round the garden with him."

"You didn't rub the earth and dead leaves in his coat then, Nat?" said my uncle.

"Oh no!" I said; "he throws himself on his side and pushes himself along, rubs his head on the ground, sometimes on one side, sometimes on the other. I think it's because he has got f—"

"Shush! Hush! my dear boy," cried my uncle, clapping his hand over my lips. "If your aunt for a moment thought that there were any insects in that dog, she would be ill."

"But I'm sure that there are some in his coat, uncle," I said, "for if you watch him when he's lying on the hearth-rug to-night, every now and then he jumps up and snaps at them, and bites the place."

"Shush! yes, my boy," he whispered; "but don't talk about it. Your aunt is so particular. It's a secret between us."

I couldn't help smiling at him, and after a moment or two he smiled at me, and then patted me on the shoulder.

"Don't do anything to annoy your aunt, my boy," he said; "I wouldn't play with Nap if I were you."

"I'll try not to, uncle," I said; "but he will come and coax me to play with him sometimes."

"H'm! yes," said my uncle thoughtfully, "and it does do him good, poor dog. He eats too much, and gets too fat for want of exercise. Suppose you only play with him when your aunt goes out for a walk."

"Very well, uncle," I said, and then he shook hands with me, and gave me half a crown.

I couldn't help it, I was obliged to spend that half-crown in something I had been wanting for weeks. It was a large crossbow that hung up in the toy-shop window in Streatham, and that bow had attracted my attention every time I went out.

To some boys a crossbow would be only a crossbow, but to me it meant travels in imagination all over the world. I saw myself shooting apples off boys' heads, transfixing eagles in their flight, slaying wild beasts, and bringing home endless trophies of the chase, so at the first opportunity I was off to the shop, and with my face glowing with excitement and delight I bought and took home the crossbow.

"Hallo, Nat!" said Uncle Joseph. "Why, what's that—a crossbow?"

"Yes, uncle; isn't it a beauty?" I cried excitedly.

"Well, yes, my boy," he said; "but, but—how about your aunt? Suppose you were to break a window with that, eh? What should we do?"

"But I won't shoot in that direction, uncle," I promised.

"Or shoot out Jane's or Cook's eye? It would be very dreadful, my boy."

"Oh, yes, uncle," I cried; "but I will be so careful, and perhaps I may shoot some of the birds that steal the cherries."

"Ah! yes, my boy, so you might," he said rubbing his hands softly. "My best bigarreaus. Those birds are a terrible nuisance, Nat, that they are. You'll be careful, though?"

"Yes, I'll be careful, uncle," I said; and he went away nodding and smiling, while I went off to Clapham Common to try the bow and the short thick arrows supplied therewith.

It was glorious. At every twang away flew the arrow or the piece of tobacco-pipe I used instead; and at last, after losing one shaft in the short turf, I found myself beside the big pond over on the far side, one that had the reputation of being full of great carp and eels.

My idea here was to shoot the fish, but as there were none visible to shoot I had to be content with trying to hit the gliding spiders on the surface with pieces of tobacco-pipe as long as they lasted, for I dared not waste another arrow, and then with my mind full of adventures in foreign countries I walked home.

The next afternoon my aunt went out, and I took the bow down the garden, leaving my uncle enjoying his pipe. I had been very busy all that morning, it being holiday time, in making some fresh arrows for a purpose I had in view, and, so as to be humane, I had made the heads by cutting off the tops of some old kid gloves, ramming their finger-ends full of cotton-wool, and then tying them to the thin deal arrows, so that each bolt had a head like a little soft leather ball.

"Those can't hurt him," I said to myself; and taking a dozen of these bolts in my belt I went down the garden, with Buzzy at my heels, for a good tiger-hunt.

For the next half-hour Streatham was nowhere, and that old-fashioned garden with its fruit-trees had become changed into a wild jungle, through which a gigantic tiger kept charging, whose doom I had fixed. Shot after shot I had at the monster—once after it had bounded into the fork of a tree, another time as it was stealing through the waving reeds, represented by the asparagus bed. Later on, after much creeping and stalking, with the tiger stalking me as well as springing out at me again and again, but never getting quite home, I had a shot as it was lurking beside the great lake, represented by our tank. Here its striped sides were plainly visible, and, going down on hands and knees, I crept along between two rows of terrible thorny trees that bore sweet juicy berries in the season, but which were of the wildest nature now, till I could get a good aim at the monster's shoulder, and see its soft lithe tail twining and writhing like a snake.

I crept on, full of excitement, for a leafy plant that I refused to own as a cabbage no longer intercepted my view. Then lying flat upon my chest I fitted an arrow to my bow, and was cautiously taking aim, telling myself that if I missed I should be seized by the monster, when some slight sound I made caused it to spring up, presenting its striped flank for a target as it gazed here and there.

Play as it was, it was all intensely real to me; and in those moments I was as full of excitement as if I had been in some distant land and in peril of my life.

Then, after long and careful aim, twang went the bow, and to my intense delight the soft-headed arrow struck the monster full in the flank, making it bound up a couple of feet and then pounce upon the bolt, and canter off at full speed towards a dense thicket of scarlet-runners.

"Victory, victory!" I cried excitedly; "wounded, wounded!" and I set off in chase, but approaching cautiously and preparing my bow again, for I had read that the tiger was most dangerous when in the throes of death.

I forget what I called the scarlet-runner thicket, but by some eastern name, and drawing nearer I found an opportunity for another shot, which missed.

Away bounded Buzzy, evidently enjoying the fun, and I after him, to find him at bay beneath a currant bush.

I was a dozen yards away in the central path, and, of course, in full view of the upper windows of the house; but if I had noted that fact then, I was so far gone in the romance of the situation that I daresay I should have called the house the rajah's palace. As it was I had forgotten its very existence in the excitement of the chase.

"This time, monster, thou shalt die," I cried, as I once more fired, making Buzzy leap into the path, and then out of sight amongst the cabbages.

"Hurray! hurray!" I shouted, waving my crossbow above my head, "the monster is slain! the monster is slain!"

There was a piercing shriek behind me, and I turned, bow in hand, to find myself face to face with my aunt.

Chapter Three.

How I Hunted the Lion in No-man's-Land and what Followed.

My aunt's cry brought out Uncle Joseph in a terrible state of excitement, and it was not until after a long chase and Buzzy was caught that she could be made to believe that he had not received a mortal wound. And a tremendous chase it was, for the more Uncle Joseph and I tried to circumvent that cat, the more he threw himself into the fun of the hunt and dodged us, running up trees like a squirrel, leaping down with his tail swollen to four times its usual size, and going over the beds in graceful bounds, till Uncle Joseph sat down to pant and wipe his face while I continued the chase; but all in vain. Sometimes I nearly caught the cat, but he would be off again just as I made a spring to seize him, while all Aunt Sophia's tender appeals to "poor Buzzy then," "my poor pet then," fell upon ears that refused to hear her.

"Oh how stupid I am!" I said to myself. "Oh, Buzzy, this is too bad to give me such a chase. Come here, sir, directly;" and I stooped down.

It had the required result, for Buzzy leaped down off the wall up which he had scrambled, jumped on to my back, settled himself comfortably with his fore-paws on my shoulder, and began to purr with satisfaction.

"I am glad, my boy," said Uncle Joseph, "so glad you have caught him; but have you hurt him much?"

"He isn't hurt at all, uncle," I said. "It was all in play."

"But your aunt is in agony, my boy. Here, let me take the cat to her."

He stretched out his hands to take the cat from my shoulder, but Buzzy's eyes dilated and he began to swear, making my uncle start back, for he dreaded a scratch from anything but a rose thorn, and those he did not mind.

"Would you mind taking him to your aunt, Natty, my boy?" he said.

"No, uncle, if you'll please come too," I said. "Don't let aunt scold me, uncle; I'm very sorry, and it was only play."

"I'll come with you, Nat," he said, shaking his head; "but I ought not to have let you have that bow, and I'm afraid she will want it burnt."

"Will she be very cross?" I said.

"I'm afraid so, my boy." And she really was.

"Oh you wicked, wicked boy," she cried as I came up; "what were you doing?"

"Only playing at tiger-hunting, aunt," I said.

"With my poor darling Buzzy! Come to its own mistress then, Buzzy," she cried pityingly. "Did the wicked, cruel boy—oh dear!"

Wur–r–ur! spit, spit!

That was Buzzy's reply to his mistress's attempt to take him from my shoulder, and he made an attempt to scratch.

"And he used to be as gentle as a lamb," cried my aunt. "You wicked, wicked boy, you must have hurt my darling terribly to make him so angry with his mistress whom he loves."

I protested that I had not, but it was of no use, and I was in great disgrace for some days; but Aunt Sophia forgot to confiscate my crossbow.

The scolding I received ought to have had more effect upon me, but it did not; for it was only a week afterwards that I was again in disgrace, and for the same fault, only with this difference, that in my fancy the garden had become a South African desert, and Nap was the lion I was engaged in hunting.

I did him no harm, I am sure, but a great deal of good, with the exercise; and the way in which he entered into the sport delighted me. He charged me and dashed after me when I fled; when I hid behind trees to shoot at him he seized the arrows, if they hit him, and worried them fiercely; while whenever they missed him, in place of dashing at me he would run after the arrows and bring them in his mouth to where he thought I was hiding.

I don't think Nap had any more sense than dogs have in general, but he would often escape from my aunt when I came home from school, and run before me to the big cupboard where I kept my treasures, raise himself upon his hind-legs, and tear at the door till I opened it and took out the crossbow, when he would frisk round and round in the highest state of delight, running out into the garden, dashing back, running out again, and entering into the spirit of the game with as much pleasure as I did.

But the fun to be got out of a crossbow gets wearisome after a time, especially when you find that in spite of a great deal of practice it is very hard to hit anything that is at all small.

The time glided on, and I was very happy still with my uncle; but somehow Aunt Sophia seemed to take quite a dislike to me; and no matter how I tried to do what was right, and to follow out my uncle's wishes, I was always in trouble about something or another.

One summer Uncle Joseph bought me a book on butterflies, with coloured plates, which so interested me that I began collecting the very next day, and captured a large cabbage butterfly.

No great rarity this, but it was a beginning; and after pinning it out as well as I could I began to think of a cabinet, collecting-boxes, a net, and a packet of entomological pins.

I only had to tell Uncle Joseph my wants and he was eager to help me.

"Collecting-boxes, Nat?" he said, rubbing his hands softly; "why, I used to use pill-boxes when I was a boy: there are lots up-stairs."

He hunted me out over a dozen that afternoon, and supplied me with an old drawer and a piece of camphor, entering into the matter with as much zest as I did myself. Then he obtained an old green gauze veil from my aunt, and set to work with me in the tool-house to make a net, after the completion of which necessity he proposed that we should go the very next afternoon as far as Clapham Common to capture insects.

He did not go with me, for my aunt wanted him to hold skeins of wool for her to wind, but he made up to me for the disappointment that evening by sitting by me while I pinned out my few but far from rare captures, taking great pleasure in holding the pins for me, and praising what he called my cleverness in cutting out pieces of card.

I did not know anything till it came quite as a surprise, and it was smuggled into the house so that my aunt did not know, Jane, according to uncle's orders, carrying it up to my bedroom.

It was a large butterfly-case, made to open out in two halves like a backgammon board; and in this, as soon as they were dry, I used to pin my specimens, examining them with delight, and never seeming to weary of noting the various markings, finding out their names, and numbering them, and keeping their proper titles in a book I had for the purpose.

I did not confine myself to butterflies, but caught moths and beetles, with dragon-flies from the edges of the ponds on Clapham Common, longing to go farther afield, but not often obtaining a chance. Then, as I began to find specimens scarce, I set to collecting other things that seemed interesting, and at last, during a visit paid by my aunt to some friends, Uncle Joseph took me to the British Museum to see the butterflies there, so, he said, that I might pick up a few hints for managing my own collection.

That visit turned me into an enthusiast, for before we returned I had been for hours feasting my eyes upon the stuffed birds and noting the wondrous colours on their scale-like feathers.

I could think of scarcely anything else, talk of nothing else afterwards for days; and nothing would do but I must begin to collect birds and prepare and stuff them for myself.

"You wouldn't mind, would you, uncle?" I said.

"Mind? No, my boy," he said, rubbing his hands softly; "I should like it; but do you think you could stuff a bird?"

"Not at first," I said thoughtfully; "but I should try."

"To be sure, Nat," he cried smiling; "nothing like trying, my boy; but how would you begin?"

This set me thinking.

"I don't know, uncle," I said at last, "but it looks very easy."

"Ha! ha! ha! Nat; so do lots of things," he cried, laughing; "but sometimes they turn out very hard."

"I know," I said suddenly.

"I know," I said, "I could find out how to do it."

"Have some lessons, eh?" he said.

"No, uncle."

"How would you manage it then, Nat?"

"Buy a stuffed bird, uncle, and pull it to pieces, and see how it is done."

"To be sure, Nat," he cried; "to be sure, my boy. That's the way; but stop a moment; how would you put it together again?"

"Oh! I think I could, uncle," I said; "I'm nearly sure I could. How could I get one to try with?"

"Why, we might buy one somewhere," he said thoughtfully; "for I don't think they'd lend us one at the British Museum; but I tell you what, Nat," he cried: "I've got it."

"Have you, uncle?"

"To be sure, my boy. There's your aunt's old parrot that died and was stuffed. Don't you know?"

I shook my head.

"It was put somewhere up-stairs in the lumber-room, and your aunt has forgotten all about it. You might try with that."

"And I'd stuff it again when I had found out all about it, uncle," I said.

"To be sure, my boy," said uncle, thoughtfully; "I wonder whether your aunt would want Buzzy and Nap stuffed if they were to die?"

"She'd be sure to; aunt is so fond of them," I said. "Why, uncle, I might be able to do it myself."

"Think so?" he said thoughtfully. "Why, it would make her pleased, my boy."

But neither Buzzy nor Nap showed the slightest intention of dying so as to be stuffed, and I had to learn the art before I could attempt anything of the kind.

Chapter Four.

The Remains of Poor Polly.

The very first opportunity, my uncle took me up with him to the lumber-room, an attic of which my aunt kept the key; and here, after quite a hunt amongst old portmanteaux, broken chairs, dusty tables, bird-cages, wrecked kennels, cornice-poles, black-looking pictures, and dozens of other odds and ends, we came in a dark corner upon the remains of one of my aunt's earliest pets. It was the stuffed figure of a grey parrot that had once stood beneath a glass shade, but the shade was broken, and poor Polly, who looked as if she had been moulting ever since she had been fixed upon her present perch, had her head partly torn from her shoulders.

"Here she is," said my uncle. "Poor old Polly! What a bird she was to screech! She never liked me, Nat, but used to call me *wretch*, as plain as you could say it yourself. It was very wicked of me, I dare say, Nat, but I was so glad when she died, and your aunt was so sorry that she cried off and on for a week."

"But she never was a pretty bird, uncle," I said, holding the stuffed creature to the light.

"No, my boy, never, and she used to pull off her feathers when she was in a passion, and call people *wretch*. She bit your aunt's nose once. But do you think it will do?"

"Oh yes, uncle," I said; "but may I pull it to pieces?"

"Well, yes, my boy, I think so," he said dreamily. "You couldn't spoil it, could you?"

"Why, it is spoiled already, Uncle Joe," I said.

"Yes, my boy, so it is; quite spoiled. I think I'll risk it, Nat."

"But if aunt would be very cross, uncle, hadn't I better leave it?" I said.

"If you didn't take it, Nat, she would never see it again, and it would lie here and moulder away. I think you had better take it, my boy."

I was so eager to begin that I hesitated no more, but took the bird out into the tool-house, where I could make what aunt called "a mess" without being scolded, and uncle put on his smoking-cap, lit his pipe, and brought a high stool to sit upon and watch me make my first attempt at mastering a mystery.

The first thing was to take Polly off her perch, which was a piece of twig covered with moss, that had once been glued on, but now came away in my hands, and I found that the bird had been kept upright by means of wires that ran down her legs and were wound about the twig.

Uncle smoked away as solemnly as could be, while I went on, and he seemed to be admiring my earnestness.

"There's wire up the legs, uncle," I cried, as I felt about the bird.

"Oh! is there?" he said, condescendingly.

"Yes, uncle, and two more pieces in the wings."

"You don't say so, Nat!"

"Yes, uncle, and another bit runs right through the body from the head to the tail; and—yes—no—yes—no—ah, I've found out how it is that the tail is spread."

"Have you, Nat?" he cried, letting his pipe out, he was so full of interest.

"Yes, uncle; there's a thin wire threaded through all the tail feathers, just as if they were beads."

"Why, what a boy you are!" he cried, wonderingly.

"Oh, it's easy enough to find that out, uncle," I said, colouring. "Now let's see what's inside."

"Think there's anything inside, Natty, my boy?"

"Oh yes, uncle," I said; "it's full of something. Why, it's tow."

"Toe, my boy!" he said seriously, "parrot's toe?"

"T-o-w. Tow, uncle, what they use to clean the lamps. I can stuff a bird, uncle, I know."

"Think you can, Natty?"

"Yes, to be sure," I said confidently. "Why, look here, it's easy to make a ball of tow the same shape as an egg for the body, and then to push wires through the body, and wings, and legs; no, stop a moment, they seem to be fastened in. Yes, so they are, but I know I can do it."

Uncle Joe held his pipe in his mouth with his teeth and rubbed his hands with satisfaction, for he was as pleased with my imagined success as I was, and as he looked on I pulled out the stuffing from the skin, placing the wings here, the legs there, and the tail before me, while the head with its white-irised glass eye was stuck upon a nail in the wall just over the bench.

"I feel as sure as can be, uncle, that I could stuff one."

"Ha! ha! ha!" he laughed. "*Wretch! wretch! wretch*! That's what Polly would say if she could speak. See how you've pulled her to pieces."

I looked up as he spoke, and there was the head with its queer glass eyes seeming to stare hard at me, and at the mess of skin and feathers on the bench.

"Well, I have pulled her to pieces, haven't I, uncle?" I said.

"That you have, my boy," he said, chuckling, as if he thought it very good fun.

"But I have learned how to stuff a bird, uncle," I said triumphantly.

"And are you going to stuff Polly again?" he asked, gazing at the ragged feathers and skin.

I looked at him quite guiltily.

"I—I don't think I could put this one together again, uncle," I said. "You see it was so ragged and torn before I touched it, and the feathers are coming out all over the place. But I could do a fresh one. You see there's nothing here but the skin. All the feathers are falling away."

"Yes," said my uncle, "and I know—"

"Know what, uncle?"

"Why, they do the skin over with some stuff to preserve it, and you'll have to get it at the chemist's."

"Yes, uncle."

"And I don't know, Natty," he said, "but I think you might try and put poor old Polly together again, for I don't feel quite comfortable about her; you have made her in such a dreadful mess."

"Yes, I have, indeed, uncle," I said dolefully, for the eagerness was beginning to evaporate.

"And your aunt was very fond of her, my boy, and she wouldn't like it if she knew."

"But I'm afraid I couldn't put her together again now, uncle;" and then I began to tremble, and my uncle leaped off his stool, and broke his pipe: for there was my aunt's well-known step on the gravel, and directly after we heard her cry:

"Joseph! Nathaniel! What are you both doing?" And I knew that I should have to confess.

Chapter Five.

How my Uncle and I put Humpty Dumpty together again.

My uncle stood by me very bravely when Aunt Sophia entered the tool-house with an exclamation of surprise. For a few minutes she could not understand what we had been about.

"Feathers—a bird—a parrot!" she exclaimed at last. "Why, it is like poor Polly."

I looked very guiltily at my uncle and was about to speak, but he made me a signal to be silent.

"Yes, my dear," he faltered, "it—it was poor Polly. We—we found her in the lumber-room—all in ruins, my dear, and we—we have been examining her."

"I don't believe it," said my aunt sharply. "That mischievous boy has been at his tricks again."

"I assure you, my dear," cried my uncle, "I had to do with it as well. I helped him. Nat wants to understand bird-stuffing, and we have been to the museum and then we came home."

"Well, of course you did," said my aunt tartly; "do you suppose I thought you stopped to live in the museum?"

"No, my dear, of course not," said my uncle, laughing feebly. "We are studying the art of taxidermy, my dear, Nat and I."

He added this quite importantly, putting his eyeglasses on and nodding to me for my approval and support.

"Bless the man! Taxi what?" cried my aunt, who seemed to be fascinated by Polly's eyes; and she began to softly scratch the feathers on the back of the head.

"Taxi-dermy," said my uncle, "and—and, my dear, I wouldn't scratch Polly's head if I were you; the skins are preserved with poison."

"Bless my heart!" exclaimed my aunt, snatching back her hand; and then holding out a finger to me: "Wipe that, Nat."

I took out my handkerchief, dipped a corner in the watering-pot, and carefully wiped the finger clear of anything that might be sticking to it, though, as my own hands were so lately in contact with Polly's skin, I don't believe that I did much good; but it satisfied my aunt, who turned once more to Uncle Joe.

"Now then, Joseph; what did you say?"

"Taxi-dermy, my dear," he said again importantly; "the art of preserving and mounting the skins of dead animals."

"And a nice mess you'll both make, I dare say," cried my aunt.

"But not indoors, my dear. We shall be very careful. You see Polly had been a good deal knocked about. Your large black box had fallen right upon her, and her head was off, my dear. The glass shade was in shivers."

"Poor Polly, yes," said my aunt, "I had her put there because of the moths in her feathers. Well, mind this, I shall expect Natty to repair her very nicely; and you must buy a new glass shade, Joseph. Ah, my precious!"

This was to Nap, who, in reply to her tender speech, made three or four bounds to get to me, but aunt caught him by the ear and held him with the skin of his face pulled sidewise, so that he seemed to be winking at me as he lolled out his thin red tongue, and uttered a low whine.

"But mind this, I will not have any mess made indoors."

As she spoke my aunt stooped down and took Nap in her arms, soiling her handsome silk dress a good deal with the dog's dirty feet. Then she walked away saying endearing things to Nap, who only whined and struggled to get away in the most ungrateful fashion; while my uncle took off his glasses, drew a long breath, and said as he wiped his face with his red silk handkerchief:

"I was afraid she was going to be very cross, my boy. She's such a good woman, your dear aunt, my boy, and I'm very proud of her; but she does upset me so when she is cross."

"I was all of a fidge, uncle," I said laughing.

"So was I, Nat, so was I. But don't laugh, my boy. It is too serious a thing for smiles. It always puts me in such a dreadful perspiration, Nat, for I don't like to be angry too. Never be angry with a woman when you grow up, Nat, my boy; women, you see, belong to the weaker sex."

"Yes, uncle," I said wonderingly; and then he began to beam and smile again, and rubbed his hands together softly as he looked at our work.

"But you will have to put Polly together again, Nat," he said at last.

"Put her together again, uncle!" I said in dismay. "Why, it's like Humpty Dumpty sat on a wall—all the king's horses and all the king's men—"

"Couldn't put Humpty Dumpty together again," said my uncle quite seriously. "But we must put Polly together again, Natty. There's your aunt, you know."

"Yes, uncle, there's Aunt Sophia," I said ruefully; "but the feathers are all out of the skin, and the skin's all in pieces. I'm afraid she will never look decent, try how I may."

My uncle rubbed his head softly.

"It does look as if it would be a terrible job, Nat," he said; "but it must be done, and I'm afraid if you made her look as well as she did when we found her, your aunt wouldn't be satisfied."

"I'm sure I couldn't make her look as well as she did then, uncle," I replied despairingly; "but I'll try."

"Yes, do, my boy. That's right, try. And look here, Nat—I'll help you."

I was very glad to hear Uncle Joseph say that, though I did not think he would be able to help me much; and so as to lose no time we began at once to think the matter out, and uncle said *yes* to all I proposed to do, which was his idea of helping me; for he said I drove in the nails and he clinched them.

After a bit of thinking I came to the conclusion that I have since learned was the very best one I could have arrived at, that the proper thing to do was to fix on Polly's wire legs as neatly made a body as I could, and then to stick the feathers all over it in their proper places. But then what was the body to be made of? Clay or putty could be easily moulded into shape, but they would be too heavy. Papier-mâché would have been the thing, but I did not know how to make it, so at last I decided to cut out a body from a piece of wood.

"The very thing, Nat," said my uncle. "Stop a minute, my boy, till I've lit my pipe, and then we'll begin."

I waited till my uncle said he was ready, and then we did begin, that is to say, he went on smoking while I sawed off a piece of wood that I thought would do.

I need not tell you all about that task; how laboriously I carved away day after day at that piece of wood with my pocket-knife, breaking one in the work; how I mounted the piece of wood at last on wires, and then proceeded, by the help of a little glue-pot that my uncle bought on purpose, to stick Polly's feathers on again. By the way, I think I fastened on her wings with tin tacks. It was a very, very long job; but at every stage my uncle sat and expressed his approval, and every spare hour was spent in the tool-house, where I patiently worked away.

I grew very tired of my task, but felt that I must finish it, and I have often thought since what a splendid lesson it proved.

And so I worked on and on, sticking little patches of skin here, feathers there, and I am afraid making such blunders as would have driven a naturalist frantic, for I am sure that patches of feathers that belonged to the breast were stuck on the back, and smooth back feathers ornamented Polly's breast. The head was tolerably complete, so that was allowed to hang on the nail in the wall, where it seemed to watch the process of putting together again; but the tail was terrible, and often made me feel ready to give up in despair.

But here my uncle really did help me, for when ever he saw me out of heart and tired he used to say:

"Suppose we give up now for a bit, Nat, and have a run."

Then when the time came for another try at Polly we used to laugh and say that we would have another turn at Humpty Dumpty.

At last—and I don't know how long it took—the time had come when Polly's head was to cease from staring down in a ghastly one-eyed way at her body, and it was to come down and crown the edifice.

I remember it so well. It was a bright, sunny half-holiday, when I was longing to be off fishing, but with Humpty Dumpty incomplete there was no fishing for me, especially as Aunt Sophia had been asking how soon her pet was to be finished.

"Come along, Nat," said Uncle Joseph, "and we'll soon finish it."

I smiled rather sadly, for I did not feel at all sanguine. I made the glue-pot hot, however, and set to work, rearranging a patch or two of feathers that looked very bad, and then I stared at uncle and he gazed at me.

I believe we both had some kind of an idea that the sort of feather tippet that hung from Polly's head would act as a cloak to hide all the imperfections that were so plain. Certainly some such hopeful idea was in my brain, though I did not feel sanguine.

"Now then, my boy, now then," cried my uncle, as at last I took Polly's head from the nail, and he rubbed his hands with excitement. "We shall do it at last."

I fancy I can smell the hot steaming glue now as I went about that day's work, for I kept on stirring it up and thinking how much I ought to put in the bird's neck and upon its skull to keep from soiling and making sticky all its feathers. It took some consideration, and all the while dear Uncle Joe watched me as attentively as if I were going to perform some wonderful operation. He even held his breath as I began to glue the head, and uttered a low sigh of relief as I replaced the brush in the pot.

Then as carefully as I could I fixed the head in its place, securing it the more tightly by driving a long thin stocking-needle right through the skull into the wood.

And there it was, the result of a month's spare time and labour, and I drew back to contemplate this effort of genius.

I can laugh now as I picture the whole scene. The rough bench on which stood the bird, the wall on which hung the garden tools, Uncle Joe with his pipe in one hand, his other resting upon his knee as he sat upon an upturned tub gazing straight at me, and I seem to see my own boyish self gazing at my task till I utterly broke down with the misery and vexation of my spirit, laying my head upon my arms and crying like a girl.

For a few minutes Uncle Joe was so taken aback that he sat there breathing hard and staring at me.

"Why, Nat—Nat, my boy," he said at last, as he got down off the tub and stood there patting my shoulders. "What is the matter, my boy; are you poorly?"

"No—no—no," I sobbed. "It's horrid, horrid, horrid!"

"What's horrid, Natty?" he said.

"That dreadful bird. Oh, uncle," I cried passionately, "I knew I couldn't do it when I began."

"The bird? What! Humpty Dumpty? What! Polly? Why, my boy, she's splendid, and your aunt will be so—"

"She's not," I cried, flashing into passion. "She isn't like a bird at all. I know how soft and rounded and smooth birds are; and did you ever see such a horrid thing as that? It's a beast, uncle! It's a regular guy! It's a—oh, oh!"

In my rage of disappointment at the miserable result of so much hard work I tore the lump of feathered wood from the bench, dashed it upon the ground, and stamped upon it. Then my passion seemed to flash away as quickly as it had come, and I stood staring at Uncle Joe and Uncle Joe stared at me.

Chapter Six.

A Piece of Deceit that was not carried out.

For a few minutes neither of us spoke. Uncle Joe seemed to be astounded and completely taken off his balance. He put on his glasses and took them off over and over again. He laid down his pipe and rubbed his hands first and then his face with his crimson silk handkerchief, ending by taking off his glasses and rolling them in the handkerchief, flipping them afterwards under the bench all amongst the broken flower-pots. And all the time I felt a prey to the bitterest remorse, and as if I had done something so wicked that I could never be forgiven again.

"Oh, uncle! dear Uncle Joe," I cried passionately. "I am so—so sorry."

"Sorry, Nat!" he said, taking my outstretched hands, and then drawing me to his breast, holding me there and patting my back with both his hands. "Sorry, Nat! yes, that's what I felt, my boy. It was such a pity, you know."

"Oh, no, Uncle Joe," I cried, looking down at my work. "It was horrible, and I've been more ashamed of it every day."

"Have you, Nat, my boy?" he said. "Oh, yes, uncle, but I kept on hoping that—that somehow—somehow it would come better."

"That's what I've been hoping, my boy," he said, "for you did try very hard."

"Yes, uncle, I tried very, very hard, but it never did come better."

"No, my boy, you are quite right; it never did come any better, but I hoped it would when you put on its head."

"So did I, uncle, but it only seemed to make it look more ridiculous, and it wasn't a bit like a bird."

"No, my boy, it wasn't a bit like a bird," he said weakly.

"Then why did you say it was capital, uncle?" I cried sharply.

"Well, my boy, because—because I—that is—I wanted to encourage you, and," he cried more confidently, "it was capital for you."

"Oh, Uncle Joe, it was disgraceful, and I don't know what aunt would have said."

"I don't know what she will say now," said my uncle ruefully, as he gazed down at Humpty Dumpty's wreck, where it lay crushed into the dust. "I'm afraid she'll be very cross. You see I half told her that it would be done to-day, and I'm afraid—"

"Oh, uncle, why did you tell her that?" I said reproachfully.

"Well, my boy, you see she had been remonstrating a little about our being out here so much, and I'm afraid I have been preparing her for a surprise."

"And now she'll be more cross than ever, uncle," I said, picking up the bird.

"Yes, my boy, now she'll be more cross than ever. It's a very bad job, Nat, and I don't like to see you show such a temper as that."

"I'm very sorry, Uncle Joe," I said humbly. "I didn't mean to fly out like that. It's just like Jem Boxhead at our school."

"Does he fly out into tempers like that, Nat?"

"Yes, uncle, *often*."

"It's a very bad job, my boy, and I never saw anything of the kind before in you. It isn't a disease, temper isn't, or I should think you had caught it. You couldn't catch a bad temper, you know, my boy. But don't you think, Natty, we might still manage to put Humpty Dumpty together again?"

"No, uncle," I said, "it's impossible;" and I know now that it was an impossibility from the first, for my hours of experience have taught me that I had engaged upon a hopeless task.

He took out his crimson handkerchief, and reseating himself upon the tub began wiping his face and hands once more.

"You've made me very hot, Natty," he said. "What is to be done?"

"I don't know, uncle," I said dolefully. "But are you very cross with me?"

"Cross, my boy? No. I was only thinking how much you are like my poor sister, your dear mother, who would go into a temper like that sometimes when we were boy and girl."

"Please, uncle," I said, laying my hand upon his arm, "I'll try very hard not to go into a temper again like that."

"Yes, yes, do, my boy," he said, taking my hand in his and speaking very affectionately. "Don't give way to temper, my boy, it's a bad habit. But I'm not sorry, Nat, I'm not a bit sorry, my dear boy, to see that you've got some spirit in you like your poor mother. She was so different to me, Nat. I never had a bit of spirit, and people have always done as they pleased with me."

I could not help thinking about my aunt just then, but I said nothing, and it was Uncle Joe who began again about the parrot.

"So you think we could not put Humpty Dumpty together again, Nat?"

"No, uncle," I said despairingly, "I'm sure we could not. It's all so much lost time."

"There's plenty more time to use, Nat, for some things," he said dreamily, "but not for doing our work, and—and, my boy, after your aunt has let us be out here so much, I'm afraid that I dare not tell her of our failure."

"Then what's to be done, uncle?" I said.

"I'm afraid, my boy, we must be very wicked and deceitful."

"Deceitful, uncle?"

"Yes, my boy, or your aunt will never forgive us."

"Why, what do you mean, uncle?" I said.

"I've been thinking, my boy, that I might go out somewhere and buy a grey parrot—one already stuffed. I dare not face her without."

I felt puzzled, and with a strong belief upon me that we were going to do a very foolish thing.

"Wouldn't it be better to go and tell Aunt Sophia frankly that we have had an accident, and spoiled the parrot, uncle?"

"Yes, my boy, much better," he said, "very much better; but—but I dare not do it, Nat, I dare not do it."

I felt as if I should like to say, "I'll do it, uncle," but I, too, shrank from the task, and we were saved from the underhanded proceeding by the appearance of my aunt at the tool-house door.

My unfortunate attempt at restuffing poor Polly made me less a favourite than ever with Aunt Sophia, who never let a day pass without making some unpleasant allusion to my condition there. My uncle assured me that I was in no wise dependent upon them, for my mother's money gave ample interest for my education and board, but Aunt Sophia always seemed to ignore that fact, so that but for Uncle Joe's kindness I should have been miserable indeed.

The time slipped away, and I had grown to be a tall strong boy of fifteen; and in spite of my aunt's constant fault-finding I received sufficient encouragement from Uncle Joe to go on with my natural history pursuits, collecting butterflies and beetles, birds' eggs in the spring, and stuffing as many birds as I could obtain.

Some of these latter were very roughly done, but I had so natural a love for the various objects of nature, that I find the birds I did in those days, rough as they were, had a very lifelike appearance. I had only to ask my uncle for money to buy books or specimens and it was forthcoming, and so I went on arranging and rearranging, making a neatly written catalogue of my little museum in the tool-house, and always helped by Uncle Joe's encouragement.

I suppose I was a strange boy, seeking the companionship of my school-fellows but very little, after my aunt had refused to let any of them visit me, or to let me go to their homes. I was driven thus, as it were, upon my own resources, and somehow I did not find mine to be an unhappy life; in fact so pleasant did it seem that when the time came for me to give it up I was very sorry to leave it, and felt ready to settle down to aunt's constant fault-finding for the sake of dear tender-hearted old Uncle Joe, who was broken completely in spirit at my having to go.

"But it's right, Nat, my boy, quite right," he said, "and you would only be spoiled if you stayed on here. It is time now that you began to think of growing to be a man, and I hope and pray that you'll grow into one of whom I can be proud."

Chapter Seven.

The Return of the Wanderer.

One day when I came home from school I was surprised to find a tall dark gentleman in the drawing-room with my uncle and aunt. He was so dark that he looked to me at first to be a foreigner, and his dark keen eyes and long black beard all grizzled with white hairs made him so very different to Uncle Joseph that I could not help comparing one with the other.

"This is Master Nathaniel, I suppose," said the stranger in a quick sharp way, just as if he was accustomed to order people about.

"Yes, that's Joseph's nephew," said my aunt tartly, "and a nice boy he is."

"You mean a nasty one," I said to myself, as I coloured up, "but you needn't have told a stranger."

"Yes," said Uncle Joseph, "he is a very nice boy, Richard, and I'm very proud of him."

My aunt gave a very loud sniff.

"Suppose we shake hands then, Nathaniel," said the stranger, whom I immediately guessed to be my Aunt Sophia's brother Richard, who was a learned man and a doctor, I had heard.

He seemed to order me to shake hands with him, and I went up and held out mine, gazing full in his dark eyes, and wondering how much he knew.

"Well done, youngster," he said, giving my hand a squeeze that hurt me ever so, but I would not flinch. "I like to see a boy able to look one full in the face."

"Oh! he has impudence enough for anything," said my aunt.

"Oh! has he?" said our visitor smiling. "Well, I would rather see a boy impudent than a milksop."

"Nat was never impudent to me," said my uncle, speaking up for me in a way that made my aunt stare.

"I see—I see," said our visitor. "You never were fond of boys, Sophy."

"No, indeed," said my aunt.

"Cats and dogs were always more in your way," said our visitor. "Get out!"

This was to Nap, who had been smelling about him for some time, and he gave him so rough a kick that the dog yelped out, and in a moment the temper that I had promised my uncle to keep under flashed forth again, as I caught at Nap to protect him, and flushing scarlet—

"Don't kick our dog," I said sharply.

I've often thought since that my aunt ought to have been pleased with me for taking the part of my old friend and her favourite, but she turned upon me quickly.

"Leave the room, sir, directly. How dare you!" she cried. "To dare to speak to a visitor like that!" and I had to go out in disgrace, but as I closed the door I saw our visitor laughing and showing his white teeth.

"I shall hate him," I said to myself, as I put my hands in my pockets and began to wander up and down the garden; but I had hardly gone to and fro half a dozen times before I heard voices, and I was about to creep round by the side path and get indoors out of the way when Mr Richard Burnett caught sight of me, and shouted to me to come.

I went up looking hurt and ill-used as he was coming down the path with Uncle Joe; but he clapped me on the shoulder, swung me round, and keeping his arm half round my neck, walked me up and down with them, and I listened as he kept on telling Uncle Joseph about where he had been.

"Five years in South America, wandering about away from civilisation, is a long time, Joe; but I shall soon be off again."

I pricked up my ears.

"Back to South America, Dick?"

"No, my dear boy, I shall go in another direction this time."

"Where shall you go this time, sir?" I said eagerly.

"Eh? where shall I go, squire?" he said sharply. "Right away to Borneo and New Guinea, wherever I am likely to collect specimens and find new varieties."

"Do you collect, sir?" I said excitedly.

"To be sure I do, my boy. Do you?" he added with a smile.

"Yes, sir, all I can."

"Oh yes! he has quite a wonderful collection down in the tool-house, Richard. Come and see."

Our visitor smiled in such a contemptuous way that I coloured up again, and felt as if I should have liked to cry, "You sha'n't see them to make fun of my work." But by that time we were at the tool-house door, and just inside was my cabinet full of drawers that uncle had let the carpenter make for me, and my cases and boxes, and the birds

I had stuffed. In fact by that time, after a couple of years collecting, the tools had been ousted to hang in another shed, and the toolhouse was pretty well taken up with my lumber.

"Why, hallo!" cried our visitor; "who stuffed those birds?"

I answered modestly enough that it was I.

"And what's in these drawers, eh?" he said, pulling them out sharply one after the other, and then opening my cases.

"Nat's collections," said my uncle very proudly. "Here's his catalogue."

"Neatly written out—numbered—Latin names," he said, half to himself. "Why, hallo, young fellow, I don't wonder that your Aunt Sophia says you are a bad character."

"But he isn't, Dick," said Uncle Joe warmly; "he's a very good lad, and Sophy don't mean what she says."

"She used to tell me I should come to no good in the old days when I began to make a mess at home, Joe," he said merrily. "Why, Nat, my boy, you and I must be good friends. You would like to come and see my collection, eh?"

"Will you—will you show it to me, sir?" I said, catching him in my excitement by the sleeve.

"Well, I don't know," he said drily; "you looked daggers at me because I kicked your aunt's pet."

"I couldn't help it, sir," I said; "Nap has always been such good friends with me that I didn't like to see him hurt."

"Then I beg Nap's pardon," he said smiling. "I thought he was only a useless pet; but if he can be a good friend to you he is a better dog than I thought for."

"He'd be a splendid dog to hunt with, sir, if he had a chance."

"Would he? Well, I'm glad of it, and you shall come and see my collection, and help me catalogue and arrange them if you like. Here, hi! stop a minute: where are you going?"

"Only to fetch my cap, sir," I said excitedly, for the idea of seeing the collections of a man who had been five years in South America seemed to set me on fire.

"Plenty of time yet, my boy," he said, showing white teeth in a pleasant smile; "they are in the docks at Southampton, on board ship. Wait a bit, and you shall see all."

Chapter Eight.

I find myself a Brother Naturalist.

I stood looking very hard at our visitor, Doctor Burnett, and thought how very different he was to Aunt Sophia. Only a little while before, I had felt as if I must hate him for behaving so badly to Nap, and for talking to me in such a cold, contemptuous way. It had seemed as if he would join with Aunt Sophia in making me uncomfortable, and I thought it would have been so much pleasanter if he had stayed away.

But now, as I stood watching him, he was becoming quite a hero in my eyes, for not only had he been abroad seeing the wonders of the world, but he had suddenly shown a liking for me, and his whole manner was changed.

When he had spoken to me in the house it had been in a pooh-poohing sort of fashion, as if I were a stupid troublesome boy, very much in the way, and as if he wondered at his sister and brother-in-law's keeping me upon the premises; but now the change was wonderful. The cold distant manner had gone, and he began to talk to me as if he had known me all my life.

"Shall we go round the garden again, Dick?" said my uncle, after standing there nodding and smiling at me, evidently feeling very proud that his brother-in-law should take so much notice of the collection.

"No," said our visitor sharply. "There, get your pipe, Joe, and you can sit down and look on while I go over Nat's collection. We naturalists always compare notes—eh, Nat?"

I turned scarlet with excitement and pleasure, while Uncle Joseph rubbed his hands, beaming with satisfaction, and proceeded to take down his long clay pipe from where it hung upon two nails in the wall, and his little tobacco jar from a niche below the rafters.

"That's what I often do here, Dick," he said; "I sit and smoke and give advice—when it is asked, and Nat goes on with his stuffing and preserving."

"Then now, you may sit down and give advice—when it is asked," said our visitor smiling, "while Nat and I compare notes. Who taught you how to stuff birds, Nat?"

"I—I taught myself, sir," I replied.

"Taught yourself?" he said, pinching one of my birds—a starling that I had bought for a penny of a man with a gun.

"Yes, sir; I pulled Polly to pieces."

"You did what?" he cried, bursting into a roar of laughter. "Why, who was Polly—one of the maids?"

"Oh no, sir! Aunt Sophy's stuffed parrot."

"Well, really, Nat," he said, laughing most heartily, "you're the strangest boy I ever met."

"Am I, sir?" I said, feeling a little chilled again, for he seemed to be laughing unpleasantly at me.

"That you are, Nat; but I like strange boys. So you pulled Polly to pieces, eh? And found out where the naturalists put the wires, eh?"

"Yes, sir."

"And how do you preserve the skins?"

"With arsenical soap, sir."

"That's right; so do I."

"But it's very dangerous stuff, sir," I said eagerly.

"Not if it is properly used, my boy," he said, taking up bird after bird and examining it carefully. "A fire is a very dangerous thing if you thrust your hand into it, and Uncle Joe's razors are dangerous things if they are not properly used. You see I don't trouble them much," he added smiling.

"No, indeed, sir," I said, as I glanced at his long beard.

"I don't have hot water for shaving brought to me, Nat, when I'm at sea, my boy, or out in the jungle. It's rough work there."

"But it must be very nice, sir," I said eagerly.

"Very, my boy, when you lie down to sleep beneath a tree, so hungry that you could eat your boots, and not knowing whether the enemy that attacks you before morning will be a wild beast, a poisonous serpent, or a deadly fever."

"But it must be very exciting, sir," I cried.

"Very, my boy," he said drily. "Yes: that bird's rough, but I like the shape. There's nature in it—at least as much as you can get by imitation. Look, Joe, there's a soft roundness about that bird. It looks alive. Some of our best bird-stuffers have no more notion of what a bird is like in real life than a baby. What made you put that tomtit in that position, Nat?" he said, turning sharply to me.

"That?—that's how they hang by the legs when they are picking the buds, sir," I said nervously, for I was quite startled by his quick, sudden way.

"To be sure it is, Nat, my boy. That's quite right. Always take nature as your model, and imitate her as closely as you can. Some of the stuffed birds at the British Museum used to drive me into a rage. Glad to see you have the true ring in you, my boy."

I hardly knew what he meant by the "true ring", but it was evidently meant kindly, and I felt hotter than ever; but my spirits rose as I saw how pleased Uncle Joe was.

"You can stuff birds, then, sir?" I said, after a pause, during which our visitor made himself very busy examining everything I had.

"Well, yes, Nat, after a fashion. I'm not clever at it, for I never practise mounting. I can make skins."

"Make skins, sir?"

"Yes, my boy. Don't you see that when I am in some wild place shooting and collecting, every scrap of luggage becomes a burden."

"Yes, sir; of course," I said, nodding my head sagely, "especially if the roads are not good."

"Roads, my boy," he said laughing; "the rivers and streams are the only roads in such places as I travel through. Then, of course, I can't use wires and tow to distend my birds, so we make what we call skins. That is to say, after preparing the skin, all that is done is to tie the long bones together, and fill the bird out with some kind of wild cotton, press the head back on the body by means of a tiny paper cone or sugar-paper, put a band round the wings, and dry the skin in the sun."

"Yes, I know, sir," I cried eagerly; "and you pin the paper round the bird with a tiny bamboo skewer, and put another piece of bamboo through from head to tail."

"Why, how do you know?" he said wonderingly.

"Oh! Nat knows a deal," said Uncle Joe, chuckling. "We're not such stupid people as you think, Dick, even if we do stay at home."

"I've got a skin or two, sir," I said, "and they were made like that."

As I spoke I took the two skins out of an old cigar-box.

"Oh! I see," he said, as he took them very gently and smoothed their feathers with the greatest care. "Where did you get these, Nat?"

"I bought them with my pocket-money in Oxford Street, sir," I said, as Uncle Joe, who had not before seen them, leaned forward.

"And do you know what they are, my boy?" said our visitor.

"No, sir; I have no books with pictures of them in, and the man who sold them to me did not know. Can you tell me, sir?"

"Yes, Nat, I think so," he said quietly. "This pretty dark bird with the black and white and crimson plumage is the rain-bird—the blue-billed gaper; and this softly-feathered fellow with the bristles at the side of his bill is a trogon."

"A trogon, sir?"

"Yes, Nat, a trogon; and these little bamboo skewers tell me directly that the birds came from somewhere in the East."

I looked at him wonderingly.

"Yes, Nat," he continued, "from the East, where the bamboo is used for endless purposes. It is hard, and will bear a sharp point, and is so abundant that the people seem to have no end to the use they make of it."

"And have you seen birds like these alive, sir?"

"No, Nat, but I hope to do so before long. That blue-billed gaper probably came from Malacca, and the trogon too. See how beautifully its wings are pencilled, and how the bright cinnamon of its back feathers contrasts with the bright crimson of its breast. We have plenty of trogons out in the West; some of them most gorgeous fellows, with tails a yard long, and of the most resplendent golden metallic green."

"And humming-birds, sir?"

"Thousands, my boy; all darting through the air like living gems. The specimens brought home are very beautiful, but they are as nothing compared to those fairy-like little creatures, full of life and action, with the sun flashing from their plumage."

"And are there humming-birds, sir, in the East?" I cried, feeling my mouth grow dry with excitement and interest.

"No, my boy; but there is a tribe of tiny birds there that we know as sun-birds, almost as beautiful in their plumage, and of very similar habit. I hope to make a long study of their ways, and to get a good collection. I know nothing, however, more attractive to a man who loves nature than to lie down beneath some great plant of convolvulus, or any trumpet-shaped blossom, and watch the humming-birds flashing to and fro in the sunlight. Their scale-like feathers on throat and head reflect the sun rays like so many gems, and their colours are the most gorgeous that it is possible to conceive. But there, I tire you. Why, Joe, your pipe's out!"

"Please go on, sir," I said in a hoarse whisper, for, as he spoke, I felt myself far away in some wondrous foreign land, lying beneath the trumpet-flowered tree or plant, gazing at the brilliant little creatures he described.

"Do you like to hear of such things, then?" he said smiling.

"Oh! so much, sir!" I cried; and he went on.

"I believe some of them capture insects at certain times, but as a rule these lovely little birds live upon the honey they suck from the nectaries of these trumpet-shaped blossoms; and their bills are long and thin so that they can reach right to the end. Some of these little creatures make quite a humming noise with their wings, and after darting here and there like a large fly they will seem to stop midway in the air, apparently motionless, but with their wings all the while beating so fast that they are almost invisible. Sometimes one will stop like this just in front of some beautiful flower, and you may see it hang suspended in the air, while it thrusts in its long bill and drinks the sweet honey that forms its food."

"And can you shoot such little things, sir?" I asked.

"Oh, yes, my boy; it is easy enough to shoot them," he replied. "The difficulty is to bring them down without hurting their plumage, which is extremely delicate. The Indians shoot them with a blow-pipe and pellets and get very good specimens; but then one is not always with the Indians; and in those hot climates a bird must be skinned directly, so I generally trust to myself and get my own specimens."

"With a blow-pipe, sir?"

"No, Nat; I have tried, but I never got to be very clever with it. One wants to begin young to manage a blow-pipe well. I always shot my humming-birds with a gun."

"And shot, sir?"

"Not always, Nat. I have brought them down with the disturbance of the air or the wad of the gun. At other times I have used sand, or in places where I had no sand I have used water."

"Water!" I exclaimed.

"Yes, and very good it is for the purpose, Nat. A little poured into the barrel of the gun after the powder is made safe with a couple of wads, is driven out in a fine cutting spray, which has secured me many a lovely specimen with its plumage unhurt."

"But don't it seem rather cruel to shoot such lovely creatures, Dick?" said Uncle Joe in an apologetic tone.

"Well, yes, it has struck me in that light before now," said our visitor; "but as I am working entirely with scientific views, and for the spread of the knowledge of the beautiful occupants of this world, I do not see the harm. Besides, I never wantonly destroy life. And then, look here, my clear Joe, if you come to think out these things you will find that almost invariably the bird or animal you kill has passed its life in killing other things upon which it lives."

"Ye–es," said Uncle Joe, "I suppose it has."

"You wouldn't like to shoot a blackbird, perhaps?"

"Well, I don't know," said Uncle Joe. "They are the wickedest thieves that ever entered a garden; aren't they, Nat?"

"Yes, uncle, they are a nuisance," I said.

"Well, suppose you killed a blackbird, Joe," continued our visitor; "he has spent half his time in killing slugs and snails, and lugging poor unfortunate worms out of their holes; and it seems to me that the slug or the worm is just as likely to enjoy its life as the greedy blackbird, whom people protect because he has an orange bill and sings sweetly in the spring."

"Ye–es," said my uncle, looking all the while as if he were terribly puzzled, while I sat drinking in every word our visitor said, feeling that I had never before heard any one talk like that.

"For my part," continued our visitor, "I never destroy life wantonly; and as for you, young man, you may take this for a piece of good advice—never kill for the sake of killing. Let it be a work of necessity—for food, for a specimen, for your own protection, but never for sport. I don't like the word, Nat; there is too much cruelty in what is called sport."

"But wouldn't you kill lions and tigers, sir?" I said.

"Most decidedly, my boy. That is the struggle for life. I'd sooner kill a thousand tigers, Nat, than one should kill me," he said laughing; "and for my part—"

"Joseph, I'm ashamed of you. Nathaniel, this is your doing, you naughty boy," cried my aunt, appearing at the door. "It is really disgraceful, Joseph, that you will come here to sit and smoke; and as for you, Nathaniel, what do you mean, sir, by dragging your un—, I mean a visitor, down into this nasty, untidy place, and pestering him with your rubbish?"

"Oh, it was not Nathaniel's doing, Sophy," said our visitor smiling, as he rose and drew aunt's arm through his, "but mine; I've been making the boy show me his treasures. There, come along and you and I will have a good long chat now. Nat, my boy, I sha'n't forget what we said."

Chapter Nine.

Uncle Dick's Boxes.

"I'm afraid we've made your aunt very cross, Nat, my boy," said Uncle Joe, rubbing his hands softly, and looking perplexed and troubled. "Do you think, Nat, that I have been leading you wrong?"

"I hope not, uncle," I said, "and I don't think so, for it has been very nice out here in the toolshed, and we have enjoyed ourselves so."

"Yes, my boy, we have, very much, indeed, but I'm afraid your aunt never forgave us for not putting Humpty Dumpty together again."

"But, uncle," I said, "isn't it unreasonable of Aunt Sophia to expect us to do what all the king's horses and all the king's men could not do?"

He looked at me for a few minutes without speaking, and then he began to smile very slightly, then a little more and a little more, till, instead of looking dreadfully serious, his face was as happy as it could be. Then he began to laugh very heartily, and I laughed too, till the tears were in our eyes.

"Of—of course it was, Nat," he cried, chuckling and coughing together. "We couldn't do what all the king's horses and all the king's men didn't manage, Nat, and—yes, my dear, we're coming."

Uncle Joe jumped up and went out of the tool-house, for my aunt's voice could be heard telling us to come in.

"Hush!" he whispered, with a finger on his lips. "Make haste in, Nat, and run up to your room and wash your hands."

I followed him in, and somehow, whenever Doctor Burnett was in the room, my aunt did not seem so cross, especially as her brother took a good deal of notice of me, and kept on asking me questions.

I soon found, to my great delight, that he was going to stay with us till he started for Singapore, a place whose name somehow set me thinking about Chinese people and Indian rajahs, but that was all; the rest was to me one great mystery, and I used to lie in bed of a night and wonder what sort of a place it could be.

Every day our visitor grew less cool and distant in his ways, and at last my aunt said pettishly:

"Well, really, Richard, it is too bad; this is the third morning this week you have kept that boy away from school by saying you wanted him. How do you expect his education to get on?"

"Get on?" said Doctor Burnett; "why, my dear sister, he is learning the whole time he is with me; I'll be bound to say that he has picked up more geography since he has been with me than he has all the time he has been to school."

"I don't know so much about that," said my aunt snappishly.

"Then I do," he said. "Let the boy alone, he is learning a great deal; and I shall want him more this next week."

"You'd better take him away from school altogether," said my aunt angrily.

"Well, yes," said the doctor quietly; "as it is so near his holidays, he may as well stop away the rest of this half."

"Richard!" cried my aunt as I sat there pinching my legs to keep from looking pleased.

"He will have to work hard at helping me with my collections, which are on the way here, I find, from a letter received this morning. There will be a great deal of copying and labelling, and that will improve his writing, though he does write a fair round hand."

"But it will be neglecting his other studies," cried my aunt.

"But then he will be picking up a good deal of Latin, for I shall explain to him the meaning of the words as he writes them, and, besides, telling him as much as I know of natural history and my travels."

"And what is to become of the boy then?" cried my aunt. "I will not have him turn idler, Richard."

"Well, if you think I have turned idler, Sophy," he said laughing, and showing his white teeth, "all I can say is, that idling over natural history and travelling is very hard work."

"But the boy must not run wild as—"

"I did? There, say it out, Sophy," said her brother. "I don't mind, my dear; some people look upon everything they do not understand as idling."

"I think I understand what is good for that boy," said my aunt shortly.

"Of course you do," said the doctor, "and you think it will do him good to help me a bit, Sophy. Come along, Nat, my boy, we are to have the back-room for the chests, so we must make ready, for they will be here to-morrow."

"Oh, Doctor Burnett," I cried as soon as we were alone.

"Suppose you call me Uncle Richard for the future, my boy," he said. "By and by, when we get to know each other better, it will be Uncle Dick. Why not at once, eh?"

"I—I shouldn't like to call you that, sir," I said.

"Why not?"

"I—I hardly know, sir, only that you seem so clever and to know so much."

"Then it shall be Uncle Dick at once," he said, laughing merrily; "for every day that you are with me, Nat, you will be finding out more and more that I am not so clever as you think."

So from that day it was always Uncle Dick, and as soon as the great chests arrived we set to work.

I shall never forget those great rough boxes made of foreign wood, nor the intense interest with which I watched them as they were carried in upon the backs of the stout railway vanmen and set carefully in the large back-room.

There were twenty of them altogether, and some were piled upon the others as if they were building stones, till at last the men's book had been signed, the money paid for carriage, and Uncle Joe, Uncle Dick, and I sat there alone staring at the chests and wondering at their appearance.

For they were battered, and bruised, and chipped away in splinters, so that they looked very old indeed, though, as my uncle told me, there was not one there more than five years old, though they might have been fifty.

Every one had painted upon it in large white letters:

"Dr Burnett, FZS, London," and I wondered what FZS might mean. Then I noticed that the chests were all numbered, and I was longing intensely for them to be opened, when Uncle Dick, as I suppose I must call him now, made me start by crying out:

"Screw-driver!"

I jumped up and ran to Uncle Joe's tool-box for the big screw-driver, and was back with it in a very short time, Uncle Dick laughing heartily as he saw my excitement.

"Thank you, Nat, that will do," he said. "It will be nice and handy for me to-morrow morning."

"Ha—ha—ha!" he laughed directly after, as he saw my blank disappointed face. "Did you think I was going to open the cases to-day, Nat?"

"I did hope so, sir," I said stoutly.

"Then I will," he cried, "for your being so frank. Now then, which shall it be?"

"I should begin with number one, sir," I said.

"And so we will, Nat. Nothing like order. Look here, my boy. Here is my book for cataloguing."

He showed me a large blank book ruled with lines, and on turning it over I found headings here and there under which the different specimens were to be placed.

But I could not look much at the book while "our great traveller", as Uncle Joe used to call him to me, was busy at work with the screw-driver, taking out the great screws, one after another, and laying them in a box.

"Now, Nat," he said, "suppose after going through all my trouble I find that half my specimens are destroyed, what shall I do?"

"I don't know, uncle," I said. "I know what I should do."

"What, my boy?"

"Go and try and find some more."

"A good plan," he said laughing; "and when it means journeying ten or twelve thousand miles, my boy, to seek for more, it becomes a serious task."

All this while he was working away at the screws, till they were half out and loose enough for me to go on turning them with my fingers, and this, after the first two or three, I did till we came to the last, when my uncle stopped and pretended that it was in so tight that it would not turn.

"Let me try, uncle," I cried.

"You? Nonsense! boy. There, I think we shall have to give up for to-day."

He burst out laughing the next moment at my doleful face, gave the screw a few rapid twists; and in a few more moments it was out, and he took hold of the lid.

"Ready?" he exclaimed.

"Yes, quite ready," said Uncle Joe, who was nearly as much excited as I was myself; and then the lid was lifted and we eagerly looked inside.

There was not much to see, only what looked like another lid, held in its place by a few stout nails. These were soon drawn out though, the second lid lifted, and still there was nothing to see but cotton-wool, which, however, sent out a curious spicy smell, hot and peppery, and mixed with camphor.

Then the treat began, for Uncle Dick removed a few layers of cotton-wool, and there were the birds lying closely packed, and so beautiful in plumage that we—that is, Uncle Joe and I—uttered a cry of delight.

I had never before seen anything so beautiful, I thought, as the gorgeous colours of the birds before me, or they seemed to be so fresh and bright and different to anything I had seen in the museum, Uncle Dick having taken care, as I afterwards found, to reject any but the most perfect skins; and these were before me ready to be taken out and laid carefully upon some boards he had prepared for the purpose, and as I helped him I kept on asking questions till some people would have been answered out. Uncle Dick, however, encouraged me to go on questioning him, and I quickly picked up the names of a good many of the birds.

Now it would be a magnificent macaw all blue and scarlet. Then a long-tailed paroquet of the most delicate green, and directly after quite a trayful of the most lovely little birds I had ever seen. They were about the size of chaffinches for the most part; but while some were of the richest crimson, others were blue and green and violet, and a dozen other shades of colour mixed up in the loveliest way.

"Now what are those, Nat?" said my uncle.

"I don't know, sir," I very naturally said.

"What would they be if they were in England and only plain-coloured?"

"Why, I should have said by their beaks, uncle, that they were finches, and lived on seed."

"Finches they are, Nat, and you are quite right to judge them by their beaks."

"But I didn't know that there were finches abroad, Uncle Dick," I said.

"Then you know now, my boy, and by degrees you will learn that there are finches all over the world, and sparrows, and thrushes, and cuckoos, and larks, and hawks, crows, and all the other birds that you find in England."

"Why, I thought they were all different, uncle," I said.

"So most people think," he said, as he went on unpacking the birds; "the difference is that while our British finches are sober coloured, those of hot countries are brilliant in plumage. So are the crow family and the thrushes, as you will see, while some of the sparrows and tits are perfect dandies."

"Why, I thought foreign birds were all parrots and humming-birds, and things like that."

"Well, we have those birds different abroad, Nat," he replied, "and as I tell you the principal difference is in the gorgeous plumes."

"But such birds as birds of paradise, uncle?" I said.

"Well, what should you suppose a bird of paradise to be?"

"I don't know," I said.

"Well, should you think it were a finch, Nat?"

"No, uncle," I said at once.

"Well, it isn't a pheasant, is it?"

"Oh no!"

"What then?"

I stood with a tanager in one hand, a lovely manakin in the other, thinking.

"They couldn't be crows," I said, "because—"

"Because what?"

"I don't know, uncle."

"No, of course you do not, my boy, for crows they really are."

"What! birds of paradise with their lovely buff plumes, uncle?"

"Yes, birds of paradise with their lovely buff and amber plumes, my boy; they are of the crow family, just as our jays, magpies, and starlings are. You would be surprised, my boy, when you came to study and investigate these matters, how few comparatively are the families and classes to which birds belong, and how so many of the most gorgeous little fellows are only showily-dressed specimens of the familiar flutterers you have at home. Look at that one there, just on the top."

"What! that lovely orange and black bird, uncle?" I said, picking up the one he pointed at, and smoothing its rich plumage.

"Yes, Nat," he said; "what is it?"

Uncle Joe took his pipe from his lips, and looked at it very solemnly.

"'Tisn't a parrot," he said, "because it has not got a hooky beak."

"No, it isn't a parrot, uncle," I exclaimed; "its beak is more like a starling's."

"If it were a starling, what family would it belong to?"

I stopped to think, and then recollected what he had said a short time before.

"A crow, uncle."

"Quite right, my boy; but that bird is not one of the crows. Try again."

"I'm afraid to try, uncle," I said.

"Why, my boy?"

"Because I shall make some silly mistake."

"Then make a mistake, Nat, and we will try to correct it. We learn from our blunders."

"It looks to me something of the same shape as a thrush or blackbird, sir," I said.

"And that's what it is, my boy. That bird is an oriole—the orange oriole; and there is another, the yellow oriole. Both thrushes, Nat, and out in the East there are plenty more of most beautiful colours, especially the ground-thrushes. But there is someone come to call us to feed, I suppose. We must go now."

"Oh!" I exclaimed, "what a pity! we seem to have just begun."

All the same we had been at work for a very long time, so hands were washed, and we all went in to dinner.

Chapter Ten.

All amongst the Bird Skins.

My aunt waylaid me with a very unpleasant task directly after dinner, but Uncle Dick saw my disappointment, and said that he must have me, so I escaped, and, to my great delight, we went at once to his room to go on unpacking the birds, my excitement and wonder increasing every minute. I was rather disappointed with some of the skins, for they were as plain and ordinary looking as sparrows or larks; but Uncle Dick seemed to set great store by them, and said that some of the plainest were most valuable for their rarity.

Uncle Joe sat and looked on, saying very little, while Uncle Dick and I did the unpacking and arranging, laying the beautiful skins out in rows upon the boards and shelves.

"They wanted unpacking," said Uncle Dick, "for some of them are quite soft and damp with exposure to the sea air. Well, Nat, what is it?"

"I was hoping to find some birds of paradise, uncle," I replied.

"Then your hopes will be disappointed, my boy, for the simple reason that my travels have been in Florida, Mexico, Central America, Peru, and Brazil, with a short stay of a few months in the West Indies."

"And are there no birds of paradise there, uncle?"

"No, my boy, nor yet within thousands of miles. Birds of paradise, as they are called, are found in the isles of the eastern seas, the Aru Isles and New Guinea."

"Oh! how I should like to go!" I cried.

"You?" he said laughing. "What for, Nat?"

"To shoot and collect, sir," I cried; "it must be grand."

"And dangerous, and wearisome," he said smiling. "You would soon want to come back to Uncle Joe."

"I shouldn't like to leave Uncle Joe," I said thoughtfully; "but I should like to go all the same. I'd take Uncle Joe with me," I said suddenly. "He'd help me ever so."

Uncle Dick laughed, and we went on with our task, which never seemed to weary me, so delighted was I with the beauty of the birds. As one box was emptied another was begun, and by the time I had finished the second I thought we had exhausted all the beauty of the collection, and said so, but my uncle laughed.

"Why, we have not begun the chatterers yet, Nat," he said. "Let me see—yes," he continued, "they should be in that box upon which your uncle's sitting."

Uncle Joe solemnly moved to another case and his late seat was opened, the layers of cotton-wool, in this case a little stained with sea-water, removed, and fresh beauties met my gaze.

"There, Nat," said Uncle Dick; "those are the fruits of a long stay in Central America and the hotter parts of Peru. What do you think of that bird?"

I uttered an exclamation of delight as I drew forth and laid gently in my hand a short stumpy bird that must in life have been about as big as a very thick-set pigeon. But this bird was almost entirely of a rich orange colour, saving its short wings and tail, which were of a cinnamon-brown, and almost hidden by a fringe of curly, crisp orange plumes, while the bird's beak was covered by the radiating crest, something like a frill, that arched over the little creature's head.

"Why, nothing could be more beautiful than that, uncle," I cried. "What is it?"

"The rock manakin, or chatterer," he replied; "an inhabitant of the hottest and most sterile parts of Central America. Here is another kind that I shot in Peru. You see it is very similar but has less orange about it, and its crest is more like a tuft or shaving-brush than the lovely radiating ornament of the other bird. That is almost like a wheel of feathers in rapid motion."

"And as orange as an orange," said Uncle Joe, approvingly.

"I thought we could not find any more beautiful birds in your boxes, uncle," I said.

"Oh! but we have not done yet, my boy; wait and see."

We went on with our task, the damp peculiar odour showing that it was high time the cases were emptied.

"Now, Nat, we are coming to the cuckoos," he said, as I lifted a thin layer of wool.

"It does seem curious for there to be cuckoos in America," I said.

"I don't see why, Nat," he replied, as he carefully arranged his specimens. "You remember I told you it was a cuckoo, probably from Malacca, that you showed me you had bought; well, those you are about to unpack are some of the American representatives of the family. You will see that they are soft-billed birds, with a very wide gape and bristles like moustaches at the sides like thin bars to keep in the captives they take."

"And what do they capture, sir?" I asked.

"Oh, caterpillars and butterflies and moths, Nat. Soft-bodied creatures. Nature has given each bird suitable bills for its work. Mind how you take out that bird. No: don't lift it yet. See, that top row must come out after the whole of that layer which is arranged all over the top row's tails."

"What! do their tails go right along the box, uncle?" I cried.

"Yes, some of them, my boy. Be careful: those are very tender and delicate birds."

I lifted one, and held it out to Uncle Joe, who came down from his seat to examine the glories of the bird I had in my hands.

It was something like the cinnamon-brown and crimson bird I had bought, but much larger. Its breast was of a vivid rosy crimson, and its back and head one mass of the most brilliant golden-green. Not the green of a leaf or strand of grass, but the green of glittering burnished metal that flashed and sparkled in the sunshine. It seemed impossible for it to be soft and downy, for each feather looked harsh, hard, and carved out of the brilliant flashing metal, while turn it which way I would it flashed and looked bright.

"Well, Nat," said Uncle Dick, "what do you say to that?"

"Oh, uncle," I cried; "it is wonderful! But that cannot be a cuckoo."

"Why not, Nat? If cuckoos are slaty coloured here and have breasts striped like a hawk, that is no reason why in the hot climates, where the sun burns your skin brown, they should not be brightly coloured in scarlet and green. You have seen that the modest speckled thrush of England has for relatives thrushes of yellow and orange. What has the poor cuckoo done that his hot country friends should not be gay?"

"But do these lovely creatures suck all the little birds' eggs to make their voices clear?"

"And when they cry 'cuckoo' the summer draws near, eh, Nat? No, my boy, I think not. To begin with, I believe that it is all a vulgar error about the cuckoo sucking little birds' eggs. Doubtless cuckoos have been shot with eggs in their mouths, perhaps broken in the fall, but I think the eggs they carried were their own, which, after laying, they were on their way to put in some other bird's nest to be hatched, as it is an established fact they do; and because they are very small eggs people think they are those of some other bird that the cuckoo has stolen."

"Are cuckoos' eggs small, uncle?" I said.

"Very, my boy, for so large a bird. I have seen them very little larger than the wagtail's with which they were placed. Then as to their crying 'cuckoo' when summer draws near. I have heard their notes, and they live in a land of eternal summer. But go on emptying the case."

I drew out specimen after specimen, some even more beautiful than the first I had taken from the case, though some were far more sober in their hues; but I had not taken out one yet from the top row. When at last I set one of these free, with his tail quite a yard in length, my admiration knew no bounds.

In colouring it was wonderfully like the first which I have described, but in addition it had a golden-green crest, and the long feathers of the tail were of the same brilliant metallic colour. It seemed to me then—and though now I find beauties in sober hues I do not think I can alter my opinion—one of the loveliest, I should say one of the most magnificent, birds in creation, and when fourteen of these wonderful creatures were laid side by side I could have stopped for hours revelling in their beauties.

"Well, Nat," said my uncle, who quite enjoyed my thorough admiration, "I should make quite a naturalist of you if I had you with me."

"Oh, if I could go!" I cried in an excited tone, at which he merely laughed. "I'd give anything to see those birds alive."

"It requires some work and patience, my boy. I was a whole year in the most inaccessible places hunting for those trogons before I got them."

"Trogons! Yes, you said they were trogons."

"*Trogon resplendens*. Those long-tailed feathers are fitly named, Nat, for they are splendid indeed."

"Glorious!" I cried enthusiastically; and though we worked for some time longer my help was very poor, on account of the number of times I kept turning to the splendid trogons to examine their beauties again and again.

Chapter Eleven.

My Hopes.

It was a long task, the emptying of those cases, even to get to the end of the birds, and I could not help thinking, as day after day crept by, what a wonderfully patient collector my Uncle Richard must have been. Certainly he had been away for years and had travelled thousands of miles, but the labour to obtain all these birds, and then carefully skin, prepare, and fill them with wool, must have been tremendous.

"And did you shoot them all, uncle?" I asked one day.

"With very few exceptions, my boy," he replied, laying down his pen for a minute to talk. "I might have bought here and there specimens of the natives, but they are very rough preservers of birds, and I wanted my specimens to be as perfect as could be, as plenty of poor ones come into this country, some of which are little better than rubbish, and give naturalists a miserable idea of the real beauty of the birds in their native homes. But no one can tell the immense amount of labour it cost me to make this collection, as you will see, Nat, when we open this next case."

Uncle Dick was right. I was astonished as we emptied the next case, which was full of tiny specimens, hundreds upon hundreds of humming-birds, with crests and throats like beautiful precious stones, and all so small that it seemed wonderful how they could have been skinned and preserved.

The more I worked with Uncle Dick the more I wondered, and the stronger grew my desire to follow in his steps. So when we had all the birds out so that they could dry in the warm air of the room, there were the cases full of beetles of all kinds, with glistening horny wing-cases; butterflies so large and beautiful that I used to lean over them, feast my eyes on their colours, and then go into day-dreams, in which I pictured to myself the wonderful far-off lands that produced such creatures, and think and think how it would be possible to go out there all alone, as my uncle had gone, and spend years in collecting these various objects to bring home.

Then I used to wake up again and work hard with my uncle, writing out names in his lists, all as carefully as I could, but of course making plenty of mistakes in the Latin names, while Uncle Joe used to sit and smoke and look on, rarely speaking for fear of interrupting us, till Uncle Dick looked up and started a conversation by way of a rest.

Then all the different birds when thoroughly dry had to be repacked in the boxes, with plenty of camphor and other preservative spices and gums to keep the various insects away, and quite a couple of months had slipped away before we were nearly done.

I ought to have been back at school, but Uncle Dick would not hear of my going, and he seemed to have such influence over my aunt that his word was quite law.

"No, Sophy, I have not half done with him," he said one evening. "I don't want to flatter the boy, but he is very valuable to me. I could easily get a clerk or copyist to make out my lists and help me select and rearrange my specimens; but he would do it mechanically. Nat takes an interest in what he is doing, and is a naturalist at heart."

"But he ought to be going on with his studies," said Aunt Sophia. "It is quite time he was back at school."

"He is learning a great deal more than he would at school," said Uncle Dick; "and his handwriting is a good deal improved. It is more free and quicker."

"But there are his other studies," said Aunt Sophia, who was in a bad humour.

"Well, Sophy, he has picked up a great deal of Latin since he has been helping me; knows ten times as much as he did about America and the West Indian Islands, and has picked up a host of little natural history facts, for he is always asking questions."

"Oh yes," said my aunt tartly, "he can ask questions enough! so can all boys."

"But not sensible questions, my dear," said Uncle Dick smiling; but my aunt kept looking angrily at me as I sat hearing all that was going on.

"Sensible questions, indeed!" she said; "and pray, of what use is it going to be to him that he knows how to stick a pin through a butterfly and leave the poor thing to wriggle to death."

"Naturalists do not stick pins through butterflies and leave them to wriggle to death," said Uncle Dick, looking at me and smiling. "Suppose they did, Nat, what would happen?"

"It would be very cruel, uncle, and would spoil the specimen," I said promptly.

"To be sure it would, Nat."

"It's all waste of time, Richard, and the boy shall go back to school."

"I have not done with Nat yet, Sophy, and I shall be obliged by your ceasing to talk nonsense. It worries me."

This was said in so quiet and decided a way, and in the voice of one so accustomed to command, that my aunt said:

"Well, Richard, I suppose it must be as you wish."

"Yes, if you please," he said quietly. "I have the boy's interest at heart as much as you."

As the time went on my aunt and Uncle Dick had two or three little encounters over this, in all of which Aunt Sophy was worsted; Uncle Dick quietly forcing her to let him have his own way in everything.

This set me thinking very much about the future, for I knew that in less than two months' time Uncle Dick would be off upon his new expedition; one that was to be into the most unfrequented regions of the East Indian Islands, though he had said very little about it in my presence.

"I should like to know all about where you are going, Uncle Dick," I said one afternoon, as we were working together.

"Why, my boy?"

"Because it is so interesting to know all about foreign lands, uncle."

"Well, my boy, I think of going from here straight away to Singapore, either with or without a stay at Ceylon. From Singapore I mean to traverse most of the islands along the equator, staying longest at such of them as give me plenty of specimens. Then I shall go on and on to New Guinea, collecting all the time, spending perhaps four or five years out there before I return; that is, if the Malays and Papuans will be kind enough to leave me alone and not throw spears at me."

"You will go where all the most beautiful birds are plentiful, uncle?" I said.

"Yes, my boy, collecting all the time."

"Shall you go alone, uncle?" I ventured to say after a pause.

"Yes, my boy, quite alone, except that I shall engage one or two native servants at the places where I stay, and perhaps I shall buy a boat for my own special use to cruise from island to island. Why, what are you sighing about, boy?"

"I was thinking about your going out there, uncle, all alone."

"Well, my boy, do you suppose I shall be frightened?"

"No, uncle, of course not; but won't you be dull?"

"I shall be too busy to be dull, my boy. The only likely time for me to be dull is of an evening, and then I shall go to sleep."

He went on with his work until it grew dark, and then at his request I lit the lamp, placed it down close to his writing, and remained standing there by his elbow wanting to speak but not daring to do so, till he suddenly turned round and looked me in the face.

"Why, Nat, my boy, what's the matter? Are you unwell?"

"No, uncle," I said slowly.

"What then? Is anything wrong?"

"I—I was thinking about when you are gone, uncle."

"Ah! yes, my boy; you'll have to go back to school then and work away at your ciphering and French. I shall often think about you, Nat, when I am busy over the birds I have shot, skinning and preserving them; and when I come back, Nat, you must help me again."

"When you come back?" I said dolefully.

"Yes, my lad. Let me see—you are fourteen now. In four or five years you will have grown quite a man. Perhaps you will not care to help me then."

"Oh, uncle!" I cried; for I could keep it back no longer. It had been the one great thought of my mind night and day for weeks now, and if my prayer were not gratified the whole of my future seemed to be too blank and miserable to be borne.

"Why, what is it, my boy?" he said. "Nat, my lad, don't be afraid to speak out. Is anything wrong?"

"Yes, uncle," I panted; for my words seemed to choke me.

"Speak out then, my boy, what is it?"

"You—you are going away, uncle."

"Well, Nat, you've known that for months," he said, with a smile.

"Yes, uncle; but don't go by yourself," I cried. "Take me with you; I won't want much to eat—I won't give you any trouble; and I'll work so very, very hard to help you always, and I could be useful to you. Pray—pray, uncle, take me too."

He pushed his chair away from the table and sat gazing at me with a frown upon his face, then he jumped up and began walking swiftly up and down the room.

"I would hardly let you know that I was with you, uncle, and there should be nothing you wanted that I would not do. Don't be angry with me for asking to go, for I do want to go with you so very, very much."

"Angry, my boy! No, not angry," he cried; "but no, no; it is impossible."

"Don't say that, uncle," I cried; "I would work so hard."

"Yes, yes, my boy, I know that; but it would not be just to you to drag you away there to those wild lands to live like a savage half your time."

"But I should like that, uncle," I cried excitedly.

"To expose you to risks of voyaging, from the savages, and from disease. No, no, Nat, you must not ask me. It would not do."

"Oh, uncle!" I cried, with such a pitiful look of disappointment on my face, that he stopped and laid his hand upon my shoulder.

"Why, Nat, my boy," he said in a soft, gentle way, very different to his usual mode of speaking, "nothing would be more delightful to me than to have you for my companion; not for my servant, to work so hard, but to be my friend, helpmate, and counsellor in all my journeyings. Why, it would be delightful to have you with me, boy, to enjoy with me the discovery of some new specimen."

"Which we had hunted out in some wild jungle where man had never been before, uncle!"

"Bird or butterfly, it would be all the same, Nat; we should prize it and revel in our discovery."

"Yes, and I'd race you, uncle, and see which could find most new sorts."

"And of an evening we could sit in our tent or hut, and skin and preserve, or pin out what we had found during the day, Nat, eh?"

"Oh, uncle, it would be glorious!" I cried excitedly. "And I say— birds of paradise! We would make such a collection of all the loveliest kinds."

"Then we should have to hunt and fish, Nat, for the pot, for there would be no butchers' and fishmongers' shops, lad."

"Oh! it would be glorious, uncle!" I cried.

"Glorious, my boy!" he said as excitedly as I; "why, we should get on splendidly, and—tut, tut, tut! what an idiot am I! Hold your tongue, sir, it is impossible!"

"Uncle!"

"Here have I been encouraging the boy, instead of crushing the idea at once," he cried impatiently. "No, no, no, Nat, my boy. It was very foolish of me to speak as I did. You must not think of it any more."

"Oh! uncle, don't talk to me like that," I cried. "Pray, pray take me with you."

"I tell you no, boy," he said impatiently. "It would be unjust to you to encourage you to lead such a vagabond life as mine. Say no more about it, sir," he added harshly. "It is impossible!"

A deep sigh escaped my lips, and then I was silent, for my uncle turned to his writing again, and for the next week he was cold and distant to me, while I went on with my task in a dull, spiritless manner, feeling so miserable that I was always glad to go and hide myself away, to sit and think, and wonder what I should do when my uncle had gone.

Chapter Twelve.

Uncle Dick Says "Yes!"

It was about a fortnight after this conversation, during the whole of which time Uncle Dick seemed to have kept me so at arm's-length that my very life had become wretched in the extreme, when, being in the drawing-room one evening, my aunt, who had been talking to him about his preparations for going away in three weeks' time, suddenly drew his attention to me.

"Do you see how ill and white this boy has turned, Richard? Now it's of no use you denying it; he's quite upset with your nasty birds and stuff."

"No, he is not," cried Uncle Dick suddenly; and his whole manner changed. "The boy is fretting."

"Fretting!" cried my aunt; "with plenty to eat and drink, and a good bed to sleep on! What has he to fret about?"

"He is fretting because he has taken it into his head that he would like to go with me."

"Like to go with you, Dick?" cried Uncle Joe, laying hold of the arms of his easy-chair.

"Yes, Joe, I'm afraid I have turned his head with my descriptions of collecting abroad."

To my utter astonishment, as I sat there with my face burning, and my hands hot and damp, Aunt Sophy did not say a word.

"But—but you wouldn't like to go with your Uncle Richard, Nat, would you?" said Uncle Joe.

"I can't help it, uncle," I said, as I went to him; "but I should like to go. I don't want to leave you, but I'd give anything to go collecting with Uncle Dick, anywhere, all over the world."

Uncle Joe took out his red handkerchief and sat wiping his face.

"I have turned it over in my mind a dozen times," said Uncle Dick, "and sometimes I have thought that it would be an injustice to the boy, sometimes I have concluded that with his taste for natural history, his knowledge of treating skins and setting out butterflies and moths, it would be a shame not to give him every encouragement."

"How?" said my aunt, drily.

"By taking him with me and letting him learn to be a naturalist."

"Humph!" said my aunt; "take him with you right away on your travels?"

"Yes," said my Uncle Dick.

"But I don't think it would be right," said Uncle Joseph softly.

"Don't be stupid, Joe," said my aunt sharply; "why shouldn't the boy go, I should like to know?"

"Oh, aunt!" I cried excitedly.

"Yes, sir, and oh, aunt, indeed!" she cried, quite mistaking my meaning. "Do you suppose that you are to stay here idling away your time all your life—and—"

"That will do," cried Uncle Dick quickly. "Nat, my boy, I have held off from taking you before; but if your Uncle Joseph will give his consent as your guardian, you shall come with me as my pupil, companion, and son, if you will, and as far as in me lies I will do my duty by you. What say you, Joe?" he continued, as I ran to him and took his extended hands.

My aunt looked at me as if she were going to retract her permission; but she was stopped, I should say, for the first and last time in her life, by Uncle Joseph, who waved his hand and said sadly:

"It will be a great grief to me, Dick, a great grief," he said, "and I shall miss my boy Nat very, very much; but I won't stand in his light, Dick. I know that I can trust you to do well by the boy."

"I will, Joe, as well as if he were my own."

"I know it, Dick, I know it," said Uncle Joe softly; "and I can see that with you he will learn a very, very great deal. Nat, my boy, you are very young yet, but you are a stout, strong boy, and your heart is in that sort of thing, I know."

"And may I go—will you take me, Uncle Dick? Say you will."

"Indeed I will, my boy," he cried, shaking my hand warmly; "only you will have to run the same risks as I do, and stick to me through thick and thin."

"But I don't think it would be possible for him to be ready," said my aunt, who evidently now began to repent of her ready consent.

"Nonsense, Sophy!" cried Uncle Dick; "I'll get him ready in time, with a far better outfit than you could contrive. Leave that to me. Well, Nat, it is to be then. Only think first; we may be away for years."

"I don't mind, sir; only I should like to be able to write to Uncle Joe," I said.

"You may write to him once a week, Nat, and tell him all our adventures, my boy; but I don't promise you that you will always be able to post your letters. There, time is short. You shall go out with me this morning."

"Where to, uncle?" I said.

"To the gunsmith's, my boy. I shall have to fit you up with a light rifle and double shot-gun; and what is more, teach you how to use them. Get your cap and let's go: there is no time to spare."

Chapter Thirteen.

How I learned to shoot.

I did not know where we were going, or how we got there, in my state of excitement; but I found myself as if in a dream handling guns and rifles that my uncle placed before me, and soon after we were in a long passage place with a white-washed target at the end, and half a dozen guns on a table at my side.

"Look here, Nat," said Uncle Dick, "time soon steps by, my boy, and you will grow older and stronger every day, so I shall let you have both gun and rifle a little too heavy for you. You must make shift with them at first, and you will improve in their use day by day."

"Yes, uncle," I said as I looked at the beautifully finished weapons from which we were to choose.

"Did you ever fire off a gun?" said my uncle.

"No, uncle."

"You will not be afraid?"

"Will it hurt me, uncle?"

"No."

"Then I'm not afraid," I said.

He liked my confidence in his word, and nodded approval.

Just then the man with us took up one of the guns to load it, but my uncle stopped him.

"No," he said; "let him load for himself. Look, Nat, this is one of the Patent breech-loading rifles. I pull this lever and the breech of the gun opens so that I can put in this little roll, which is a cartridge—do you see?"

"Yes, uncle."

"Now I close it, and the rifle is ready to fire. Next I reopen, take out the cartridge, and close again. Try if you can do the same."

I took the rifle, and, with the exception of being too hurried and excited, did nearly as my uncle had done.

"Now, my boy," he said, "the piece is loaded, and a loaded gun or rifle is a very dangerous thing. Never play with your piece; never trifle in any way; never let your barrel be pointed at those who are with you. Remember those bits of advice."

"Yes, uncle."

"There, now, put the piece to your shoulder, aim at that white target, and pull the trigger."

"But there is no cap on," I said.

"Caps are things of the past, Nat," he said smiling, "except that they are inclosed in the cartridge. Now, then, hold your piece tightly to your shoulder, take careful aim—but quickly—and fire."

I tried to obey him exactly, but the rifle seemed very heavy to hold up firmly, and the sight at the end of the barrel seemed to dance about; but I got it pretty steady for the moment, drew the trigger, there was a sharp report, and the stock of the piece seemed to give me a thump on the shoulder as I heard a dull *clang*.

"Well done, Nat; a good beginning, boy. There, your bullet has hit the target just on the extreme edge."

"What, that black star? Is that the place, uncle?"

"To be sure it is, my boy. I thought that rifle would be too heavy for you; but if you can do that the first time, it decides me to keep it."

The man smiled approval, and my uncle took the rifle in his hand.

"Brush!" shouted the man, and a brush started out of a hole in the wall, and touched the target over with white-wash.

"Now for the double gun," said my uncle. "Try this one, Nat."

I took the gun and put it to my shoulder, aiming at the target; but it seemed heavier than the rifle, and the sight wavered about.

"Try this one, Nat," said my uncle; and he handed me another with rather shorter barrels.

"I like this one, uncle," I said. "It's ever so much lighter."

"No, sir," said the man smiling; "it's half a pound heavier. It is the make. The weight of the gun is more central, and it goes up to the eye better."

"Yes," said my uncle; "it is a handy little gun. Load that the same as you did before."

I found the construction so similar that I had no difficulty in loading both barrels of the gun, and it seemed such easy work to just slip in a couple of little rolls of brown paper as compared to the way in which I had seen men load guns with a ramrod.

"Now, Nat," said my uncle in a quick businesslike way; "once more, you must remember that a gun is not a plaything, and though you are a boy in years you must begin to acquire the serious ways of a man. To handle a gun properly is an art, perfection in which means safety to yourself and friends, durability to the gun, and death quick and painless for the object at which you fire. Now then. No hesitation, boy: raise your gun quickly to your shoulder, take a sharp aim, and fire right and left barrels at those two targets."

My heart beat fast as I did as my uncle bade me, feeling two sharp thuds on my shoulder, and then as I stared through the smoke I expected to see the two white targets covered with shot marks.

"Better luck next time, Nat," said my uncle smiling.

"Haven't I hit them, uncle?" I said in dismay.

"No, my boy; one charge ploughed up the sawdust below the target on the right, and the other scored the white-washed wall three feet to the left of the second target."

"But do you think it is a good gun, uncle? I aimed quite straight."

"We'll see, Nat," he replied, taking the gun from my hand, and reloading it with a quick cleverness of hand that fascinated me.

Then raising the gun he fired both barrels in rapid succession, hardly seeming to take aim, and as the smoke rose above our heads we all walked towards the targets, which looked like currant dumplings.

The man with us rubbed his hands with satisfaction, saying that it was a capital close pattern, which my uncle afterwards explained to me meant that the shot marks were very close and regular all over the targets, instead of being scattered irregularly, which he said was a great disadvantage in a gun.

"I don't think, sir, that you'll find many guns do better than that, sir; and, if you'll excuse me for saying so, I don't think many gentlemen would have made two such clever shots."

"There is no cleverness in it," said my uncle quietly. "When a man spends all his days with a gun in his hand it becomes like second nature to him to hit that at which he aims. Yes, I like the gun. Now, Nat, what do you say—which was in fault last time?"

"I was, uncle," I said rather ruefully. "I thought it would be so easy to shoot."

"So it is, my boy, when you have had practice. Now come back and we will not lose any more time in selecting pieces. You shall have that gun and that rifle, and we will have a couple of hours' practice at loading and firing."

We walked back to the table, and as we did so I saw a man thrust a long-handled brush from a loophole at the side of the wall and whiten the targets once more.

"You decide upon those two pieces, then, sir," said the gunmaker; and my uncle bowed his head.

I noticed then how quiet he seemed when away from home, speaking very little but always to the purpose; a habit, I suppose, acquired from his long and solitary life abroad.

He then said that we had an abundant supply of cartridges, and took a chair beside me.

"Now, Nat," he said, as soon as we were alone, save that a man was behind the loophole ready to thrust out his long-handled brush to whiten the target. "Now, Nat, my boy, fire away all that ammunition. It will not be wasted, for it will make you used to your gun. We will leave the rifle practice till we get to sea. Now, then, begin, and mind this, when you have fired keep your eye upon the object at which you aimed. I'll tell you why. If it is a bird, say a valuable specimen, that we have been seeking for weeks, you may have hit the object, but it flies a short distance before it drops, and if you have lost sight of it for a moment all our trouble is wasted, for it is sometimes labour in vain to seek for small objects in a dense, perhaps impenetrable jungle."

"I'll remember that, uncle."

"Another thing, my boy—a very simple thing, but one which you must learn to do, for your eyes are too valuable when we are collecting for them to do anything but look out for the treasures we seek. Now mind this: you raise your gun, take aim, and fire—not hurriedly, mind, but with quick ease. Then either before or after you have fired your second barrel, according to circumstances, but with your eyes still fixed upon the bird or animal at which you shot, open the breech of your gun, take out the spent cartridge, and reload."

"Without looking, uncle?"

"Certainly: your fingers will soon manage all that with a little education."

I could not help a little nervous haste as I began to load and fire at the targets, but after two or three shots I grew more used to what I was doing, and to my great delight found that I had hit the target.

Then after a little more practice I found it so much easier that I generally saw one or two little spots on the white discs; and by the time that the ammunition was all gone—that was after I had fired forty-eight times—I had once or twice made a respectable show upon the target, but I finished off with four misses, and as my head was now aching badly from the concussion and the noise, I turned with a very rueful face to my uncle.

"Time we left off that," he said smiling. "You are tired, and your hands are getting unsteady."

"I'm afraid I shall never shoot, Uncle Dick," I said dolefully.

"Nonsense, my boy!" he cried, clapping me on the shoulder; "you shot very badly indeed, but better than I expected, and you steadily improved until you grew tired. All these matters take time."

Chapter Fourteen.

How to manage a boat.

The time was short before we were to start on our long journey, but Uncle Dick was determined to make the best of it, and he steadily went on with what he called my education, as well as fitting me out with proper necessaries for my voyage.

These last were very few and simple.

"For you see, Nat," he said, smiling, "we must not encumber ourselves with anything unnecessary. You must bid good-bye to collars and cuffs, and be content with flannels, one to wear and one for your knapsack; and this you will have to wash and dry whenever you get a chance. We'll take some socks, but after a time we shall have to be content with nothing but good boots. We must not have an ounce of luggage that we can do without."

It was a delicious time of adventure to me as I went about with Uncle Dick buying the necessaries for our trip, and very proud I felt of my flannels and stout drill breeches and Norfolk jackets, with belt to hold cartridges, and a strong sheathed knife.

Every day I had a long practice with my gun with what uncle said were satisfactory results; and matters had been going on like this for about a fortnight when my uncle said one day:

"Now, Nat, we must have a bit more education, my boy. We shall very often be left to our own resources, and travel from island to island in a boat, which we shall have to manage; so come along and let me see if I cannot make a sailor of you before we start."

In order to do this he took me down to Gravesend, where, in spite of its being a rough day, he engaged a sailing-boat.

"Bit too rough for that, mister, isn't it?" said a rough-looking sailor who stood by with his hands in his pockets.

"It is rough, my man," said my uncle quietly. "Jump in, Nat."

I felt afraid, but I would not show it, and jumped into the boat, which was pushed off, and my uncle at once proceeded to hoist the lug-sail.

"That's right, Nat," he said encouragingly. "I saw that you felt a bit nervous, for your cheeks were white; but that is the way: bravely meet a terror and it shrinks to half its size. I can remember feeling as timid as could be on entering an open boat and pulling off in a choppy sea; but now I know the danger, and how to meet it, I feel as calm and comfortable as you will after a trip or two. Now then, lay hold of that rope and give a pull when I cry 'haul', and we'll soon have a little sail upon her."

I did as he bade me, and, pulling at the rope, the sail was hoisted part of the way with the effect that it ballooned out in an instant, and the boat went sidewise.

"Mind, uncle," I shouted; "the boat's going over;" and I clung to the other side.

"No, it isn't, Nat," he said coolly. "We could heel over twice as much as that without danger. I'll show you. Take another pull here."

"No, no, uncle," I cried, "I'm satisfied; I believe you."

"Take hold of the rope and haul," he shouted; and I obeyed him, with the boat heeling over so terribly that I felt sure that the water would rush over the side.

He laughed as he made fast the rope, and bade me go to the rudder, for I had taken tight hold of the side of the boat.

There was something so quick and decided about Uncle Dick's way of ordering anyone that I never thought of disobeying him, and I crept to the rudder, while he took his place beside me as the boat danced up and down upon what I, who had never seen the open sea, thought frightful waves.

"Now, Nat," he said, "you see this rope I have here."

"Yes, uncle."

"This is the sheet, as it is called, of the sail, and it runs through that block to make it easier for me to give or take as I want. Now, my boy, here is your first lesson in managing a sailing-boat whether the wind is rough, or as gentle as a breath. Never fasten your sheet, but hold it loose in your hand."

"Why, uncle?" I said, as it seemed to me that it would have saved all the trouble of holding it if it had been tied to the side.

"That's why," he said, as just then the wind increased, so that I clung once more to the side, for the sail was blown so hard that the boat would have gone over enough for the water to rush in if Uncle Dick had not let the rope run swiftly through his hands, making the sail quite loose, and the boat became upright once more.

"I brought you out on a roughish day, Nat," he continued, "so as to give you a good lesson. Look here, Nat,—if an unskilful rider mounted a spirited horse he would most likely be thrown; and if a person who does not know how to manage a sailing-boat goes out in one on a windy day, the chances are that the boat is capsized, fills, and goes to the bottom. Now, if I had not had hold of the sheet then, and eased off the sail—let it go, as a sailor would call it,—we should have been capsized, and then—"

"What then, uncle?" I said, feeling very nervous indeed.

"We should have gone to the bottom, my boy, and been drowned, for I don't think I could have swum ashore from here in my clothes and taken you as well."

"Then—then, hadn't we much better go ashore at once, uncle?" I said, looking at him nervously.

"Yes, Nat, I'll take you ashore at once if you feel afraid; but before doing so I will tell you that I brought you out here to give you a severe lesson in what boat-sailing with me is likely to be; and I tell you besides, Nat, that I know well how to manage a boat. You have had enough of it, I see, and we will go back."

He made a motion to take the tiller out of my hands, for I was steering as he told me to steer, but I pushed his hand back.

"I thought you were frightened, Nat," he said; and then there was a pause, for I wanted to speak, but the words would not come. At last, though, they did.

"I am frightened, uncle, very much frightened; and this going up and down makes me feel sick."

"All right, then, Nat, we'll go back," he said kindly; but he was watching me all the while.

"No," I gasped, "we won't, and—and," I cried, setting my teeth fast, "I won't be sick."

"But it is dangerous, Nat, my boy," he said; "and we are going straight away into rougher water. Let us go back."

"No," I said, "you brought me out to try me, uncle, and I won't be a coward, not if I die."

He turned his head away for a few minutes, and seemed to be looking at the distant shore, and all the while the little boat rushed through the water at a tremendous rate, the sail bellying out and the gunwale down dangerously near the waves as we seemed to cut our way along.

The feeling of sickness that had troubled me before now seemed to go off, as if my determination had had something to do with it; and in spite of the sensation of dread I could not help liking my position, and the way in which we mastered the waves, as it were, going head on to one that seemed as if it would leap into the boat, but only for us to rise up its slope and then plunge down to meet another, while the danger I had feared minute after minute floated away astern.

When my uncle turned his head he said quietly:

"Nat, my boy, it was dangerous work to come out here with me; but, my boy, it is far more dangerous work to go out on that long voyage with me amongst savages, perhaps; to sail on unknown seas, and to meet perils that we can not prepare to encounter. Do you not think, my boy, you have chosen badly? Come, Nat, speak out. I will not call you a coward, for it would only be natural for you to refuse to go. Come, speak to me frankly. What do you say?"

"Was it dangerous to come out to-day, uncle, in this little boat?"

"Decidedly, my boy. You heard what that old boatman said."

"Yes, uncle. Then why did you come?"

He stared at me for a moment or two, and then said quietly to me, leaning forward so that he could look straight into my eyes.

"To give you a lesson, my boy."

"But you knew you could manage the boat, uncle?"

"Yes, my boy. I have had a good deal of experience in boat-sailing on the great American rivers, and on the sea."

"And you would not mind coming out at a time like this, uncle?"

"No, my boy, certainly not. I have been out years ago with the Yarmouth boatmen in very rough seas indeed."

There was a pause for a time, and then he said again, "Well, Nat, will you give up?"

"No, uncle," I said excitedly, "I don't feel half so frightened. I couldn't help it then."

"You'd have been a strange boy, Nat, if you had helped it," he said laughing; "and I am very glad we came. Now, let me tell you that we are in a very small boat in water quite rough enough to be very dangerous; but knowing what I do, possessing, as I do, the knowledge which is power, Nat, there is not the least danger whatever, and you may rest perfectly assured that we will get back quite safe."

"Then I've been terribly cowardly, and afraid for nothing, uncle," I said, as I felt horribly ashamed.

"Yes, my boy, but that is generally the case," he said smiling. "You were afraid because you were ignorant. Once you know well what you are about, you feel ashamed of your old cowardice."

"But it's very shocking to be like that, uncle," I said.

"Not at all, my boy. It is the result of ignorance. The more ignorant and uncultivated people are, the greater cowards they seem. They are superstitious, and believe in ghosts and goblins and imps and fairies; and as for savages in far-off regions, they are sometimes the greatest cowards under the sun."

"I feel very much ashamed of myself, uncle," I said, and the tears stood in my eyes.

He looked at me very kindly as I spoke.

"I wish I was not so ignorant."

"For my part, Nat," he said, "I feel very proud of you, my boy; and let me tell you that you have no cause to be ashamed at all. Now take hold of the sheet here, and give and take as I tell you. Don't be afraid to let it slip through your hands fast if there is a heavy squall. I'll steer. The sea is heavier out in this long reach. Tell me when you'd like to put back."

"I don't want to go back, uncle," I said; "let's go on."

He nodded, and away we dashed, scudding along and riding over the waves, while he showed me how he steered, and why he did this and that; how, by a little pressure on the tiller, he could check our speed, and even turn the little vessel so that we were facing where the wind blew from, and now the sail flapped angrily; but we made no progress at all, only were tossed about on the waves.

I told him that I thought we could only go along with the wind straight behind us, but he showed me how we could sail with the wind on either side, and sometimes with it almost facing us, by what he called tacking, which I found meant that, if the wind came from straight before us, say at a certain point in front, we could get there at last by zigzagging through the water, now half a mile to the left, now half a mile to the right, a common way of progressing which brought us nearer and nearer every time.

"The sea is rougher than I thought," he said, "for I suppose we may call it sea out here, Nat, this being the estuary of the Thames, so I think I'll make that do for to-day."

"Don't go back for me, uncle," I said, as a wave broke over the bow of the boat, splashing us from top to toe.

"I am going back for both our sakes, Nat, for we shall soon be wet through. It is a day for india-rubber coats; but this has been a glorious sail, and a splendid lesson for you, Nat."

"Yes, uncle," I said, "and I feel hardly frightened a bit now."

"THE LITTLE BOAT RUSHED THROUGH THE WATER"

"No, my boy, it has given you far more confidence than you had before. It is live and learn, Nat; you believe more in me and I believe more in you."

He gave me one of his nods as he said this, and then took the rope from my hand.

"Now, Nat, steer us home, my boy; I'll tell you what to do. By and by you and I will have a native boat, perhaps, with a matting sail, to manage, sailing about near the equator."

"But is it rough out there, uncle, amongst the islands?" I said.

"Very, at times, my boy; but with a light, well-built boat like this I should not be afraid to go anywhere. See how like a duck she is in shape, and how easily she rides over the waves. I should like to have one exactly the same build but twice as large, and with the fore part and poop decked over or covered in with canvas; and I don't know but what it would be wise to take out such a boat."

Then he went on giving me explanations about the sail, and which was a lug-sail, what was meant by fore-and-aft rig, and a dozen other things, showing me the while too how to steer.

The result was that, drenched with spray, but all in a glow with excitement, we got safely back, and for my part feeling that I had had a lesson indeed, and ready to put out any time with my uncle in far rougher seas.

Chapter Fifteen.

Saying "Good-Bye!"

Days of practice with my gun followed, and then two or three more afternoons in the mouth of the Thames, my uncle always selecting the roughest days for that purpose; but after a time or two I quite got over my dread of the water, and was ready enough to hold the sheet or take the tiller, picking up very rapidly a knowledge of how to steer so as to ease the boat over the waves that would take us on the beam; learning how to tack and go about: and a dozen other little matters highly necessary for one who attempts the management of a boat.

And then the day of parting came, for Uncle Dick had made all his preparations, which were after all very simple, consisting as they did of two or three changes of clothes, plenty of ammunition, tools for skinning birds and animals, an abundant supply of preserving paste, and some medicines.

It was arranged that we were to go by one of the French steamers from Marseilles, to catch which we had of course to cross France, and then we intended to travel by one of the Peninsular and Oriental steamers to Singapore after crossing the Isthmus of Suez, for this was long before Monsieur de Lesseps had thrust spade into the sand.

"Get the good-byes over quickly, Nat," said Uncle Dick; and this I did as far as my Aunt Sophy was concerned, though she did kiss me and seem more affectionate than usual.

But it was different with poor Uncle Joseph, and had I known how he would take it to heart I'm afraid that I should have thought twice over before making up my mind to go.

"I can hardly believe it, Nat, my boy," he said in a husky voice. "It don't seem natural for you to be going away, my boy, and I don't know how I shall get on without you."

As he spoke he held my hands in his, and though he was pretending to be very cheerful, I could see that he was greatly troubled, and after all his kindness to me I felt as if I was behaving cruelly and ungratefully in the extreme.

"But I'm not going to grieve about you, Nat, my boy," he said quite cheerfully, "and here's your knife."

As he spoke he drew a splendid great jack-knife out of his pocket, hauling out a quantity of white cord to which it was attached, and proceeding to fasten it round my waist.

"There, Nat, my boy," he said, "it was the best I could get you; and the man says it is a splendid bit of stuff. Do you like it, Nat—do you like it?"

"Oh, uncle," I said, "it is too kind of you!"

"Not a bit, my boy, not a bit; and now make good use of it, and grow strong and big, and come back as clever a man as your uncle, and I know you will."

There is a bit of history to that knife, for it was only the day before that he and I and Uncle Dick were together, and Uncle Joe wanted to make me a present.

"There, Nat," said Uncle Joe, drawing his heavy gold watch out of the fob by its watered-silk ribbon with the handsomely chased gold key and large topaz seal at the end, "I shall give you that watch, my boy, for a keepsake. Take it, Nat, and put it in your pocket; keep it out of sight, my boy, till you have gone. I shall tell your aunt afterwards, but she mightn't like it, you know, and it would be a little unpleasant."

"But I don't like to take your watch, uncle," I said, glad as I should have been to have it, for it seemed too bad to take it away.

"Quite right, Nat," said Uncle Dick; "don't take it."

"Not take it!" said Uncle Joe in a disappointed tone.

"No; he does not want a watch, Joe. Where he is going he must make the sun his watch."

"Yes," said Uncle Joe quickly, "but how about the night?"

"Then he'll have to sleep and rest himself for the next day's work."

"And how about getting up in good time?"

"Daylight's the good time for getting up, Joe," said Uncle Dick; "and the sun will tell him the time."

"Ah!" cried Uncle Joe triumphantly, "but the sun does not always shine."

"No, not here," replied Uncle Dick. "You have too much smoke and fog. We are going where he shines almost too much. Here, put away your watch, Joe. It is of no use to a boy who will be journeying through the primeval forest, plunging through thorny undergrowth or bog, or fording rivers and letting his clothes dry on him afterwards."

"But I should have liked him to have the watch," said Uncle Joe, rubbing one side of his nose softly with the case.

"Leave it for him in your will, then, my boy," said Uncle Dick. "He wants nothing that will encumber him, and your watch would only be a nuisance when the water had soaked in. Leave it to him in your will."

"Yes," said Uncle Joseph, "but I should have liked to give him something else to make him always remember me when he's away."

"Why, Uncle Joe," I cried, with a curious choking feeling coming in my throat, "you don't think I could ever forget you?"

"No, my boy, no," he said, shaking my hand very heartily, and then laying the watch down, as if he didn't care to take to it again.

"It's very kind of you, Joe," said Uncle Dick, for he saw how his brother-in-law seemed hurt; "but don't you see, my dear boy, we are going to lead the roughest of rough lives, and what we carry at a time when every extra ounce will be a trouble, must be the barest necessities. I've often had to leave behind valuable things, solely because I could not carry them. Here, I tell you what: you go into the city to-morrow, and buy him one of the best, and biggest, and strongest jack-knives you can find; one of those with a steel loop so that it can hang handily from a lanyard, ready for any purpose from cutting his breakfast to hacking a way through the canes, or skinning a wild beast. You could not give him a better present than that."

"To be sure," cried Uncle Joe, brightening up, "I will. What kind of a handle would you like, Nat?"

"Never mind the handle, Joe; look to the blade. Let it be a thoroughly good bit of stuff, the best you can buy."

"To be sure. Yes; to be sure," cried Uncle Joe; and taking up his watch he lowered it so carelessly into its place that it missed the fob, and ran down the right leg of his trousers into his Wellington boot.

I had to turn boot-jack and drag the boot off before the watch could be recovered, Uncle Dick laughing heartily the while.

And now this was the knife the good, amiable old fellow had got for me, and certainly it was one that would stand me in good stead for any length of time.

"Good-bye, Joe, old fellow," said Uncle Dick, gripping his hand fast. "I'll take care of Nat."

"Yes, yes, you will, won't you?" he cried.

"Indeed I will, Joe, indeed I will; and now once more good-bye, old fellow, I'm off. Till we meet again. Come after me soon, Nat."

Uncle Dick went away so as to leave us together, and no sooner were we alone than Uncle Joe hesitated for a moment, and then hugged me to his breast.

"Good-bye; God bless you, my boy!" he cried. "It's all for the best, and I won't worry about your going; only come back to me as soon as you can, and mind you write."

I can remember that there was a curious dim look about everything just then, and that Uncle Dick was very quiet in the cab; and so he was in the train, speaking to me hardly at all, and afterwards he read to himself nearly all the way to Paris, after which he suddenly seemed to turn merry and bright, and chatted to me in the heartiest way.

Chapter Sixteen.

Out on the Blue Water.

Everything was so new to me that, on embarking at Marseilles, I was never tired of inspecting the large steamer, and trying, with only moderate success, to talk to the French sailors, who, on learning our destination, were very civil; but, after the first day or two, began to joke me about never coming back any more.

It was comical work trying to make out what they meant as they began to talk to me about the terrible wild beasts I should meet, and, above all, about the orang-outangs, which they assured me were eight or nine feet high, and would look upon me, they assured me, as a *bonne bouche*.

The third day out on the beautiful blue water, as some of the passengers had guns out, and were shooting at the sea-birds for amusement merely, a practice that I should have thought very cruel but for the fact that they never once hit anything, Uncle Dick came up to me on the poop deck and clapped me on the shoulder.

"Now, Nat," he said, "there's plenty of room out here for a rifle ball to go humming away as far as it likes without danger to anyone; so get out your rifle and you shall have a practice."

"At the sea-gulls, uncle?" I said.

"No, no; nonsense!" he said; "we don't shoot sea-gulls with a rifle. I shall start you with a target."

"A target, uncle?" I said; "but if you do, we shall leave it all behind in a very short time."

"To be sure we shall," he replied, laughing; "and then we'll have another."

I ran down and got my rifle out of the cabin, feeling half ashamed to go on deck again when I had fastened on my belt full of cartridges; but I got over my modesty, and joined my uncle, whom I found waiting for me with half a dozen black wine bottles, and as many bladders blown out tightly, while the bottles were empty and firmly corked.

"Now, Nat," he said, "here are your targets, and I reckon upon your having half a dozen shots at each before the steamer takes us too far away, unless you manage to sink it sooner."

I looked at my uncle to see if he was laughing at me, but he was quite serious, and, in obedience to his order, I loaded and stood ready.

"Now, look here, my boy," he said; "this will be rather a difficult task, for both your target and you are in motion. So you must aim as well as you can. I should draw trigger just as the bladder is rising."

"But how shall we know if I hit it?"

"You are not very likely to hit it, Nat," he said smiling; "but if you do, the bladder will collapse—the bottle be shivered to fragments, and sink. Now let us see."

It made me feel nervous to see so many people collect about me, one and all eager to witness my skill, and I knew enough French to understand a good many of their remarks. Some said I must be a very skilful shot, others that I could not shoot at all; and one way and another they disconcerted me so that, when my uncle threw the first bladder over the side, and I saw it floating away, I felt so confused that I let it get some distance before I fired.

"Reload," said my uncle; and I did so, and fired again.

"Reload," he said; and, having obeyed him, I waited till the bladder was on the top of a wave, and again fired without result.

"Again," said my uncle; "don't hesitate, and fire sharply."

The bladder was now getting a long way astern and looking very small, so small that I knew I should not hit it, and consequently I felt no surprise that it should go floating away.

"Don't lose time, Nat," my uncle continued, just as if it was quite a matter of course that I should go on missing shot after shot.

So once more I prepared to fire, and as I did so I saw that two of the French passengers had their telescopes fixed upon the object at which, after taking very careful aim, speck as it seemed, I fired.

To my utter astonishment, as the smoke rose I saw no bladder was floating on the waves, a fact of which the lookers-on had already informed me by a round of applause.

"He would not hit them when they were close," cried one passenger. "I said, he would not try. It was un grand shot, messieurs, un coup merveilleux."

I felt scarlet in the face, and grew the more and more ashamed as first one and then another insisted upon shaking hands with me.

"Now, Nat," said my uncle in a low voice, "after that you will lose your character if you do not hit some more."

"Pray, don't send out another, uncle," I whispered.

"Why not, boy? What does it matter if you do miss? Keep on practising, and never mind what people say. Are you ready?"

"Yes, uncle."

"Fire, then, as soon as you get a good view of the bladder."

I waited until it was about forty yards away, and rising slowly to the top of a wave, when, calculating the distance as well as I could, I fired, and the bladder disappeared.

I could not believe it, and expected each moment to see it come back to the surface; but no, there was no bladder visible; and, having reloaded, my uncle sent another afloat, bidding me wait till it was farther away before I fired.

I obeyed him and missed. Fired again and missed, but the third time the bladder collapsed and sank, and my reputation as a marksman was made.

The French passengers would have petted and spoiled me had not my uncle interfered; and when we were once more alone he began to talk of my success.

"You quite exceeded anything I expected, Nat," he said smiling. "How you managed it, my boy, I cannot tell. The first time I set it down to pure accident; but when you repeated it again and again, all I can say, my boy, is that your eyes must be wonderfully good, and your aim and judgment even better. I doubt with all my practice whether I could have been more successful."

"I think it must have been chance, uncle," I said, "for I seemed to have no time to aim, and the vessel heaved up so just then."

"No, my boy," he replied, "it was not chance, but the result in a great measure of your practice with your gun; but you will not always shoot so well as that. When you come to be out with me in the wilds of one of the islands we visit, and have perhaps been tramping miles through rough forest, you will find it hard work to hit the object at which you aim."

"But it will be easier to shoot from the ground than from on shipboard, uncle, will it not?"

"For some things yes, my boy, for others no. But wait a bit, Nat, and we shall see."

The practice was kept up all through our voyage, and I became quite an adept at breaking floating bottles and other objects that were sent over the side, for the bladders soon came to an end; but our voyage was very uneventful. It was always enjoyable, for there was so much that was fresh to see. I never complained about the heat, which was very great, although people were lying about under awnings, while I used to get into the chains, or the rigging below the bowsprit, so as to gaze down into the wonderfully clear water and watch the dolphins and bonita as they darted through the sunlit depths with such ease and grace.

Sometimes I have wished that I could be a fish, able with a sweep or two of my powerful tail to dart myself through the water just as I pleased, or float at any depth, keeping up with the huge steamer as it was driven on.

Then a change would come over me, and I would think to myself: Well, I'm very glad I'm not a fish; for just as I would be watching some lovely mackerel-like fellow with a flashing back of mottled blue and purple, some monster ten times his size would make a dart at him and engulf him in his capacious throat. And as I watched the larger fish seize their food, it seemed to me that once they could get within easy range they seemed to suck their prey into their jaws, drawing it in with the great rush of water they sent through their gills.

It was not tempting at such times and above all when one used to see a thin grey fellow, six or eight feet long, seeming to sneak by the side of the ship, or just astern, where there was an eddy. Every now and then it would turn half over and show the pale under parts as it made a snatch at something that looked good to eat; and after a good many tries the sailors managed to catch one by means of a hook baited with a piece of ham that had been condemned as high.

It was only about six feet long, and when it lay on the wet deck thrashing about with its tail I thought that after all a shark was not such a dangerous-looking creature as I expected, and I said so to my uncle.

"Think not, Nat?" he said.

"Why, no, uncle, I don't think I should be afraid of a shark; I think I could catch such a fellow as that with a rod and line."

"Ah! Nat, some of them run up to fifteen or twenty feet in length," he said; "and they are awfully savage brutes. Such a one as this would be enough to kill a man."

"He don't look like it, uncle," I said. "Why, look here!"

I ran to where the shark lay, and stooping down, seized it with both hands by the thin part just before where the tail forked, meaning to give it a shake and drag the brute along the deck; but just as I got tight hold the creature seemed to send a wave down its spine, and with one flip I was sent staggering across the deck to fall heavily at full length, the crew and passengers around roaring with laughter at my discomfiture.

I was so angry and mortified that I jumped up, opened my great jack-knife, and was rushing at the shark, when my uncle laid his hand upon my arm.

"Don't be foolish, Nat, but take your lesson like a man. You will not despise the strength of a shark for the future."

"Why, it was like touching a great steel spring, uncle," I said.

"If anything I should say that the backbone of a shark has more power in it when set in motion than a steel spring, Nat," he said. "There, now, our friend is helpless, and we can examine him in peace."

For, after thrashing the deck with a series of tremendous blows with his tail, the shark had his quietus given to him with a few blows of a hatchet, and as he lay upon the deck my uncle pointed out to me the peculiarity of the monster's structure, and after we had examined his nasty sharp triangular teeth in the apparently awkwardly placed mouth, I was shown how it was that a shark had such wonderful power of propelling itself through the water, for in place of having an ordinary fin-like tail, made up of so many bones with a membrane between, the shark's spine is continued right along to the extremity of the upper curve of its propeller, the other curve being comparatively small.

The flying-fish in the Red Sea have been described too often for it to be necessary for me to say anything about the beauty of these fishy swallows, but we saw hundreds of them dart out of the sea, skim along for a distance, and then drop in again. Then there were glimpses had in the deep clear blue—for that was the colour I found the Red Sea—of fishes with scales of orange, vermilion, and gold, bright as the gorgeous sunsets that dyed sea and sky of such wondrous hues evening after evening before darkness fell all at once, and the great stars, brighter, bigger, and clearer than I had ever seen them before, turned the heavens into a vast ocean of gems.

Day and night seemed to me to follow one another with wonderful rapidity, till one morning, as the steamer was panting and throbbing on its way, my uncle pointed to what looked like a low distant haze far away on our right.

"Do you see those mountains, Nat?" he said.

"Mountains, uncle! Are these mountains?"

"Yes, my boy, in a land that I could find it in my heart to visit, only that is not quite wild enough for our purpose."

"What place is it, then?" I said, gazing eagerly at the faint distant line.

"Sumatra, Nat;" and as he spoke the long-shaped island, so familiar on the maps at school, rose before my eyes, and with it came Java, Celebes, Borneo, and New Guinea, places that were before long to be the objects of our quest.

Chapter Seventeen.

The Malay Kris in strange Lands.

Three days later we were lying in Singapore harbour, and I had one or two runs ashore to have a good look at the town, with its busy port full of all kinds of vessels, from the huge black-sided steamer and trim East Indiaman, to the clumsy high-sterned, mat-sailed, Chinese junk, and long narrow Malay prahu.

I could have stayed there a month staring about me at the varied scenes in the bright sunshine, where hundreds of Chinamen in their blue cotton loose clothes and thick-soled shoes were mingled with dark-looking Hindoostanees, Cingalese, and thick-lipped, flat-nosed, fierce-looking Malays, every man in a gay silk or cotton sarong or kilt, made in plaids of many colours and with the awkward-looking, dangerous kris stuck at the waist.

I say I could have stopped here for a month, enjoying the change, and wondering why the Malays should be so constantly chewing betel-nut and pepper leaves. I learned, too, that there was much to be seen in the island, and that there were tigers in the jungle near the plantations; but my uncle said there was no time to waste, and we must get on.

"We don't want civilisation, Nat, or the works of man; we want to go far away into the wilds."

"But don't you mean to go to Malacca, uncle?" I said. "That is where so many birds come from."

"I did think of going there, Nat; but I want to get to less-frequented spots, and I have found to-day a great prahu that is going right away to the Ké Islands, which will be well on our route to Aru and New Guinea. The Malay captain says he will take us, and tow our boat behind."

"Our boat, uncle?"

"Yes, Nat; while you have been staring about at the heathen I have been busy looking out for a boat, and I have found one that I think will do. Come and see."

I went with him to a creek outside the busiest part of the town, where the principal part of the people seemed to be fishermen, and here, after threading our way amongst dozens of clumsy-looking boats, my uncle showed me one that I should have thought would be the last to suit us.

"Why, you don't admire my choice, Nat!" he said smiling.

"It is such a common-looking thing, and it isn't painted," I replied.

"No, my boy, but it is well varnished with native resin. It is Malay built, very strong, and the mast and sails are well-made, though rough; better still, it will carry us, and a man or two for crew if we like, and give plenty of room for our treasures as well."

"But it is differently rigged to the boats on the Thames, uncle," I said disparagingly.

"Naturally, my boy," he said laughing; "but the sails will require the same management."

"And what an anchor, uncle!" I said. "Why, it is made of bamboo and a stone."

"We can easily buy a small grapnel and some cord, Nat," he said smiling; "and when you have found out how our boat will sail, you will think better of it, I am sure."

On the following day but one we were on board the prahu surrounded by fierce-looking Malays, every man being armed with his kris, and looking as bloodthirsty a lot as I thought I had ever seen. Our boat was towing behind as the men used long oars to get us out of the port, and then the great matting sails were hoisted, and we began to go swiftly through the surging sea.

"There, Nat," said my uncle gleefully, "good-bye to civilisation, for we are fairly off. How do you feel now?"

"I was thinking, uncle, suppose that, now they have us safely on board, and away from all help—"

"They were suddenly to rise up, draw their knives, which are said to be poisoned, Nat."

"Yes, uncle, and stab us."

"Rob us," he said laughing.

"And throw us overboard, uncle."

"Ah! Nat; suppose they did. What would Uncle Joe say?"

"It would kill him, uncle," I said, with tears in my eyes.

"And Aunt Sophy?" he said.

"Well, I don't know about Aunt Sophy," I replied; "but I hope she would be very sorry."

"Ah! well, you needn't be nervous, Nat, for I don't think the Malays are such bloodthirsty fellows as people say; and our captain here, in spite of his fierce aspect, is very gentlemanly and pleasant."

I could not help looking at our captain, whom Uncle Dick called gentlemanly, for to my eyes he seemed to be a fierce savage, with his scarlet kerchief bound round his head, beneath which his dark eyes seemed to flash angrily.

"Shall you keep your loaded gun with you always, uncle, while we are with these people?" I said.

"No, my boy, certainly not," he replied; "and you may take it for granted, Nat, that even the most savage people are as a rule inoffensive and ready to welcome a white man as a friend, except where they have been ill-treated by their civilised visitors. As for the Malays, I have met several travellers who have been amongst then and they all join in saying that they are a quiet superior race of people, with whom you may be perfectly safe, and who are pleased to be looked upon as friends."

"But I thought, uncle," I said, "that they were very dangerous, and that those krises they wore were poisoned?"

"Travellers' tales, my boy. The kris is the Malay's national weapon that everyone wears. Why, Nat, it is not so very long since every English gentleman wore a sword, and we were not considered savages."

We had rather a long and tiresome voyage, for the prahu, though light and large, did not prove a very good sea-boat. When the wind was fair, and its great sail spread, we went along swiftly, and we were seldom for long out of sight of land, coasting, as we did, by the many islands scattered about the equator; but it was through seas intersected by endless cross currents and eddies, which seemed to seize upon the great prahu when the wind died down, and often took us so far out of our course one day, that sometimes it took the whole of the next to recover what we had lost.

So far, in spite of the novelty of many of the sights we had seen, I had met with nothing like that which I had pictured in my boyish dreams of wondrous foreign lands. The sea was very lovely, so was the sky at sunrise and sunset; but where we had touched upon land it was at ports swarming with shipping and sailors of all nations. I wanted to see beautiful islands, great forests and mountains, the home of strange beasts and birds of rare plumage, and to such a place as this it seemed as if we should never come.

I said so to Uncle Dick one day as we sat together during a calm, trying to catch a few fish to make a change in our food.

"Wait a bit, Nat," he said smiling.

"Yes, uncle, but shall we see wonderful lands such as I should like?"

"You'll see no wonderful lands with giants' castles, and dwarfs and fairies in, Nat," he replied smiling; "but before long I have no doubt that I shall be able to show you beauties of nature glorious enough to satisfy the most greedy imagination."

"Oh! of course I did not expect to see any of the nonsense we read of in books, uncle," I said; "only we have been away from home now three months, and we have not got a single specimen as yet, and I want to begin."

"Patience, my boy, patience," he said. "I am coming all this distance so as to get to quite new ground. So far we have not landed on a tropic island, for I shall not count civilised Singapore; but very soon we shall take to our own boat and coast along here and there, landing where we please, and you shall have nature's wonders and natural history to your heart's content. Look there," he said softly; "there is a beginning for you. Do you see that?"

He pointed down into the gloriously blue clear water, illumined by the sunshine, which made it flash wherever there was the slightest ripple.

"Yes, I can see some lovely little fish, uncle," I said. "Why, they are all striped like perch. There's one all blue and scarlet. Oh! I wish I could catch him."

"No, no; farther down there, where those pink weeds are waving on that deep-brown mass of coral. What's that?"

"Why, it's a great eel, uncle. What a length! and how thin! How it is winding in and out amongst the weed! Is it an eel?"

"No, Nat; it is a snake—a sea-snake; and there is another, and another. They are very dangerous too."

"Are they poisonous, then?" I said.

"Extremely. Their bite is often fatal, Nat, so beware of them if ever you see one caught."

We had a fine opportunity for watching the movements of these snakes, for several came into sight, passing through the water in that peculiar waving manner that is seen in an eel; but a breeze springing up soon after, the sail filled out, and once more we glided rapidly over the beautiful sea.

I call it beautiful sea, for those who have merely looked upon the ocean from our own coasts have no conception of the grandeur of the tropic seas amongst the many islands of the Eastern Archipelago, where the water is as bright as lapis lazuli, as clear as crystal, and the powerful sun lights up its depths, and displays beauties of submarine growth at which the eye never tires of gazing.

It used to worry me sometimes that we had not longer calms to enable me to get down into the little boat and lie flat, with my face as close to the water as I could place it, looking into what was to me a new world, full of gorgeous corals and other Zoophytes, some motionless, others all in action. Scarlet, purple, blue, yellow, crimson, and rich ruddy brown, they looked to me like flowers amongst the singular waving weeds that rose from the rocks below.

Here fishes as brilliant in colours, but more curious in shape, than the pets of our glass globes at home, sailed in and out, chasing the insects or one another, their scales flashing every now and then as they turned on one side or dashed up towards the surface and leaped clean out of the water.

In some places the sand was of a beautiful creamy white and as pure as could be, Uncle Dick saying that it was formed out of the corals which were being constantly pounded up by the waves.

But whenever the breeze rose I had to be quickly on board again, and on we sailed till, after a long dreamy voyage, we came one morning in sight of some mountains; and as we drew nearer I could see that the rocks rose straight up from the sea, which, calm as it was, sent up columns of spray where the waves broke upon the solid stone.

"There, Nat," said my uncle, "that is our present destination."

"What! that rocky place, uncle?" I said, with a tone of disappointment in my voice.

"Yes, my quick young judge," he said laughing. "Wait till we get closer in," he continued, using his glass; "or no, you can see now; look, Nat."

He handed me the glass, and as I looked through, my heart seemed to give a great throb, for the lovely picture I gazed upon seemed to more than realise my dreams.

For what at a distance looked to be a sunlit rocky shore, proved through the glass to be a land with lovely shaped trees growing to the edges of the cliffs, which were covered with wonderful shrubs and creepers. Even the rocks looked to be of beautiful colours, and every here and there I could see lovely little bays and nooks, edged with glistening white sand, upon which the crystal water played, sparkling like diamonds and sapphires in the sun.

"Oh, uncle!" I cried.

"Well, Nat, will that place do for a beginning?"

"How soon can we get ashore?" I cried excitedly in answer.

"In a couple of hours, now, Nat; but I said will this place do?"

"Oh, uncle!" I cried, "it was worth coming all the way to see. I could wander about there for months. Shall I get the guns out of the cases?"

"Gently, gently," he said laughing; "let's get into harbour first."

Chapter Eighteen.

I find the Black Ways Strange.

We were not very long in getting to the harbour, a snug landlocked cove where the great prahu in which we had come could lie well protected from the rollers. Our passage in was made easy, as the great sails were lowered by the men in a couple of canoes, who paddled out, shouting and singing, and splashing the water; and then, after ropes had been made fast to their sterns, they paddled away again, drawing us steadily inshore.

I began to wonder directly whether these would be anything like the savages who came to Robinson Crusoe's island; but a moment's reflection told me that Juan Fernandez was supposed to be his island, and that was on the other side of the world.

"Well, Nat, what do you think of our visitors?" said my uncle, as I leaned over the prow of our vessel and watched the men in the canoe.

"I was thinking, uncle, that it can't cost them much for clothes," I said, laughing.

"No, Nat," he replied, joining in my mirth; "but do you see how different they are to our sailors here?"

"Yes, they are blacker, uncle, and have different shaped noses, and their hair curls instead of being straight."

"Good!" he exclaimed; "that's the way to become a naturalist. Observe everything. You are quite right; we are going to leave one race of men now, Nat, the Malays, to travel amongst the Papuans, a people who are wonderfully different in every way."

I felt a little nervous at first on going ashore, for we were surrounded by quite a crowd of fierce-looking blacks, all chattering, gesticulating, and pressing on us in their eagerness to get close up, but I soon found that it was only excitement and delight at seeing us among them, and that they wanted to barter ornaments and shells, for tobacco and sugar, or knives.

They were just like children, and though, had they been so disposed, they could have overpowered us and taken possession of everything we possessed in an instant, nothing seemed farther from their thoughts.

The captain of the prahu came ashore with us, and we explained to one of the chief men that we wanted to have a hut on shore and stay with them for a time, and his countenance expanded into a broad grin of pleasure, one which seemed to increase as we both shook hands with him, and uncle gave him a handful of tobacco, and I a small common one-bladed knife.

He looked at both in turn, and then seemed puzzled as to what he ought to give us in exchange, while, when he was made to understand that they were presents and nothing was wanted back, he attached himself to us, and very soon we found ourselves the possessors of a very dark, little well-thatched hut, with no windows, and nothing to close the door, but it answered our purpose in giving us shelter, and to it the chief willingly helped with a couple of dozen of his men, in getting our chests, boxes, and stores.

The next thing was to find a place for our boat, which was towed ashore behind a canoe; and on the chief understanding the want, he very soon pointed out to us a shady nook where it could be run ashore and beached in safety, away from the waves, he helping himself to make the rope fast to a large cocoa-nut tree.

This done, the chief walked, or rather strutted, round our boat, and looked under it, over it, and about it in all directions, making grimaces expressive of his disgust, and ending by kicking its sides and making derisive gestures, to show that he thought it a very poor boat indeed.

AT BREAKFAST WITH A NEW FRIEND

The prahu was going away the next day, so a busy scene of trading went on till night, when the captain sought us out, and in his broken English enquired very earnestly whether we had landed everything, including sundry stores which my Uncle Dick had purchased of the Scotch merchants at Singapore, they being able to tell him what was most likely to find favour amongst the savages with whom we should have to deal.

In answer to a question, the Malay captain assured us that we might feel quite safe amongst the Ké islanders, and also with those in the Aru and neighbouring isles; but he said that he would not trust the men of New Guinea, unless it was in a place where they had never seen white men before.

He promised to be on the look-out for us as he was trading to and fro during the next year or two, for my uncle assured him that we should be about that time among the islands, and with the promise to meet us here in a year's time if we did not meet before, and to come from Singapore provided with plenty of powder and shot for our use, and ready to take back any cases of specimens we might have ready, he parted from us with the grave courtesy of a Mohammedan gentleman. The next time we saw him was in the morning, as he waved his scarlet headkerchief to us from the deck of his prahu, which was floating away on the current, there being barely wind enough to fill the sails.

Some very beautifully shaped canoes filled with the naked black islanders paddled out for some little distance beside the prahu, singing and shouting, and splashing the sea into foam with their paddles, making it sparkle like diamonds in the glorious morning sunshine.

But after a while my uncle and I, in spite of the delightful sensation of being ashore in such a glorious climate, began to feel so very human that we set to and made a fire; then I fetched water from a spring in the rock that ran over in a cascade towards the sea, and after rigging up three pieces of bamboo, gypsy fashion, the kettle soon began to sing, the coffee was measured out, a box dragged outside the hut door to act as a table, and just as the canoes approached the shore we began upon biscuit, a couple of toasted red herrings, of which we got a couple of boxes at Singapore, and what seemed to me the most delicious cup of coffee I had ever tasted.

"There," uncle said to me at last, "we are regularly launched now, Nat. Those Malays were not savages, but people of law and order. Now we are left alone in the wilds indeed."

"Yes, uncle, and here come the black fellows," I said with my mouth full of biscuit.

In fact, as soon as they had run their beautiful canoes up on to the sands they were starting in a body to come and look at us; but there was a loud shout and some gesticulating, and we saw one tall savage flourishing a spear, when they all went off in other directions, while the savage with the spear came sidling towards us in a slow, awkward way, keeping his face turned in the opposite direction, but gradually coming nearer.

"I hope he does not mean to throw that spear at us, Nat," said my uncle. "Where did the others go?"

"They seemed to go into the woods there," I said.

"Humph! And they might get round to the back of our hut," said my uncle, looking rather uneasy. "But we will not show any distrust. Have you recognised that chief this morning?"

"I think this is he, uncle," I said, "but I can't see his face."

"Well, we will soon see," said my uncle, as we went on with our breakfast, and kept on watching the black till he came about fifty yards away, apparently searching for something amongst the shrubs and plants with the handle of his spear.

"Shout at him, Nat," said my uncle.

"Eh?"

The savage must have seen us from the first, but he looked up, then down, then turned himself and *gazed* in every direction but that in which we were; and I shouted again, but still he would not look our way.

"He is shamming, Nat, like a very bashful boy," said Uncle Dick. "He wants us to ask him to breakfast. Hallo! Get my rifle, Nat; I can see a lot of heads in the trees there. No, sit still; they are only boys."

The savage evidently saw them at the same moment, for he made a rush towards the dark figures that were stealing from tree trunk to tree trunk, and we saw them dash away directly out of sight, after which the savage came sidling in our direction again.

"Hi!" I shouted, as the childish pantomime went on, and the savage stared in all directions as if wonder-stricken at a strange noise coming he knew not whence, and ending by kneeling down and laying his ear to the ground.

"Hi!" I shouted again; but it was of no use, he could not possibly see either us, our chest, our fire, or the hut, but kept sidling along, staring in every direction but the right.

"Go and fetch him, Nat, while I toast another bloater. We'll give him some breakfast, and it will make him friendly."

I got up and went off, wondering what Uncle Joe and Aunt Sophia would have said to see me going to speak to that great spear-armed savage, and for a moment I wondered what would happen if he attacked me.

"Uncle Dick would shoot him dead with his rifle," I said to myself by way of comfort, and I walked boldly on.

Still he would not see me, but kept sidling on till I got close up to him and gave him a smart spank on his naked shoulder.

In an instant he had spun round, leaped to a couple of yards away, and poised his spear as if to hurl. Then, acting his astonishment with great cleverness, his angry countenance broke up into a broad smile, he placed his spear into the hollow of his left arm, and stepped forward to shake hands, chattering away eagerly, though I could not understand a word.

"Come and have some breakfast," I said, and he chattered again. "Come and have some breakfast," I shouted; and then to myself: "How stupid I am! He can't understand."

So I took him by the arm, and pointed towards where my uncle was watching us with his rifle leaning against the table; and I knew that he must have been looking after my safety.

The savage stared here and there and everywhere, but he could not see my uncle till I dragged him half-way to the fire and pointed again, when he uttered a shout of surprise, as much as to say, "Well, who would have thought of seeing him there!"

He then walked up with me, grinning pleasantly, shook hands, and looked astonished as we pointed to the ground for him to sit down.

He seated himself though, at last, after sticking his spear in the sandy earth, and then watched us both as I spread some salt butter out of a pot on a piece of biscuit, and then handed him over some hot coffee, which I made very sweet, while my uncle, after shaking hands, had gone on toasting the bloater upon a stick of bamboo.

"Don't give him the coffee too hot, Nat," said my uncle. "There, that's done, I think."

"I could drink it myself, uncle," I replied, and we placed the food before our guest, pointing to it, but he kept on shaking his head, and put his hands behind him.

"Perhaps he thinks it is not good, uncle," I said, after we had several times partaken of our own to set him an example.

"Or that it is poisoned," said my uncle. "Taste it to show him it is good, Nat."

I took up the tin mug of coffee and tasted it twice, then broke a piece off the biscuit, put a little of the herring upon it, and ate it, the savage watching me closely the while.

Then his face broke into a broad smile once more, and he made believe to have suddenly comprehended that the food was meant for him, for, taking a good draught of the coffee, he leaped up, tossing his arms on high, and danced round us, shouting with delight for quite a minute before he reseated himself, and ate his breakfast, a good hearty one too, chattering all the while, and not troubling himself in the least that we could not understand a word.

"I'm sorry about one thing, Nat," my uncle said. "He would not eat that food because he was afraid that it was poisoned."

"Well, wasn't that right of him, uncle?" I said, "as we are quite strangers."

"Yes, my boy; but it teaches us that he knows what poison is, and that these savages may make use of it at times."

Our black guest looked at us intently whenever we spoke, and seemed to be trying to comprehend what we said, but began to laugh again as soon as he saw that we observed him, ending by jumping up and shaking hands again, and pointing to the rifle, seizing his spear, holding it up to his shoulder, and then making a very good imitation of the report with his mouth.

He then pointed to a bird flying at a distance, and laughed and nodded his head several times.

"That relieves us of a little difficulty, Nat," said my uncle. "The Malay captain seems to have told him why we have come; but there is another difficulty still, and that is about leaving our stores."

"It seems to me, uncle, that what we ought to do first is to learn the language."

"Yes, Nat, and we must. It would be more useful to us now than your Latin and French."

"Yes, uncle, and we shall have to learn it without books. Hallo! what's he going to do?"

Chapter Nineteen.

Our Very Black friend.

The reason for my exclamation was that our visitor suddenly began to drag the chest we had used for a table into the hut, and after this he carried in the kettle, and two or three other things that we had had out, the rifle included; after which, as we watched him, he patted us both on the chest to call our attention to what he was going to do, and, picking up his spear, he thrust it down into the ground close up to the doorway, its point standing up above the thatch.

"What does he mean by that, uncle?" I asked.

"I think I know, Nat," he replied; "but wait a minute. This fellow is no fool."

For after calling our attention to what he was going to do, he ran off into the jungle; and as we watched the spot where he had disappeared, he peered at us from behind a tree trunk, then from another, and another, popping up in all sorts of out-of-the-way places where we least expected to see him, and then suddenly creeping out on hands and knees from among some bushes, raising his head every now and then as if looking to see if he was watched, and again crawling on towards the hut.

Just in the midst of the pantomime he became aware of what we had seen before, about a dozen boys coming cautiously through the forest, when, jumping up in a rage, he dashed at them, and they disappeared, he after them, to come back panting and continue his performance, hiding and creeping out again, and going nearer and nearer to the hut.

"I say, uncle, isn't this all nonsense?" I said.

"No, my boy. He can't talk to us to make us understand, so he is trying to show us something by signs."

As he spoke the black crept on and on, rising to his knees and peering round to see if he was watched, and at last, having arrived within half a dozen yards of the hut, he rose and made a dash for the door, making believe to see the spear, stuck up there like a sentry, for the first time, and then stopping short, uttering a howl of dread, and shivering all over as he crept crouching away, holding out his hands behind him as if to ward off a blow.

Then suddenly springing up, he ceased acting, looked at us, and laughed.

"Why, what does he mean, uncle?" I said.

"I know," said Uncle Dick quickly; and pointing to some of the savages down on the shore he went up to the door of the hut, and made as if to go in, but stopped and pointed again to the savages at a distance.

The black nodded and laughed, danced about with delight, and then pointing to the savages himself he ran to the door, and came shivering and crouching away once more as if too much alarmed to go in.

"It is all right, Nat," said my uncle; "he is evidently a chief, and he means that no one will dare go into the hut while his spear is stuck there. We have made a friend."

All this time the savage was looking sharply from one to the other, as if to make sure that we comprehended him; and then, seeing that we did, he made signs for us to follow him, talking excitedly the while.

We walked with him to a grove of cocoa-nut trees, passing a number of the people as we passed through, but no one attempted to follow us; and after about a quarter of an hour's walk he led us to a roughly-built palm-thatched shed, where we could hear the sounds of chopping and hammering, and on entering we found, to our surprise, that the shed was far larger than we had expected, and that in it were four men busy at work making a boat similar to one that lay there evidently but lately built.

Our new friend pointed to the finished boat, and we looked it over at once to find that it was beautifully made and perfect, with its oars, anchor, mast, and sail, and finished with such neatness that I began to wonder what tools the man must use, while my wonder was increased upon my uncle pointing out to me the fact that there was not a single nail in the whole boat, which was entirely put together by means of wooden pegs, and fastened with thin bands of rattan cane.

The black noticed our appreciation of the boat, and had we felt any doubt before of his power, it was silenced at once, for, giving his orders, the boat was half carried, half run down over the soft sand out into the pure blue water, when he signed to us to enter, leaped in afterwards, and we were run right out by the men.

The breeze was light, but strong enough for the boat, and the sail being hoisted, away we went upon the long rollers, rising and falling so easily that I could not help thinking how clever these islanders must be.

"Why, Nat," said my uncle, "we ought to have waited until we came here, for this boat is worth a dozen of the one I bought. It is so light and buoyant, and suited to the seas we are on. It will hold quite as much as our own, and be stronger and far easier to manage."

All this time the black was watching him intently, striving to understand his words, but shaking his head in a disappointed manner from time to time.

We had a fair trial of the boat, and became each minute better satisfied. Sometimes my uncle steered, sometimes I, and always to find that the light vessel went over the roughest rollers like a cork, and without shipping a drop of water.

My uncle managed as well that we should run along the coast, so as to see something of the country, with the result that I grew quite excited by my desire to land and see some of the wonders of the place; and at last the boat's head was put about and we ran back.

Now, however, the black chief took the rudder in hand, and ran us ashore on the top of a great roller, which left us high and dry upon the soft white sand, our companion jumping out and pulling us beyond reach of the next wave with the greatest ease.

The spot he had chosen was close to the boat we had brought from Singapore, up to which our companion had walked, kicking it with a look of contempt; and I must say that I could not help feeling ashamed of the rough, common, clumsy-looking thing, after our ride in that from which we had just disembarked.

Just then our companion shouted, and half a dozen blacks came racing and clattering to our side, taking charge of the boat, while we walked up to the hut, not without some misgivings as to the state of its contents.

It was quite evident, though, that no one had been near it, and our companion, with a look of consequence that was very comical in a naked savage, took up his spear and stood aside while we entered and obtained our guns and ammunition.

At this, however, he made signs indicative of his displeasure, shaking his head and pointing to the boat and then to our stores.

"I shall have to trade for the boat," said my uncle; "and to tell the truth, Nat, I don't feel at all unwilling."

So setting to, there was a long pantomime scene, in which my uncle offered the black chief our heavy, clumsy boat for the new, light, canoe-like vessel we had tried.

The offer was refused with a show of disgust, but not so great as I expected; for, as I afterwards found, there were iron and copper fittings in our boat that were looked upon by the islanders as a great acquisition. So then my uncle proceeded to lay in the boat a bit at a time the additions that he would give in exchange, his offerings consisting of showy cloth, brass wire, and axes, till the chief was satisfied and the boat was our own, after which he made signs for us to get our guns, and we started inland for our first shooting expedition, I with my pulses throbbing, and every nerve in a state of tension as I wondered what would be the first gloriously feathered trophy that I should secure.

Chapter Twenty.

Amongst Nature's Treasures.

It was a land of marvels to me, as now for the first time I saw in all their beauty the tall cocoa-nut trees and other palms, like vast ferns, towering up on their column-like stems and spreading their enormous feathery leaves so gracefully towards the earth. Then after a few steps we came upon bananas, with their long ragged leaves and mighty clusters of curiously-shaped fruit, with hundreds of other trees, such as I had never even heard of before, and among which, every now and then, we heard the sharp harsh cry of some bird of the parrot tribe.

These cries set us both on the *qui vive*, but though we walked for some little distance we did not obtain a shot nor see a single bird, but we found that there was plenty of forest land full of vast trees with here and there patches of beautiful undergrowth, so that, as Uncle Dick said, it was only a matter of time.

"I feel as excited over it, Nat, as you seem to be, my boy; for it is intensely interesting always to me, this search for unknown birds. What's that?"

We stopped to listen, but could not make out what the noise was that kept falling upon our ears. It was a kind of soft pleasant croak, ending in a kind of deep hum, sometimes coming from one direction, sometimes from another.

"It can't be a bull-frog, Nat, for we are not near any marsh or water as far as I can see."

"Are there tree bull-frogs, uncle?" I said, "because that noise comes out of one of the tall trees. Oh! look, there's a big bird," I cried, and raising my gun I took quick aim and fired, when far above us there was a heavy flapping noise of wings amongst the trees, and then silence.

"A miss, or a hit too weak to bring him down, Nat," said my uncle smiling. "Better luck next time. Load again, my boy."

I hastily reloaded, and we went on again, rising higher and higher over very difficult ground; and then we entered another grove of high trees and heard the same soft croaking noise as before.

"Pigeons, Nat, without doubt," said my uncle. "No other birds, I think, would have made that curious flapping of the wings."

"But that bird I shot at was too big for a pigeon, uncle," I replied.

"You'll find pigeons out here, Nat, four times as big as you have seen at home. Look, my boy, on the top branches of that great tree there is quite a cluster of them. Steal up softly; you round that way, I will go this. We shall one of us get a shot, I dare say."

I made a little circuit in obedience to my uncle's orders, and we crept up softly towards where a huge tree rose like a pillar to a tremendous height before sending out a branch, and there, just dimly seen in the soft twilight beneath the canopy of leaves, were several huge birds, which took flight with a great rattle of wings as we came near.

There was the quick report of my uncle's gun, closely followed by mine, and one bird fell heavily to the ground, the others disappearing from view beyond the trees; but just then our companion uttered a shout and dashed on ahead, to return in a few minutes with a second bird which his quick eyes had detected as wounded, and he had seen it drop into a tree some distance off, and then fall, to lead him a long chase before he secured it and brought it back.

Meanwhile we were both kneeling beside the first, which had fallen in a patch of open ground where the sun came down, and I shall never forget the delight with which I gazed at its wonderfully beautiful plumage.

"A pigeon, you see, Nat," said my uncle; "and a fine one too."

"Is that a pigeon, uncle?" I said wonderingly.

"To be sure it is, my boy, and —"

Crack!

"That was a thrush, if I am not mistaken."

I ran and picked up a bird that he shot in the middle of his speech, as it flew over some low bushes, and brought it back in triumph.

"No, uncle, it is not a thrush," I cried. "It is a lovely blue and grey bird."

"What is it, then, Nat?" he said, smiling. "Have you forgotten all I told you about the representatives of our home birds being bright in colour?"

"But I did not think a thrush could be all of a lovely pale blue, uncle," I said; "and I never saw such a pigeon as that. Why, its back and wings are almost as green as those cuckoos—the trogons—and what beautiful feet and eyes! Oh! uncle," I said, "I am glad we came."

He smiled as he knelt down and carefully smoothed the feathers of the great pigeon, thrusting a little cotton-wool into its beak to soak up any moisture that might escape and damage the feathers.

"We shall, I believe, find plenty of magnificent pigeons out here, Nat," he said, as I eagerly watched his acts, so as to know what to do next time.

"But I never expected to find pigeons, uncle, with gold and violet reflections on their feathers."

"Why not, Nat," he replied laughing, "when in dull, foggy old England, where there is so little sunshine, the pigeons and doves have beautiful iris-like reflections on their necks and breasts? Now for the thrush. There, Nat, that is a beauty. I should have felt that I had done a good day's work if I had only secured that dainty prize with its delicately harmonious coat of soft grey and blue."

"And it is a thrush, uncle?"

"Certainly. Look at the beak. This is one of the Pittas or ground-thrushes, Nat, of which there are a good many out in these islands. Some of them are, I believe, much more brightly coloured than this; but bright plumage is not all we want, my boy; it is new specimens, Nat. We must be discoverers as well as collectors."

By this time the lovely thrush was hung with the two pigeons carefully by the beaks to a long bamboo, and after we had explained to our black companion, by means of a little dumb-show, that he must carry the bamboo carefully, a task which, after a few skips and bounds to show his delight, he undertook to perform. We went on again, trusting to him to find the way back through the wilderness of great tree trunks, some of which rose, without a branch, to a vast height above our heads, but only to make up for it afterwards, for the branches then clustered so thickly that all the sunshine was shut out, and we walked in the deep shadow, save where here and there we found an opening which looked quite dazzling by contrast. Here it was that we found flowers growing, and saw traces enough of insects to make us determine to bring collecting-boxes another time, on purpose to obtain the glorious beetles and butterflies that we saw here and there.

"Look, uncle," I cried; "there's another, and another. Oh, if I had my butterfly-net!"

For I kept seeing beetles of dazzling lustre, and butterflies marked with such brilliant colours, that I was ready to throw down my gun and rush off in chase.

"Yes, this is a better collecting ground than Clapham Common, Nat," said my uncle. "We ought to have plenty of pinning out to do to-morrow night. To-day I hope to be busy enough making skins. Hist! Look at the black."

I had just time to save the bamboo with the birds from being thrown down upon the ground by our companion, who went upon hands and knees, and crawled forward a short distance to the shelter of some bushes at the edge of a bright opening, where the sun poured down like showers of silver light.

"He has found something," I whispered.

"Then you run forward, Nat, and see. Be cool, and take a good quick aim. I'll mind the birds."

He took the bamboo, and I ran forward to where the black was waving me on; but went more cautiously as I drew nearer, and a few moments later I was crouching in the shadow of the bushes at the edge of the opening, watching the objects at which the black was pointing.

I knew by means of my ears what birds he had found, before I caught sight of them, for every now and then a harsh shrill scream was uttered, and before long I could see across the opening quite a little flock of beautiful scarlet lories busily feeding on the clustering fruit of a tall forest tree, which, being close to the sunny opening, was covered with leaves and twigs, from the top to the very ground.

I was so utterly taken up by the beauty of the sight that I forgot all about my gun, but knelt there watching the lovely little long-tailed birds, climbing by the help of their beaks, in and out amongst the branches, sometimes hanging by their strong curved bills, sometimes head downwards by one or both legs, and always busily hunting for food.

I had seen stuffed specimens before, but they seemed so poor and common-looking beside the velvety softness and brilliant colouring of these smooth-feathered, lively, rounded birds, and I kept on enjoying the sight to so great an extent that I am sure the flock would have escaped had not my black companion shook my arm violently, and pointed to my gun, when, recalling the object of my journey, I raised it, took careful aim, and fired.

There was a shrill cry from the birds, and the flock took flight, but not until I had managed to get another shot, the result being that I secured three very beautiful specimens to take back to my uncle, showing them to him with a glow of pride.

"I want to be of some use, uncle," I said, for I had been afraid that he would think I could not shoot.

"Use, Nat! why, you shot one of those pigeons this morning."

"Did I, uncle?" I said.

"To be sure, my boy. At all events I did not, so it must have been you."

He was delighted with the three specimens I had secured, and saying that these would be as many as he could comfortably preserve that day, we went on exploring more than collecting, in what was to me quite a fairyland of wonders.

Perhaps long confinement on shipboard had something to do with it; but all the same, every place we came to had its beauties of some kind or another. Now it was a noisy stream leaping from the rocks in a feathery cascade; at another time, a grove full of curious orchids. Every now and then some lovely butterfly would start from flower or damp spot in the openings, but it was of no use to chase them then, my uncle said, for we had no means of preserving them.

"Let's collect, Nat," he said, "and make a splendid set of cases of birds and insects; but let's have no wanton destruction. I hate to see birds shot except for a purpose."

"We shall have to look out, uncle," I said, laughing, "for it is hard enough work to walk on this ground; I don't know how we shall run."

In fact, when we got back to our hut, after shooting a couple more pigeons, our shoes were showing already how sharp the rocks were that formed a great part of the ground over which we tramped.

I almost wondered at my uncle shooting two more pigeons, as we had already a couple, but I found out the reason when we reached home, as we called it, to find that everything was in its place; no one apparently having entered the hut, from which our black guide now took his spear, and without another word hurried away.

Chapter Twenty One.

Feeding in the Wilderness.

"I hope Master Ebony is not offended," said my uncle, wiping his face. "Perhaps it is only his way. Now, Nat, get some sticks and make a good fire, while I lay the cloth and cook. That's the evil of being alone, we have to prepare and cook for ourselves; but we'll have a treat to-day."

I soon had a fire burning, and then watched Uncle Dick as with sharp knife and clever fingers he quickly skinned the four pigeons, placing their skins where they would not dry, and then busying himself over the birds.

"Won't you have some dinner first, uncle?" I said, for I was terribly hungry.

"First? No, my boy, not till we have cooked it. You don't want to eat your birds raw, do you?"

"What! are you going to eat those—those—"

"Pigeons?" he said, as I hesitated. "To be sure, Nat; why not? Do you suppose that because birds have bright feathers they are not good to eat?"

"Well, no, uncle," I replied, as I thought of pheasants, and that at one time people used to eat the peacock; "but these birds have green feathers." It was a very stupid remark, but it seemed the only thing I could then say.

"Ah! they'll be none the worse for that, my boy," he said, laughing, as he removed the birds' crops on to a great leaf which I held for him. "We'll examine those after dinner, Nat, so as to see on what the birds feed. If I'm not mistaken they eat the large fruit of the nutmeg for one thing."

"Then they ought to taste of spice, uncle," I said, laughing.

"Wait a bit, Nat, and you'll see how good these fruit-pigeons are. Now, cut with that great jack-knife of yours a good sharp pair of bamboo skewers, or spits, and we'll soon have the rascals roasting. We can't eat the insects, but we can the birds, and a great treat they will be after so much shipboard food."

"That they will be, uncle," I said, as the pigeons, each quite double or three times the size of one of our home birds, were stuck before the fire, and began to send out a nice appetising smell.

"Then you won't be too prejudiced to eat them?" he said, laughing.

"Oh, uncle!" I said, "I'm so hungry I could eat anything now."

"Well done, Nat. Well, my boy, as long as we get plenty of specimens to skin we sha'n't starve. Turn that skewer round. That's right; stick it tightly into the sand, and now let's have on a little more wood. Pick up those old cocoa-nut shells and husks, and put on, Nat."

"Will they burn well?" I said. "I was afraid of putting out the fire."

"Splendidly, my boy. The shells are full of oil, and will send out a capital heat."

We were obliged to nibble a biscuit while we waited, and anxiously watched the frizzling and browning birds, for we were terribly hungry.

"I hope they won't be long, uncle," I said.

"So do I, Nat," he replied; "but what a splendid dining-room we have got out here! Isn't it lovely, my boy, under this blue sky and shading trees?"

"Hundreds of times better than going to a picnic at Bushey Park, uncle," I said. "But you talked of eating the birds we shot. Thrushes would be good, wouldn't they?"

"Delicious, Nat, only so very small."

"But you wouldn't eat parrots, uncle, lories, and paroquets, and these sort of birds?"

"Why not?" he replied, turning his skewer, while I imitated him, it seeming to be settled that we were each to have a couple of pigeons for our dinner.

"I don't know why not, uncle," I said thoughtfully, "only it seems so queer to eat a Poll parrot;" and as I spoke I could not help thinking of poor Humpty Dumpty, and all the trouble I had had. "It seems queer," I said again.

"But why does it seem queer, Nat?" he said, smiling. "Come, my boy, you must throw aside prejudices."

"Well, you see, uncle, they have got such hooked beaks," I said, in a helpless sort of way.

"Ha! ha! ha!" he laughed. "Why, what a reason, Nat! I might as well say I would not eat snipe, or woodcock, because it has such a long straight beak. Turn your skewer, Nat. They are beginning to smell maddeningly nice. They're as fat as butter. Nothing like a walk such as ours to give you an appetite. There, take the big tin and go and fill it with Adam's ale."

I ran to the rock pool and filled the tin with the cool clear water, and came back to the fire.

"They'll soon be done, Nat," said my uncle. "Yes, my boy, I should eat parrots, and shall eat a good many, I hope. Why, look here, Nat, what do parrots eat?"

"Sop and seed and sugar," I said.

"Yes, when they are shut up in a cage at home, Nat; but fruit, my boy, in their native state. There, you may take that as a rule, that all birds that live on seed or fruit are good for food."

"And those that live on prey, uncle, are bad," I said.

"Well, no; that won't do, Nat. Parrots are delicious. I've eaten dozens. And so are some birds that live on small prey—ducks and geese, for instance, eat a great many live things; and the birds that live on insects are, some of them, very good. I think we may say birds of light diet are all good, and draw the line at all carrion or raptorial birds. I should not like to eat hawk, owl, or anything of the crow family; but there is no knowing, Nat, what we might do if half-starved, and that's what I am now. Nat, my boy, the birds are done. Now for a glorious feast! I'm sure I shall pick the bones of my two."

"And I'm sure I shall, uncle. I was never so hungry in my life."

"Then now to begin, my boy; give me that tin plate and say grace, if we are in the wilds. What's become of all the savages?"

"Oh, uncle!" I cried, "here comes our guide. He wasn't offended."

"Thunder!" cried Uncle Dick, with a comical look of disgust; "he has come back to dinner."

"Yes, uncle," I groaned, as I looked at the pigeons; "and he has brought two great hungry fellows with him."

"Fetch the guns, Nat," cried my uncle in comical wrath; "let's fight in defence of our prey. No, don't; we must bribe them with biscuits to go."

Uncle Dick looked at me in a miserably resigned way, and it all seemed so droll that these blacks should come up just as we were preparing for such a feast, that I leaned back against the cocoa-nut tree by the fire and laughed till I cried.

Chapter Twenty Two.

Company to Dinner.

I was wiping the tears from my eyes as Mr Ebony, as uncle called him, came up, carrying something in a great palm leaf, while his companions had something else in a basket.

Mr Ebony was grinning tremendously. Then he said something, and the two others went away, while our black guest, for that he evidently meant to be, sniffed at the pigeons, rubbed himself, and danced with delight.

But we had wronged him, for he was not going to behave shabbily, for, taking the basket, he rolled out of it a dozen great fruit, half being cocoa-nuts, the other something nearly as large that I had never seen before.

Then he nodded and grinned, and had another bit of a dance before unrolling the huge palm leaf, and showing us four good-looking fishes, each twice as big as a large mackerel, and so fresh that one was hardly now dead.

Mr Ebony grinned and danced again, nodding at us both, and saying something in his tongue which sounded to me like, "Now we'll have such a jolly tuck-out;" but of course it was not that, though it evidently meant as much.

The next minute with wonderful skill our visitor had cut some bamboos with a kind of adze he had in the cord round his waist, slit open and cleaned the fish with a sharp-pointed piece of wood, and then got each one stuck on a piece of bamboo to roast before the fire.

He was like a man on springs; he did things so jerkily and quick, jumping up and rushing off, to come back laden with wood for the fire, some of which he carefully put on, and then nodded and grinned and rubbed himself.

"Well, Mr Ebony," said my uncle, smiling, "you are really not a bad fellow after all; and as you have come to dinner in full dress I am very glad to see you, and let's fall to. By all the rules of etiquette, my dear sir, soup comes first, sir. We have no soup. Fish follows next, but, my dear carbonaceous-looking friend, the fish is not done, while the pigeons are, so sit down. Nat, my boy, give our honoured guest a tin plate and a biscuit. Monsieur Ebony—pigeon?"

As my uncle spoke he pulled up his bamboo spit, and, taking hold of the sandy end, he presented the other to our visitor, who took hold tightly, watching my uncle the while as he drew his hunting-knife, and, with a dexterous chop, divided the bamboo in two, leaving each with a pigeon.

"Come, Nat, boy, fall to. That other pigeon will have to be divided."

Then there was silence as I helped myself to the great pigeon, and we began to eat with such a sense of enjoyment as I never felt before; but when my uncle and I were half through our pigeons Mr Ebony had finished his, and was casting furtive glances at the one still frizzling and browning before the fire in company with the fishes, which our guest carefully turned.

"Give him the other pigeon, Nat," said my uncle, "and we will make up with fish;" so I offered it to our visitor, but he shook his head, and began chattering, pointing to the fish, which he kept turning; and as soon as one was done, looked with a good deal of natural politeness to see if we were ready; but as we were not, he threw his bones over his head—of course I do not mean his own bones, but the bones of the pigeon, which he had crunched up with his white teeth, like a dog, and began at once upon his fish.

Leaving the fourth pigeon stuck upon the spit, we now in our turn each tried a fish, which Uncle Dick said were a kind of perch, and very delicious they were, especially with the addition of a little pepper, of which, after the first taste, our visitor showed himself to be very fond; and taken altogether, we made a most delicious repast, without thinking of the dessert which had yet to come.

This our visitor commenced after he had eaten a second fish, chattering away to us, and opening the nuts with great skill, giving one to each of us, so that for the first time I tasted what cocoa-nut really was like. Not a hard, indigestible, sweet, oily kind of woody kernel fast round the shell, so that it was hard to get it off; but a sweet, soft pulp that we cut and scraped out like cream-cheese, while it had a refreshing slightly acid flavour that was most delicious.

I never saw anyone before like our black friend, for no sooner did he see by our looks that we enjoyed his cocoa-nuts than he jumped up and danced, laughing with pleasure, but stopping every now and then to have a taste himself, till we had finished, when he took one of the other great nuts, which I saw were thorny, and marked down the sides with seams, as if ready for opening by means of a knife.

"That is not cocoa-nut, is it, uncle?" I said, looking curiously at the great wooden fruit, as the black proceeded to split it open with his hatchet, inserting the blade very cleverly so as to get it open, with the result that a very unpleasant odour arose.

"It don't seem to be good, whatever it is," said my uncle. "Why, it must be the durian, Nat," he said eagerly. "I wanted to see that fruit."

"But it does not seem good to eat, uncle," I said, as I looked at the portion given to me, which appeared to be full of a kind of custard with big seeds inside, about as large as a chestnut.

"They say it is delicious," he replied, helping himself to a little with the blade of his knife. "Taste away."

I tasted, and he tasted, the black watching us attentively; and no sooner did he see the face I made than he became tremendously excited, jumping about, making smacking sounds with his lips, and rubbing himself to show how good it was. Then, still seeing that we did not get on, he opened another, and taking half began to eat rapidly, dancing about with delight and rolling his eyes, to explain to us that he was having a most delicious feast.

"Perhaps this is a better one," said my uncle, stretching out his hand for the untouched half, but upon tasting it he did not find it so satisfactory as that which we had, and we made a very poor dessert, as far as the durian was concerned, greatly to our friend's chagrin.

The meal being at an end, we each took a hearty draught of the pure water, and offered the tin to our guest, but he shook his head and kept on making signs as he cried out:

"Rack-rack-rack-rack!"

"What does he mean, uncle?" I said. "Look, he is pretending to pour something into the water. He means arrack."

"Yes, and he will not get any, Nat—neither arrack nor brandy. Those are for medicines, my boy; but go and get one of those small bottles of raspberry vinegar, and I'll give him some of that."

The black watched me intently as I fetched the little bottle of rich red syrup, and kept his eyes upon his host, when, after emptying all but about half a pint of water out of the tin, my uncle poured out a table-spoonful of the syrup into the clear water and stirred it up, offering it afterwards to the black, who took it, smelt it suspiciously, and then handed it to me.

I drank a portion, and found it so good that I finished it, to our guest's amazement and disgust; but the cup was soon replenished, and now he tasted eagerly, drinking it up, and then indulging in a fresh dance.

"Now for work," said my uncle. "Let's clear away, Nat;" and the remains of the dinner having been carried into the tent, the box of requisites was brought out, and with the black squatting down upon his heels to watch us attentively, I helped Uncle Dick prepare his first skins.

Chapter Twenty Three.

How to prepare Skins, and go Fishing.

The process was very simple, for he took the thrush and the lories, inserted a sharp-pointed penknife just through the skin, and then with clever fingers turned the delicate skin back, taking care not to injure the feathers either by the moisture of the bird's flesh or by handling and roughening the plumage, the result being that he skilfully turned the skin inside out after cutting through the legs and wings, cleaning the bones of flesh, and leaving in the skull, after stripping the bird right to the beak.

It was surprising how beautifully clean everything came away, so that when the fleshy side of the skin had been brushed over with moistened arsenical soap, the wing-bones tied together, the hollow of the skull and orbits of the eyes filled up with cotton-wool, and a ball of the same placed for the body, the skin being turned back over all and slightly shaken, a stranger would hardly have known that the flesh of the bird had been removed.

There was no odour except the aromatic scent of the preserving soap; and when a little sugar-paper had been twisted up into which to thrust the bird's head and shoulders to keep the neck short, and the bird had lain in the sun for a few hours, it became quite stiff and dry, exactly like the skins with which I was familiar.

Uncle Dick insisted upon my doing the thrush and one of the lories, while he did the pigeons, whose skins were so tender, and so covered with oily fat, that they required a great deal of care to keep the feathers unsullied.

I set to work then, skinning my birds pretty readily from old practice, and after a little bungling I managed to make of them respectable-looking skins.

"You'll soon improve, Nat," said my uncle, as we laid our specimens all together in the sun, the black nodding his approval at all we did; but the skins had not been lying there long, and our hands washed previous to putting on the kettle for tea, before our new friend jumped up in a great state of excitement, pointing to a reddish-brown streak that seemed to run from the wood nearly to where our specimens lay.

"Ants!" exclaimed my uncle, darting to the skins, and shaking off a few of the enemies that had come to the attack; and it was not until we had contrived to make a little channel all round one of our boxes upon which the skins were laid, and connected it with the little spring of water, so that our treasure was surrounded by a tiny moat, that we could keep the insects away.

Our black friend, who was evidently a great chief among his people, made no scruple about stopping to have some tea with us, watching the boiling of the kettle and our preparations with the greatest of curiosity, but always in a calm, composed way.

"It is rather a nuisance always having him here, Nat," said my uncle; "but we should be bothered with a good many more if he were to go, and really he does not seem a bad sort of fellow."

He certainly was not, for though he ate heartily of anything we gave him, he was as generous as could be, going off to return with men laden with fruit, fish, and a kind of sago, which was not at all bad boiled up and sweetened.

I missed a good many things such as I had been used to, but so far it all seemed to be glorious fun, and that night I lay down to rest looking through the open doorway at the stars, breathing the soft warm air, and dropping off into a delicious sleep, to dream of home, and Uncle Joe in his garden, smoking his long clay pipe.

I was awakened at daybreak by some one touching me, and on opening my eyes I started with dread as I saw a black face close to my own, and a grinning set of white teeth.

I knew directly who it was, though, and getting up I saw that my uncle was still peacefully sleeping off the previous day's fatigue.

I was going to rouse him, but Mr Ebony pulled me by the arm to come without waking him.

My next movement was to get my gun; but again our black friend objected, pulling at me half angrily, and I accompanied him outside into the cool grey morning.

I hesitated to follow him for a minute, thinking that I ought not to leave my uncle; but I could not help thinking that we were quite helpless amongst these savages if they chose to turn against us, and therefore all we could do was to cultivate their good-will.

Mr Ebony, whose black mop of hair stood out more fiercely than ever, was watching me attentively, scowling fiercely, as I thought; but as soon as I prepared to follow him he began to grin and chatter away to me, keeping on repeating the word "*Ikan-Ikan,*" till we were down in the half darkness by where the waves lapped the sand; and now I saw a good-sized canoe with half a dozen men waiting, all looking, with their paddles in their hands, like so many fierce black executioners, prepared to make an end of me.

Mr Ebony signed to me to get into the boat, and feeling that perhaps they might be going to make a prisoner of me and take me to another island, I asked myself whether I ought not to resist; but seeing how useless it would be, I resigned myself to my fate, jumped into the canoe, Mr Ebony followed; and with no singing and splashing now, but in utter silence, we pushed off over the grey sea.

"Where are we going, I wonder?" I said to myself.

"Ikan, Ikan," said Mr Ebony, shaking something in the bottom of the canoe.

"Ikan! where's that, I wonder?" I said to myself. "Why, these are fishing-lines. Ikan, fish," I exclaimed, pointing to the lines and then to the sea, making as if to throw in one of the lines.

"Ikan, Ikan," cried Mr Ebony, grinning with delight, and then he touched my hands and the lines, and patted my back—dancing about afterwards till he nearly danced overboard, after which he became a little more calm, but kept on smiling in the most satisfied way, and shouting "Ikan, Ikan;" all the others saying it after him, as if highly satisfied, and when to please them I said "Ikan, Ikan," they uttered a shout, and I felt quite at home, and delighted at having come.

I don't know how it was, but as soon as I felt satisfied that they were not going to do me any harm I began to learn how much they were all like a set of schoolboys of my own age, for big, strong, well-made men as they were, they seemed to be full of fun, and as young as they could be.

They paddled swiftly out and away from the land, working hard to send the great canoe well along over the long rollers that we seemed to climb, to glide down the other side; and, with the exception of the heaving, slow rolling motion of the sea, all being deliciously calm, I thoroughly enjoyed my ride, especially as Mr Ebony, who was evidently a very big man amongst his people, had taken a great liking to me and kept on drawing my attention to every splash on the surface of the water, and then to the busy way in which he was preparing his coarse fishing-lines.

I suppose there are some boys who never cared for fishing; but however cruel it may be as a sport, I must confess that I was always passionately fond of it, and now to be out on this tropic sea before sunrise, with the stars seen faintly here and there, the blacks keeping up a rhythmical motion of the paddles, and the water lapping up against the bow of the canoe, I felt an indescribable kind of delight that no words of mine will put on paper.

I should think we paddled about a couple of miles, and then at a word from Mr Ebony the paddles were all laid in, and a line, with its great coarsely-made hooks formed out of well-sharpened pieces of brass wire, was handed to me, my guide showing me how to throw it over the side; not that I needed showing, for it seemed to come quite natural; and I began to think, as I passed the line over, of the sticklebacks on Clapham Common, and the occasional carp that we schoolboys used to catch.

Mr Ebony grinned with satisfaction, and threw his own line over the side just as a splash behind me made me turn in time to see a rope running out rapidly, evidently attached to some kind of anchor.

This checked the canoe, which was floating along so fast that it had begun to ride over our lines, which now, however, floated away upon the swift current.

There was no noise or chattering now, but all the blacks sat or stood very quietly in the canoe, and I saw that three of them had long spears, barbed like hooks, and looking as if they were meant for catching fish.

There was a good length of line in my hands, which I kept on paying out, as the sailors call it, just as Mr Ebony was letting out his till it was nearly all gone, and I saw that the end was tied to the edge of the canoe. But still there was no sign of any fish, and I was beginning to stare about me, for just then a patch of golden light seemed to start out into view, and I could see that the tops of the mountains in the island were just catching the first rays of the sun, while the stars that had been looking so pale seemed to go out quickly one after another.

"I wonder whether Uncle Dick is awake yet," I thought to myself, "and what he will say to my being away, and —"

An exclamation from my black companion brought me back from my dreamy thoughts; not that it was necessary, for something else had roused me, and that was a sharp jerk at the line, which snatched it quite out of my hands, and had it not been fastened to the side of the boat I should have lost it.

Mr Ebony was coming to my help, but seeing me dart at it again and, catching hold, begin to haul in and struggle hard with my fish, he rubbed himself and grinned, especially when he saw that I had to hang on with all my might to keep from being dragged out of the canoe.

The next moment he had enough to do to manage a fish that had taken his bait, and to keep it from crossing my line so as to get them into a tangle.

It was quite startling for the moment to have hold of so strong a fish, one which darted here, there, and everywhere; now diving straight down, now running away out to sea, and then when I thought the line must snap, for it made tugs that cut my hands and jerked my shoulders, I uttered a cry of disappointment, for the line came in slack, and the fish was gone.

It puzzled me to see how coolly the others took it, but I supposed that they were used to losing fish from the badness of their tackle, and besides, there was evidently a big one on Mr Ebony's line to take their attention.

"I wonder whether he has taken the hook," I thought to myself as I carefully drew in the line, coiling it neatly down between my legs, yard after yard, till I had pulled in at least fifty yards of the coarse cord, when, to my utter astonishment, there was a sudden check or rush, and the line began to run rapidly out again, my fish being still there, and I saw now that it had made a rush in towards the canoe, and then lain quite still close to the bottom till I had disturbed it by jerking the line as I hauled it in.

The rest that it had had seemed to have made it stronger than ever, for it darted about at a tremendous pace, and I was still playing it, letting it run when it made fierce dashes, and hauling in the line whenever it grew a little slack, when there was a bit of a bustle by my side as Mr Ebony drew his fish close up to the side of the canoe, and one of the blacks darted a barbed spear into it and lifted it into the canoe.

It was a beautifully-marked fish about three feet long, and as I glanced at it I wondered whether mine would be as big; and then I thought it must be bigger, it pulled with such tremendous force; but at last its struggles grew less and less powerful, and twice over I was able to draw it nearly to the surface, but only for it to dart away again, and I thought it was lost.

It seemed to excite a good deal of interest amongst the savages, two of whom stood, one on either side of me, ready with their spears to make a thrust at the fish, and one of them stretched out his hand to take the line from me, but Mr Ebony uttered such a fierce exclamation, and caught so angrily at a paddle, that the man drew back, and after a long and gallant fight I at last drew my fish so close in that, just as it was in the act of dashing off again, a couple of spears transfixed it, and it was drawn over the side amidst a shout of triumph.

Mr Ebony, who was the most excited of all, patting me on the shoulders and shaking hands most eagerly with one of the savages, took out the hook, the line was thrown over again, and I had time to examine my prize, a splendid fish, flashing with glorious colours in the morning light. It was over a yard long, and very thick and round, while its glistening scales were as big as shillings at the very least; in fact I don't think I should exaggerate if I said that some in the centre rows were as large as two-shilling pieces, fluted and gilded, and some tinged with orange and glistening scarlet and green.

So great was the delight of all on board that they began to dance and sing with such vigour that the canoe rocked about, and one man went head over heels out into the sea.

I was horrified as I saw him disappear, but he was up again, grinning hugely, and slipped in over the side of the canoe like a great black eel, giving himself a shake to send the water out of his mop of hair, and then sitting down to watch us fish.

For quite half an hour now we caught nothing, but it did not seem to matter, for there was so much to look at as the glorious sun rose over the sea, turning it into orange and gold; while, when I was tired of that, the beauty of the trees and mountains on the island, with the endless changes of light and shade, made my heart beat with pleasure as I thought of what a lovely home these savages possessed, and it seemed to explain to me why it was that they were all so childlike and happy.

I caught another fish then of seven or eight pounds weight, different to the others, and Mr Ebony caught seven or eight quickly one after the other, I suppose out of a shoal, and then, laughing and chattering once again, the anchor, which proved to be a curious elbow, evidently the root of a tree, sharped at its points and weighted with a lump of coral, was hauled up, placed in the stern of the canoe, and we turned for the shore.

"What a morning for a bathe!" I thought, as we drew nearer; and starting up in the canoe when we were about a quarter of a mile from the land, I began to take off my things, meaning to swim ashore, where we were within a couple of hundred yards; but Mr Ebony stopped me, saying something I could not understand of course.

"I'm going to swim ashore," I said, making believe to leap overboard, and then striking out with my arms; but my companions all chattered angrily, and Mr Ebony, to my horror, came at me, snapping at my arms and legs with his great white teeth, and looking terribly fierce, while, as I shrunk away, one of the blacks touched me on the back, and as I turned sharply, with Mr Ebony holding on to my trouser leg and apparently trying to tear out a piece, the black behind me pointed down into the clear water, now brightly lit-up by the sun, and I saw two long grey fish gliding slowly amongst the coral rocks, and I wanted no telling that they were sharks.

I pointed to the sharks in my turn, shuddering as I thought of what an escape I had had; and not being able to express myself in language, I did what Mr Ebony had done to me, made a dash at his leg and pretended to bite it, not doing so, however, for I did not care to touch his great black limb with my teeth.

He understood me, though, and chattered with delight, getting up and relieving his feelings by a short dance before settling down again and shaking hands.

In another minute the canoe was run up on the beautiful soft sand, the savages leaping out into the shallow water and carrying it beyond reach of the waves, when I stepped out with Mr Ebony, who made one of the men pick up my fish and carry it before us in triumph to our hut, the others taking the rest of the fish towards the village.

Chapter Twenty Four.

A Butterfly Hunt.

"Why, Nat," cried my uncle, "I was beginning to be alarmed. Been fishing, eh?" he said, as he shook hands with our black friend, who had evidently made up his mind to stay breakfast; for, seizing the big fish, he snapped off a couple of great banana leaves upon which to lay it, and the man who had carried it went away; but not until I had made him show his teeth by giving him a couple of biscuits and a handful of sugar.

I explained to my uncle how I had been carried off that morning, and my feeling of alarm, and he nodded.

"I don't think there is anything to be alarmed about, Nat," he replied, "so long as we do not in any way touch upon their prejudices; but what a splendid fish, Nat, my boy! It must be a kind of mullet, I should say, by its soft mouth and the long barbs hanging from the corners of its chubby lips. Yes, that's what it must be; but I'm sorry to say that I am very ignorant about fish."

My uncle had not been idle, for he had made a good fire, the kettle was boiling, and we should have begun breakfast at once if it had not been for Mr Ebony's preparations. He had lost no time, but had slit off some great chunks of solid fish, placing them on great bamboo skewers to roast, washing his hands afterwards with great nicety, and then scooping up the dry warm sand and letting it trickle over his fingers, palms, and wrists, until they were dry.

"I have not been idle, you see, Nat," said my uncle, pointing to a newly made skin, that of a very lovely little green lory with a delicate peach-coloured head, the separation from the green feathers being marked by a deep black collar which gave the bird a neatness and beauty that was very attractive to the eye.

But Mr Ebony was not satisfied with his contribution to the breakfast, for, striking me on the breast, pointing to the fire, and saying, "Ikan, Ikan, youf, youf," several times over, I repeated them to his satisfaction, understanding that he meant I was to mind the fish, and then he went off quickly.

"Ikan," said my uncle, "that's the Malay word for fish, so I suppose they use some Malay words though their language is quite different."

"Then he said, 'youf, youf,' uncle."

"Yes: youf must mean cooking or fire, which is api in the Malay tongue. But this fresh morning air gives me an appetite, Nat. I hope he won't be long; turn the fish, my lad, it's burning."

"No, uncle, it's only brown," I replied, altering the position of the great collops; "but how beautiful it smells!"

"Yes, Nat, we want no fish sauces out here, my boy."

"Where did you shoot that beautiful lory, uncle?" I asked.

"It was in that palm-tree close to us, Nat," he replied; "and now, while we are waiting, I'll put together a few boxes and the butterfly-nets and the cyanide bottle, ready for a start directly after breakfast."

"Shall you take the guns, uncle?"

"Only one, Nat, and we'll carry it in turn," he replied. "This is to be a butterfly and beetle day, so we will not go far in any direction, but keep within reach of the camp so as to come back for food and rest. It will save us from having to carry provisions."

Just then we saw Mr Ebony coming towards us loaded with a basket of fruit, which he placed on the sand, and then after a dance round us he plumped down by the fire and picked out the skewers where the fish was most done, handing one to each, and our breakfast began.

Mr Ebony thoroughly enjoyed his coffee with plenty of sugar, for he had no distrust now, but ate and drank as we did, laughing and talking all the while, and stopping every now and then to point to butterfly or bird that went by, eating a prodigious breakfast, but mostly of fish and fruit.

Breakfast over, as soon as he saw us ready for a start he stuck his spear down again in front of the door, excited and eager to be off, and ready to draw our attention to the fact that one of us had no gun.

We pointed, however, to the butterfly-nets and that satisfied him, and when we were ready to start I suggested to my uncle that we should put the uncooked remains of the fish and the fruit inside the hut so as to have them when we came back.

"To be sure, Nat," he said, "I had forgotten them."

But at the first attempt to remove them Mr Ebony stopped me, and uttered a loud, ringing cry, whose effect was to bring about a couple of dozen little naked black boys out of the jungle, where they must have been watching us, safely hidden all the time.

To these comical-looking little objects the chief said a few words, when there was a rush, and the remains from our breakfast were carried off like magic, Mr Ebony pointing to the sea and to the trees as much as to say, "There is plenty more when we want it."

We were not long in getting to work, for no sooner were we in the denser part of the island where the foliage grew thick and moist, than we were astounded at the number of little lizards that swarmed about, darting here and there and puzzling me at first as to what colour they were. One moment they seemed to be bright green, the next like a wriggling line of the most beautiful blue.

I found out their colour, though, as soon as I had one in the butterfly-net, for while their bodies were of a brilliant green, their tails were a blue as pure as the sky.

A couple of them were consigned to the spirit bottle for preservation, and then we tramped on, growing more and more delighted with the country the farther we went.

For some time butterflies were absent, so we had to take to collecting birds, but hardly had we shot three different kinds of parrots, all of a most lovely colour, than we seemed to tumble upon the butterflies, and in the course of that one day we captured some of the most lovely specimens I had ever seen out of a museum. Blue, yellow, black, crimson, no tint was wanting to make them attractive, and we went on for hour after hour, forgetting all about our dinner in the excitement of the chase, and filling our boxes before we thought of leaving off.

Not only butterflies had been captured, but beetles of many kinds, most of them clad in armour that seemed to have been burnished, so brilliant were they in their green, purple, and violet when held up in the sun.

Chapter Twenty Five.

Why Ebony would not say Good-bye.

It was with feelings full of regret that we said good-bye to our black friend at the end of a month; for by that time the want of fresh specimens made my uncle say that it was time to be on the move. We could have gone on shooting scarlet lories, nutmeg pigeons, and pittas as long as we liked, but that would have been wanton work, and uncle discovered that the neighbouring islands would, wherever we went, give us fresh supplies and present to us birds and insects such as we had never seen before, so at last we prepared to start, and with some little difficulty made Mr Ebony understand that we wanted a good supply of sago, fruit, and fish for our voyage.

At first he could not understand that we were going right away, but as soon as he did comprehend our signs the poor fellow looked miserable, for he had regularly attached himself to us all the time of our stay, and he was inconsolable at the idea of our going.

He helped us, however, to load our boat, and would have given us fish enough for twenty people would we have taken it; and at last, just after an early breakfast, we bade farewell to the beautiful island, and waving an adieu to the people, of whom we had seen very little, we turned to shake hands with our black friend, both my uncle and I having ready a present for him; mine being a handy little hatchet, my uncle's a large two-bladed knife.

To our surprise, though, as we stood down on the sands he refused to shake hands with us, looking very serious and glum, and when we gave him our presents, thinking that they would bring a smile to his face, he took them quickly and threw them into the bottom of the boat.

"It is a pity," said my uncle, "for I do not like the idea of parting bad friends, Nat, my boy. I'd give something if I could speak to the poor fellow in his own language and tell him that we are not ungrateful for all his kindness."

"I often wish we could speak in their own tongue, uncle," I said.

"Yes, Nat, but it is next to impossible, for there are fifty or sixty different dialects spoken. There, offer to shake hands with him again. You two were always such good friends."

I offered my hand to the black chief, but he put his own behind him and pointed to the boat, as much, it seemed to me, as to say, "There, you've got all you want now; go away."

My uncle tried with no better success, and as the natives were gathering about us we reluctantly got in where the beautiful canoe lay heaving on the sands as the great rollers came in.

Everything was in readiness, our boxes snugly stowed, our provisions ready, our guns in their waterproof cases, the sail lay ready for hoisting, and all that was wanted now was to wait until a good wave came in and then shove off and ride out on it as it retired.

The canoe was so large that I wondered whether we should be able to manage it ourselves; but I had full confidence in my uncle's skill, and it seemed to me that my help now ought to be of some use. So I seized the pole that lay ready, and prepared to use it; but Mr Ebony, as we had somehow got into the habit of calling him now, said something to the little crowd on the sands, when, as he took the lead, eight or nine ran into the water, seized the boat by the sides, and ran her right out forty or fifty yards to where the water was up to their breasts, when, giving us a final thrust, away we went upon the top of a roller, my uncle hoisting the sail at the right moment, and we glided on.

I had seized a great paddle used for steering and taken care to keep the boat's head right, laughing to myself the while, and wondering what my uncle would say when he turned round, for he was hauling up the sail and too busy to notice anything but his work.

When at last he did turn round, just as we had glided lightly a good five hundred yards from the shore, he cried out: "Hallo!"

For there, just in front of me, squatting down upon his heels and with all his white teeth displayed, was Mr Ebony, apparently quite at home, and without the slightest intention of going back.

"Why, what does this mean?" said my uncle, and he pointed to the shore.

But Mr Ebony had no intention of going, and if we had not learned much of his language, he had picked up something of ours, for he began to shout, "No, no, no, no, no," till he was out of breath, and laying himself down he took tight hold of one of the thwarts of the canoe, as if to say that he meant to cling to that if we tried to throw him over.

"This is why he wouldn't shake hands, Nat," said my uncle. "He couldn't swim ashore now, for the sharks, so I suppose he means to come with us. Let's see."

My uncle pointed to the shore, but Mr Ebony shook his head, so Uncle Dick pointed right ahead eastward, in the direction we were going, and our black friend nodded, and jumping up danced about, grinning and muttering excitedly the while.

"Well, Nat," said my uncle, "what's to be done? He wants to go with us."

"Can't we take him, uncle?" I replied.

"Oh yes, Nat, we can take him," he replied; "and he would be very useful. Only it comes upon me like a surprise. It is, of course, a good thing to have a black with us, for it will teach the people we come across that we are friendly, even if we cannot make them understand, though, I dare say, Ebony here will be able sometimes to act as interpreter."

"Ebo-Nee, Ebo-Nee, Ebo-Nee," cried our passenger loudly; and he began to beat his chest to show that he comprehended whom we meant.

Then touching me on the chest he cried with great eagerness, "Nat, my boy—Nat, my boy," looking delighted when we laughed; and to give further example of his powers as a linguist, he next touched my uncle as he had touched me.

"Ung-go-Dit, Ung-go-Dit," he cried, finishing off by slapping his naked flesh, and shouting, "Ebo-Nee, Ebo-Nee."

"Very good, Master Ebo-Nee," said Uncle Dick; "since you are so apt at learning, you may as well go on and pick up our words, for I quite despair of learning yours."

The black was shrewd enough to see that we accepted his presence, and upon this he shook hands with us both twice over and then took the great paddle from my hand, steering and showing himself thoroughly skilful in the management of our canoe.

My uncle pointed east as the course he wanted to go; but our crew, as we called him, rose in mutiny directly, pointing south, and handing the paddle back to me he grew very excited, saying, "Bird, bird," flapping his arms like wings and uttering screeches, whistles, and cries, before lifting an imaginary gun to his shoulder and uttering the word "Bang!"

"That is plain enough to understand, Nat," said my uncle.

"Yes," I replied; "he means that there are plenty of parrots and other birds on some island where he will take us."

"Bird, bird," cried Ebo-Nee, as we called him henceforth, and he pointed south-west.

"It does not much matter where we go, Nat," said my uncle, "so long as we visit islands where naturalists have never been before, so I shall trust to our friend here. We can get to New Guinea at any time now, for it lies all along the north. All right, go on then," said my uncle to Ebo-Nee, and he nodded and smiled, pointing to what looked like a mist upon the water far away.

"Nat, ung, shoot," cried Ebo eagerly; "shoot, shoot, shoot."

"Why, we shall have quite an English scholar on board soon, Nat," said my uncle laughing; and then in turns we held the sheet as the swift canoe glided over the sunlit waves till the island we had left began to grow dim in the distance and its mountains to sink, as it were, beneath the wave, while the place to which we were going grew less misty and indistinct.

It was evidently very high land, and as we drew nearer we could see that right and left of it there were other islands apparently of goodly size.

Mid-day came and we made a hearty meal, the canoe, urged by the soft brisk breeze, still gliding onwards till towards evening, when we were sufficiently near the land we approached to make out that it was very bleak and bare and sterile. There was a ridge of mountains in the central portion, but as we examined the place with the glass it looked as blank and uninviting as could be.

"Not a sign of an inhabitant," said my uncle. "I'm afraid we have made a mistake, Nat; but perhaps one of the other islands may prove more inviting."

He continued his inspection and went on talking. "There are plenty of traces of sea-birds," he continued, "for the cliffs are covered with guano; but it is not their breeding season, and I cannot see a single bird. But he is not making straight for the sands. Why don't you try to land there?"

Ebo shook his head, and then laughed and said, "No," steering the canoe to the left of the island. And so we sailed on till it was so near sunset that it would be dark in half an hour, when our crew, who had evidently been here before, suddenly steered the canoe into a cove well sheltered from the rollers, and lowering the sail we ran her up on the soft sands quite clear of the sea, Ebo at once setting to work collecting dry drift-wood to make a fire.

He pointed out a sheltered spot among some heaped-up rocks where the sand had been blown up by tempests into a soft bed, and here, after a very hearty meal well cooked over the fire Ebo had made, we lay down to sleep; my uncle having climbed to the top of the rocks and swept the island with his glass, returning to say that there was not a trace of a human being.

We slept soundly and well out there in that little storm-swept island, but no storms disturbed us, and the first thing I heard after lying down was the crackling of wood as Ebo piled it up to make a good fire.

As soon as he saw me awake he beckoned me to go to the boat, and there, taking the fish we had brought out of the basket, he smelt it, made me do the same, and then threw all but one small silvery fellow into the sea.

"Hullo!" cried my uncle, "isn't that waste, Nat?" for he had advanced over the sands unheard.

"I think so, uncle, but he means to catch some fresh."

That was evidently Ebo's intentions, for he cut up the silvery fish into scraps for bait, and then signing to us to help him, we launched the canoe, paddled out half a mile, and then threw over a couple of lines, Ebo showing his teeth with delight as he drew in quickly a couple of good-sized mullet-looking fish, a couple more, and another soon coming to my line.

But Ebo was not satisfied till we had caught five or six times as many as seemed necessary. Then and then only did we paddle ashore.

It was soon evident why Ebo had wanted so many fish, for after cleaning and setting enough for our breakfasts to roast, he prepared the rest and put them to cook while we made a hearty meal.

This being ended my uncle rose.

"Well, Nat," he said, "this seems a terribly sterile place, but we may as well have a look round; one finds good specimens sometimes in unlikely spots. Let's get our guns."

Ebo was watching us intently all the time, evidently trying to comprehend us and directly after he, to our utter astonishment, shouted out: "no gun; no shoot; no gun; no bird. Boat, boat, boat, boat."

He pointed to the canoe, and then right to sea again, and seeing us laugh he burst into a hearty fit himself, ending by dancing about and putting the freshly cooked fish on board, where we followed him and once more launched upon the tropic sea.

It was plain enough that this was only a resting-place upon our way, for as soon as the sail was hoisted Ebo took the paddle and steered us south-west, leaving larger islands to right and left though nothing was visible ahead.

"I suppose we must trust him, Nat," said my uncle; "but it does look rather wild work cruising these seas in an open canoe, quite at the mercy of a savage whose language we cannot speak."

"But I think he must have been here before, uncle," I replied.

"No doubt about it, my boy."

"Nat, my boy," cried Ebo laughing, for he had caught part of my uncle's speech.

"Yes, he has been here before, and probably has touched at some place where he has seen, or thinks he has seen, plenty of birds. At any rate, if the weather holds fair it will not be such a very difficult thing to run for some island for shelter."

I had been thinking the same thing, that it seemed a very risky proceeding to sail right out to sea under the guidance of this savage; but there was so much romance and novelty in the idea of sailing away like Columbus in search of a new land, that I thoroughly enjoyed it, and the farther we sailed the more excited I grew.

It was now plain enough why Ebo had insisted upon a good supply of fish, for we dined off it and then made our evening meal of the same, no land being in sight, and when at last the lower edge of the sun seemed to touch the crimson water, sending a path of light right to our canoe, whose sail it seemed to turn to ruddy gold, there was still no land in sight.

My uncle stood up and used the glass, gazing straight before him in the direction that seemed to be our goal; but Ebo shook his head, and then closed his eyes and made believe to sleep, pointing to us in turn.

"He wants us to lie down and sleep, Nat," said my uncle, "but it is out of the question;" and he shook his head.

Ebo tried again and again to get us to lie down, but finding that we would not, he sat there laughing and looking as merry as could be, although there was no land in sight, and at last, when the sun was disappearing, he placed the paddle in my uncle's hand, pointing south-south-west as the course to be steered, after which he lay down and went off fast asleep.

I sat talking to my uncle and holding the sheet, though the breeze was so steady it seemed to be quite unnecessary, while he steered the canoe onward through the darkness, taking the stars for his compass, till the motion of the boat and the darkness combined to send me off into a deep sleep. I had closed my eyes and started up several times before, but this last time, when I opened my eyes again a was to see the black figure of Ebo seated there steering, with the sun just above the horizon, and my uncle stretched in the bottom of the canoe fast asleep.

Ebo grinned as I stared at him, and then as I looked about I found that far away to the west there was land that we must have passed in the night, but still we were sailing on as it were into space.

The water now was bright golden again, and the air felt delicious; but I began to wish that we were at our journey's end, and pointing ahead I tried to learn from our steersman how much farther he was going to take us.

His reply was to point straight ahead, and we were still speeding on, when, after five or six hours' sleep, my uncle jumped up into wakefulness, ready to partake of the waiting meal of cold fish, biscuits, and fruit; the coffee, which in a case like this I made by means of a spirit-lamp, being kept in abeyance for a time.

"Well, Nat," he said, "is our wild-goose chase nearly at an end? Is land in sight?"

"No, uncle," I said, after gazing carefully ahead. Just then Ebo pointed to the telescope, and made signs to my uncle to use it.

"Look through?" he said to the black. "All right, my friend, I will;" and placing it to his eye as he stood up in the boat he cried to me as I eagerly watched him, "Land ahead, Nat, and apparently a wooded shore!"

Chapter Twenty Six.

An Unknown Island.

By the time we had made a hearty meal Ebo pointed with triumph to the faint hazy speck in the distance, now growing minute by minute plainer to our eyes.

Ebo watched our countenances very intently, and then suddenly broke out with:

"Bird — shoot — bird."

"He seems to have brought us here under the impression that it is a good place, Nat, and I trust it will prove so," said my uncle. "I hope there will be no unpleasant savages to hinder our work."

As we drew nearer the glass was frequently brought to bear, but neither my uncle nor I could detect any sign of habitation, not even when we were within a quarter of a mile of the shore; but, to Uncle Dick's great delight, the place proved to be densely wooded in some parts, while the lofty hills looked green and park-like, with the large trees dotted here and there.

The beach was a soft white sand, upon which the waves curled gently over; and not twenty yards from the highest marks made by the tide, the tall palms, loaded with fruit, drooped their great feathery leaves.

As far as we could see the island was not large, but the interior was very mountainous, the green hills running up to a great height, for the most part well-clothed with wood; and to our great delight, as we ran the boat cautiously upon the sand, we could hear the screams of parrots and the whistling and twittering of innumerable birds.

"We may as well be prepared against danger," said Uncle Dick, loading his gun, and I followed suit; but Ebo began to chatter and expostulate with us for leaving the boat, and signed to us to help him run it up on the next wave well ashore, so that a rope could be made fast round the nearest palm stem.

This we did, and the black's next movement was to collect wood for a fire.

To humour him we waited about while he lit the fire, but kept making little incursions amongst the openings to see if we could spy out any signs of human habitation.

But look where we would we saw nothing, and it soon became evident that we were the only occupants of that part of the island.

Ebo seemed so satisfied and contented that it was very evident that there was nothing to fear; so we obeyed his signs after we had helped him to make a good fire, and followed him through an open park-like piece of the country till we were about half a mile from the sea, when his object in guiding us was plain enough, for he pointed out a little flock of half a dozen pigeons, as big, it seemed to me, as ordinary fowls, and getting within range we fired together, and shot four.

Ebo rushed forward in triumph, and I followed, to regret that I had not attended to Uncle Dick's instructions about reloading, for I could have obtained a specimen of a curious great black parrot or cockatoo, I could not quite see which, as it flew across an opening.

But we secured the birds we had shot, and going back my uncle and I set to and skinned them, handing over the bodies to Ebo to cook, while we carefully preserved the skins, admiring them all the while.

For they were of a rich warm slate colour, and each bird bore a delicate grey crest upon his head, which gave him a noble look, making each bird seem a very prince among pigeons.

Handsome as was the appearance of the birds, they were none the less delicious in the eating. No doubt our open-air life had a good deal to do with the keen enjoyment we had in eating the birds we shot; but feeding as these pigeons did on spices, nuts, and other sweet food, the flavour given to their flesh was very fine.

Dinner over, we were for an expedition; but Ebo protested loudly. Taking an axe and beckoning us to follow we accompanied him to a patch of bamboo, and helped him to cut down a good selection of stout pieces, and after them a number of lengths of rattan cane, which grew here in a wonderful way. I had seen it growing before, but never to such perfection; for it seemed to run up one tree and down another, running along over the bushes for a short distance and then ascending another, till Uncle Dick computed that some of these canes were quite a hundred yards long.

It was very evident what Ebo meant, and he was telling us all the time, though not a word could we understand, as we helped him.

"As we are to make a hut for shelter, Nat, I suppose he expects us to stay here for some time, which is a good sign, for he evidently knows that there are plenty of specimens to be had."

"Do you think any naturalist has been here before, uncle?" I said.

"I hardly dare think such a thing, Nat," he replied; "but I cannot help feeling hopeful. As I judge it this seems to be an island to which he and his fellows have sailed some time or another, and it is possible that European foot has never trodden here before."

"Let's hope it is so, uncle," I said; "and then, what a collection we shall get!"

"You will make me as sanguine as you are yourself, Nat," he said laughing; and then we began to be too hot and busy to talk much, for after carrying the bamboos and rattans to the edge of the forest, just beneath a widely spreading tree, in whose branches every now and then some beautiful lory came and perched, but only to fly off screaming, Ebo began to build. Sharpening four stout bamboos and forcing them into the soft sandy soil for the four corners of the hut, he very soon bound as many more to them horizontally about five feet from the ground, tying them in the cleverest way with the cane.

Then he tied a couple more across at each end, and laid a long stout bamboo in the forks they made for a ridge-pole, binding all as strongly as could be with an ingenious twist, and after that making rafters of smaller bamboos, so that in a couple of hours he had made the rough framework.

Towards the latter part of the time, in obedience to his instructions, which were given by word of mouth and wave of hand, Uncle Dick and I cut a great number of palm leaves of a very large size, with which Ebo rapidly thatched the hut, making by the time it was dark a very rough but very efficient shelter, where we lay down to sleep that night upon a pile of soft dry grass, of which there was any quantity naturally made into hay and close at hand.

We were so tired out that night that we did not trouble ourselves about there being no sides to the hut, being only too glad to have a roof to keep off the dew, and, trusting to there being no dangerous wild beasts, we followed Ebo's example, lying down and sleeping soundly till the sun was once more above the sea.

Chapter Twenty Seven.

Fresh Treasures.

Ebo set to work earnestly to finish the hut, binding down the palm leaves of the thatch with more long canes, which he cleverly threaded in and out, and afterwards secured their ends. Then he cut off the long ends of the bamboos so as to leave all tidy before commencing the sides.

My uncle was as anxious as I was to go upon some expedition; but as there was no shelter to be obtained here, and it became more and more evident that we were upon an uninhabited island, he saw the necessity for having our boxes and stores under a roof.

So we set manfully to work helping the black, cutting bamboos, bringing large palm leaves, fetching long rattan canes, and handing them to him; while, saving when he left off for meals, Ebo toiled like a slave, working with an industry that we should not have expected to find in an inhabitant of one of these sleepy isles.

At last, though, he finished, and his childish delight seemed to know no bounds. He danced and shouted, ran in and out, walked round the hut, and then strutted up to us full of self-satisfaction, his tongue going all the while, and evidently feeling highly delighted at our smiles and words of praise.

No time was lost in transferring our boxes and stores beneath the roof; and then, as it wanted quite three hours to sunset, my uncle proposed, by way of recompense for all our drudgery, that we should take our guns and see if we could not obtain a few specimens.

Ebo looked delighted, and, without being told, obtained a short piece of bamboo ready for carrying the birds we shot.

Then, taking his spear out of the canoe, he smiled to show how ready he was; but Uncle Dick took him by the arm and led him up to the door of the hut.

"Put your spear there, as you did before, to keep off all visitors, Master Ebo," he said; and he accompanied his request with signs to express what he wished.

Ebo understood him at once, and made as if to stick the spear in the ground before the door, but he stopped short and shook his head, ran a few yards, and peered in amongst the trees; turned round and shook his head again; ran in another direction and peeped about, coming back shaking his head again.

Ebo's motions said as plainly as could be:

"There is nobody here but ourselves," and as if to satisfy us he led the way to a high hill about a mile away, from whence we had a splendid view all but in one direction, where there lay a clump of mountains. Look which way we would there was nothing but rich plain and dense jungle, with occasional patches of park-like land. Not a sign was there of huts, and once more Ebo looked at us and shook his head, counting us afterwards in his own way—one, two, three, and then tossing his arms in the air.

"We are in luck, Nat," said my uncle. "This island must swarm with natural history specimens, and he has brought us here because he thought it a good place; so now to make the best use of our time. Look out!"

As he spoke he raised his gun and fired at a bird darting down a narrow rift between two rocks that looked as if they had been riven asunder.

I thought he had missed it, but Ebo ran ahead and returned directly with a most lovely kingfisher in glorious plumage.

"If we get nothing more in this island, Nat, I shall be satisfied," said my uncle as we gazed at the lovely creature which Ebo had brought; and seeing the satisfaction in our faces he indulged in another dance.

"Yes," continued my uncle, patting Ebo's black shoulder, "you are a treasure, Ebo, and I see we shall be greatly in your debt. Now, Nat, we must not have a feather of that bird spoiled. I feel ready to go back on purpose to prepare it."

It was indeed a lovely creature; but as I gazed upon its delicately beautiful tints I felt puzzled. It was of rich purple on the back, with azure-blue shoulders dashed and speckled with a lighter blue, while all the under parts were of a pure white, which seemed to throw out the rich colours of the back. But the great beauty of the specimen was its tail, which was long and had the two centre feathers continued almost without any plumes till the end, where they spread out like a couple of racket bats, making the little bird in all about a foot and a half long.

I felt as if I should never tire of gazing at the beautiful specimen, and quite understood my uncle's feeling about wishing to make sure of it by preserving it at once.

Just then, though, a large bird flew across, at which I fired, but it was too far distant, and the shots did no more than rattle about its feathers.

"Did you see its great beak, uncle?" I said.

"Yes, Nat, a hornbill. I daresay we shall find plenty of them here. They take the places in the East of the toucans of the West. But now, Nat, there is an easy shot for you—look! Ebo is pointing to it. There, seated on that twig. Now see he darts off after a fly and is back again. No, he is off once more. We have scared him."

But by this time I had seen the bird, and taking quick aim as it hovered and snatched at a fly of some kind, I fired and brought it down, to find that I too had got a prize in the shape of a lovely little bee-eater, with plumage rich in green and blue, brown and black, while its tail was also rendered more beautiful by the extension of its central feathers in two long thin points.

My uncle's gun spoke out again the next moment, the second barrel following quickly, and Ebo ran and picked up another of the lovely kingfishers, and one of a different kind with a rich coral-red beak, short tail, and its back beautifully barred with blue and black like the ornamental feathers in the wings of a jay.

"That is a bee-eater you have shot, Nat, and a lovely thing too. Mine are all kingfishers."

"There must be a little stream down in that hollow between those rocks, uncle," I replied.

"No, Nat, I don't suppose there is," he said, smiling. "But why do you say that?"

"Because of those kingfishers, uncle. There must be a stream or pool somewhere near."

"I daresay there is, Nat; but not on account of these birds, my lad. They are dry kingfishers, Nat. They do not live upon fish, but upon beetles, butterflies, and moths, darting down and picking them off the ground without wetting a feather."

"Why, how curious!" I said. "They have beaks just like the kingfishers at home."

"Very much like them, Nat," he said; "but they catch no fish. But come, we must get back to the hut, or we shall never get our birds turned into skins before dark. Look out!"

We fired so closely together that it sounded like one shot, and three more of the great pigeons fell heavily to the ground—part of a little flock that was passing over our head.

Ebo seized them with a grin of delight, for he knew that these meant larder, and then hastening back we had just time to strip and prepare our skins before night fell, when, work being ended, the fire was relit, the kettle boiled, and a sort of tea-supper by moonlight, with the dark forest behind and the silvery sea before us, ended a very busy day.

Chapter Twenty Eight.

A bit of a Scare.

That night as I lay in the dark, with the beach outside lit-up by the moon, and listened to the strange noises of the forest behind the hut, I felt over and over again ready to awaken my uncle or Ebo, so sure was I that I could hear wild beasts on the move.

Should there be tigers, or leopards, or even wild boars, what chance should we have if they attacked? Or it might be that one of the huge serpents of which I had read so much might creep in at the open door.

I wanted to be brave, but somehow that night I felt horribly afraid, even the humming buzz of some night-flying beetle making me start. Perhaps I was over-excited, or perhaps, as my uncle would have said, I had eaten too much. At all events, be it what it may, I could not go to sleep, but lay there turning hot and cold and wishing it was morning. The silence seemed so dreadful, and the idea of this being an uninhabited island, instead of being delightful as it had felt in the bright sunshine, now appeared horrible, and I lay thinking of our being far from all human help, and that if our boat happened to drift away we should be left to starve.

Of course this was all nonsense, for with such a clever savage as Ebo and our own ingenuity and tools we could have built another boat — not such a good one as we had arrived in, but quite strong enough to bear us over a calm sea to one or the other of the islands where trading vessels came.

Then I grew hot and seemed to be dripping with perspiration, and my horror increased. What would become of us when our food and powder and shot were gone? We should starve to death. And I began to tremble and wish I had not come, feeling as if I would give anything to be back at home in my old bedroom, with the gas outside in the road and the policeman's heavy foot to be heard now and then as he went along his beat on the look-out for burglars. I should have been ready to meet Aunt Sophia the next morning and receive the severest scolding I had ever had—anything to be away from where I was.

Then I tried to reason with myself and to think that even if our powder and shot were gone we could make bows and arrows, and set traps, and as food ran short we could always make fishing-lines and catch the scaly creatures that swarmed amongst the rocks all round the shore. Besides which there were cocoa-nuts in plenty, with abundance of other fruit.

I thought too of how when I was at home I should have revelled in the idea of being in such a place, to have an uninhabited island, and such a glorious one, far more beautiful and productive than that of Robinson Crusoe, than whom I should be far better off, for in addition to a man Friday I had my clever uncle for companion, guide, and protector.

At the thought of the last word I stretched out my hand to awaken him and tell him of my horrible feeling of dread; but I drew it back for very shame, for what was there to be afraid of?

I grew a little calmer then and lay gazing out of the open door at the brilliant moonlight, which made some leaves glisten as if they were of silver, and all beneath and amidst the thickets look dark and black and soft as velvet.

Then came a strange sighing noise from the forest behind us, which made my flesh creep as I wondered what it could be. Then there was a wild, strange cry, and soon after a heavy crash as of something falling.

After that, as I lay bathed in perspiration and oppressed by the terrible feeling of loneliness that seemed to increase, I fancied I heard the pat, pat, pat, pat of some animal running along the ground, followed by a hard breathing.

"That must be a wild beast," I said to myself; and I rose up on one elbow to listen, meaning to get hold of my gun and load it if the sound came nearer.

Then in a confused and troubled way I began to ask myself whether I ought to awaken Uncle Dick and at the same time kick Ebo to make him seize his spear and help in our defence.

But there are no big wild beasts in these islands, my uncle had said to me several times, even expressing his doubt as to there being anything very large in New Guinea.

"But there are great apes," I said to myself. "I know there are in Borneo, so why should there not be others in an island like this?" and in imagination I began to picture a hideous, great orang-outang cautiously advancing towards our cabin.

I knew they could be very fierce and that they were tremendously strong. Then, too, some travellers had described them as being quite giants of six, seven, and eight feet high, and supposing that there really were no other wild beasts in this island, undoubtedly there were these wild men of the woods, as the Malays called them, and it was one of these that was coming about the hut.

Of course; I knew now as well as if I had seen it. That crash I had heard was made by one of these monsters, and that was its hard breathing that I could hear now.

It was of no use that I tried to make myself believe that I was only listening to Ebo breathing, and every now and then indulging in a regular snore. No, I would not believe it, and lay with my feeling of horror increasing each moment till I lay so helpless now, that if I had wanted to get my gun I could not, I dared not move.

Then there was another horror in the shape of a curious lapping noise from the sea, with a splashing and wallowing as of some great beast; and I did know this, that horrible crocodiles came up the rivers and lived about their mouths, going out to sea and back, and though we had seen no river yet in this island, it was evident that this was one of the monsters crawling about on the shore, and I seemed to see it in the moonlight with its great coarse, scaly back, crooked legs, long stiff tail, and hideous head with sly cruel-looking eyes, and wide, long, teeth-armed jaws.

After a while I knew as well as could be that with its strange instinct it would scent us out and come nearer and nearer, crawling along over the soft sand and leaving a track that could easily be seen the next day. I even seemed to see its footprints with the wide-spread toes, and the long, wavy furrow ploughed by its tail.

It was all one terrible nightmare, growing worse and worse; the noise on the shore increased, the rustling and crashing in the woods; there was a strange humming and buzzing all around, and the breathing sounded closer and deeper.

At last when I felt as if I could bear it no longer, and that if I did not rouse my uncle and Ebo we should be destroyed, I tried to call out, but my voice sounded weak and faint; there was a terrible sense of oppression about me, and the humming and singing noise increased.

I contrived, however, to touch Ebo, and he muttered angrily and changed his position, the noise he made in doing so waking my uncle, who started up on one elbow as if to listen.

"He hears it all, then," I said to myself, and with a wonderful sense of relief I knew that we should be saved.

Why did I not spring up to help him? you will say.

Ah! that I could not do, for I lay there perfectly paralysed with fright and quite speechless, till to my horror I saw in the dim light of the reflected moonbeams my uncle lie down again, when I made a tremendous effort and gasped forth something or another, I cannot say what.

"Hallo!" he exclaimed. "Anything the matter, Nat?" and getting up quickly he struck a match and lit a little wax taper that he always carried in the brass match-box, part of which formed a stick.

He was kneeling by my side directly and had hold of my hand, when at his touch my senses seemed to come back to me.

"Quick!—the guns!" I panted; "wild beasts!—a crocodile, an ape, uncle. I have been hearing them come."

"Nonsense! my boy," he said, smiling.

"No, no; it is no nonsense, uncle. Quick!—the guns!"

"No, my dear boy, it is nonsense. There are no noxious or dangerous beasts here. You are quite safe from them. You have been dreaming, Nat."

"I've not been asleep," I said piteously.

"Haven't you, my lad?" he said, with one hand on my brow and the other on my wrist; "then you have been fancying all these troubles. Nat, my boy, you have got a touch of fever. I'm very glad you woke me when you did."

"Fever, uncle?" I gasped, as the horror of my situation increased, and like a flash came the idea of being ill out in that wilderness, away from all human help and comfort; and, ludicrous is it may sound, I forgot all about Uncle Dick, and began to think of Dr Portly, who had a big brass plate upon his door in the Clapham Road.

"Yes, my boy, a touch of fever, but we'll soon talk to him, Nat; we'll nip him in the bud. A stitch in time saves nine. Now you shall see what's in that little flat tin box I brought. I saw you stare at it when I packed up."

"I thought it was preserving things, uncle," I said.

"So it is, my boy, full of preserving things, one of which you shall soon have for a dose. I hope you like bitters, Nat?"

He laughed so pleasantly that he seemed to give me courage, but I glanced in a frightened way at the opening as I said that I did not much mind.

He saw my glance, and went outside with a cup in his hand, to come back in a few minutes with it full of water from a pool close by.

"No wild beasts about, Nat, my boy," he said merrily. "They were only fever phantoms."

"But I have not been to sleep, uncle," I protested.

"Sign that you are ill, Nat, because generally you drop off in an instant and sleep soundly for hours. There are no wild beasts, my boy, in these islands."

"But I'm sure I heard a great ape breathing hard, and it broke off a great branch in the forest."

"And I'm sure, Nat, that you heard Ebo snoring; and as to the branch breaking, you heard, I dare say, a dead one fall. They are always falling in these old forests. We don't notice the noise in the day, when the birds are singing, but in the night everything sounds wonderfully clear."

"But I'm certain I heard a crocodile crawling up out of the sea, and creeping towards the hut."

"And I'm certain you did not, my dear boy. We have no muddy tidal river here for them to frequent. It was all fever-born, Nat, my boy; believe me."

All the while he was talking I saw that he was busy getting something ready. First he put a little white powder in a glass, then he poured a few drops of something over it, and filled it up with water, stirring it with a little bit of glass rod before kneeling down by me.

"There, Nat," he said kindly, "drink that off."

"What is it, uncle?" I said, taking the glass with hot and trembling hand.

"A preserving thing, my boy. One of the greatest blessings ever discovered for a traveller. It is quinine, Nat, fever's deadliest enemy. Down with it at once."

The stuff was intensely bitter, but my mouth was so hot and parched, and the water with it so cool and pleasant, that I quite enjoyed it, and drew a deep breath.

"There, now, lie down again, my boy, and be off to sleep. Don't fill your head full of foolish imaginings, Nat. There is nothing to fear from wild beasts here."

"But am I going to be very ill, uncle?"

"No, certainly not. You will sleep after that till three or four hours past sunrise, and then you will waken, feeling a little weak, perhaps, but in other respects all right. Perhaps it will come back again, and if it does we will rout it out once more with some quinine. Why, Nat, I've had dozens of such attacks."

I lay back, feeling more at rest, and satisfied that uncle was right about the beasts, for there was no sound now to trouble me; only the lapping of the water, which seemed to be only the waves now beating softly upon the sand, while the heavy breathing was certainly Ebo's, that gentleman never having moved since I touched him.

Then I saw my uncle shut up his little tin case and replace it in the chest, put out the wax taper, and lie down upon his couch of dry grass, yawning slightly, and then lying gazing out of the open door, for I could see his eyes shine.

But by degrees the faintly lit-up hut, with its bamboos and roof, its chests, guns, and Ebo's spear, all seemed to grow indistinct, and then all was restful peace.

Chapter Twenty Nine.

A strange Cry in the Woods.

When I opened my eyes again the sea was dancing and sparkling, and the leaves waving gently in the soft warm breeze. I could see from where I lay that the water was rippling gently upon the sand, and not far from the hut door my uncle was busy skinning some bright-plumaged bird, while Ebo was cooking a couple of pigeons, and watching a little kettle stuck amongst the glowing ashes.

I was very comfortable, and did not feel disposed to move, for all seemed so calm and pleasant; and when I thought a little about my previous night's fancies I was ready to smile at them as being perfectly absurd.

I did not speak, but lay quite still, gazing at the lovely picture framed by the open door, and thinking how beautiful it all was, and how foolish I had been to go on fancying such dangers as I had in the night.

Then it was very pleasant, too, to watch Uncle Dick, and how very much quicker and cleverer he was at making a skin than I was. Still, I hoped by practice to get to be as quick.

He went on till he had dressed the interior of the skin with the soap preparation, and after filling certain parts with cotton-wool, and tying the wing-bones together, he turned it back, smoothed the plumage, and I saw that it was another of the short blue-barred kingfishers similar to that we had obtained before.

I could not help noticing as I lay there so quietly what great care and attention he gave to his task, seeming as if he thoroughly enjoyed his work, and felt it to be a duty to do it well.

At last, though, it was put away to dry, and after carefully washing his hands he came to the hut door very gently to see if I was awake.

"Ah, Nat," he said smiling, "how are you after your long sleep?"

"Long sleep, uncle!" I cried. "Is it very late?"

"Nearly noon, my boy. Well, how are you?"

"I—I think I'm quite well, thank you, uncle," I said, springing up, and feeling ashamed to be lying there, but turning so giddy that I should have fallen had Uncle Dick not caught my arm.

"Sit down," he said quietly. "There, that is better."

"Yes; I feel better now," I said.

"To be sure you do. Well, Nat, I think we have beaten the fever. You will feel weak for a day or two, but you will soon be all right."

And so it proved. For after two or three days of weakness, and a strange weary feeling that was quite new to me, I rapidly got better and felt no more dread of being alone at night; in fact I slept soundly as could be, and got up ready and fresh for any new work.

Uncle Dick was very kind, for until I was stronger he contented himself with shooting just about the hut, finding plenty of beautiful birds; but as soon as I was strong enough we prepared some cold provisions and started off for a longer exploration.

Ebo was delighted, and capered about in the excess of his joy, chattering in his own tongue and introducing every English word he had picked up, and these began now to be a good many; but he had very little idea of putting them to a proper use, muddling them up terribly, but keeping in the most perfect humour no matter how we laughed at him.

"It is my belief, Nat," said Uncle Dick, "that we shall find something better worthy of our notice yet if we make a good long expedition into the more wooded parts of the island."

"I thought we could not be better off, uncle," I said, "for we are getting some lovely birds."

"So we are, Nat; but one is never satisfied, and always wants more. I expect we shall find some birds of paradise, for it strikes me that the cry I have heard several times at daybreak comes from one of them."

"Birds of paradise! Here, uncle?" I cried.

"Why not, my boy? It is as likely a place as it is possible to imagine: an island near the equator, deeply wooded, and hardly ever visited by man. I should say that we must find some here."

"Oh, uncle!" I cried as my eyes glistened, and I felt my cheeks flush at the anticipation of seeing one of these noble birds before the muzzle of my gun.

"I shall be greatly disappointed if we do not find some, and I should have been in search of them before now, only I thought you would like to go, and there was plenty of work close home."

I did not say much, but I felt very grateful at his thoughtfulness, and the very next morning we were off before it was day, tramping through the thick herbage and mounting the rising ground towards the south.

"I purpose trying to get right across the island to-day, Nat," he said, "and if we are too tired to get back all the way we must contrive enough shelter and camp out for one night in the woods."

"I shall not mind, uncle," I said, and on we went.

This time we had provided ourselves with light small baskets, such as we could swing from a cord that passed over our right shoulders, and long and deep enough to hold a good many specimens. We all three bore these, Ebo's being double the size of ours, as he had no gun to use, but trotted easily by our side with his spear over his shoulder.

Before we had gone two miles several lovely birds had fallen to our guns, principally of the thrush family, for our way was amongst bushes on the rising ground.

It is impossible to describe properly the beauty of these lovely softly-feathered objects. Fancy a bird of the size of our thrush but with a shorter tail, and instead of being olive-green and speckled with brown, think of it as having a jetty head striped with blue and brown, and its body a blending of buff, pale greyish blue, crimson, and black.

We kept on, taking our prizes from the baskets, where they lay in cotton-wool, to examine and admire them again and again.

No sooner had we feasted our eyes upon these birds than something as bright of colour fell to our guns. Now it would be a golden oriole or some glittering sun-bird. Then a beautiful cuckoo with crimson breast and cinnamon-brown back. Then some beautifully painted paroquet with a delicate long taper tail; and we were in the act of examining one of these birds, when, as we paused on the edge of a forest of great trees by which we had been skirting, my uncle grasped my arm, for, sounding hollow, echoing, and strange, there rang out a loud harsh cry: "*Quauk-quauk-quauk! Qwok-qwok-qwok!*"

This was answered from a distance here and there, as if there were several of the birds, if they were birds, scattered about the forest.

"There, Nat," said my uncle; "do you hear that?"

"Yes," I said, laughing. "I could hear it plainly enough, uncle. What was it made by—some kind of crow?"

"Yes, Nat, some kind of crow."

"Are they worth trying to shoot, uncle?" I asked.

"Yes," he said with a peculiar smile; and then, as the cry rang out again, apparently nearer, he signified to Ebo that he should try and guide us in the direction of the sounds.

The black understood him well enough, and taking the lead he went on swiftly through the twilight of the forest, for it was easy walking here beneath the vast trees, where nothing grew but fungi and a few pallid-looking little plants.

And so we went on and on, with the trees seeming to get taller and taller, and of mightier girth. Now and then we caught a glimpse of the blue sky, but only seldom, the dense foliage forming a complete screen.

Every now and then we could hear the hoarse harsh cry; but though we went on and on for a tremendous distance, we seemed to get no nearer, till all at once Ebo stopped short, there was the hoarse cry just overhead, and I saw something sweep through the great branches a hundred and fifty feet away.

I had not time to fire, for my uncle's gun made the forest echo, though nothing fell.

"I missed it, Nat," he said, "for the branches were in my way; but I thought I would not let the slightest chance go by."

"What was it, uncle?" I said.

"One of your crows," he replied, laughing; and Ebo went on again.

Just then my uncle glanced at his compass, and saw that we were travelling in the right direction—due south—so it did not matter how far we went; but though we kept hearing the cries of the crow-birds, as I eventually called them, we saw no more, and felt disappointed for a time, but not for long; there were too many fresh objects for our notice.

At last daylight appeared ahead, and we came out from amongst the trunks, which had risen up on every side of us like pillars, into a beautiful open valley dotted with trees, some of which were green with luxuriant branches right to the ground.

We did not spend many moments gazing at the beautiful landscape, so lovely that I half expected to see houses there, and that it was the result of clever gardening; but it was nature's own work, and in every tree there were so many birds, and of such lovely kinds, that we seemed to have come to the very place of all in the world to make our collection.

"There, Nat, look!" said my uncle, pointing to where, in the full sunshine, a great bird with a train of soft amber plumage flew across the opening, to disappear amongst the trees; "there goes one of your crows."

"That lovely buff bird, uncle?" I said; "why, it looked like what I should think a bird of paradise would be."

"And that's what it was, undoubtedly, Nat," he said, "though I never before saw one on the wing."

"But you said crow, uncle," I said. "Oh! of course, you said the birds of paradise belonged to the crow family. I wish you could have shot it."

"It would have required a rifle to hit it at that distance, Nat; but wait a bit. We have learned one thing, and that is the fact that we have birds of paradise here, and that satisfies me that we cannot do better than keep to our present quarters. This place exceeds my highest hopes for a collecting ground. There, look at that bird by the great hollow-looking tree."

"I was looking at it, uncle. It is one of those great birds with the big bill and a thing upon it like a deck-house."

"Yes," said my uncle, "and there is something more. Look, Ebo has gone on. He seems to understand by our looks when he cannot make out our words."

For Ebo had trotted forward towards the tree that had taken our attention, where the great hornbill had flown to a dead trunk some ten-feet from the ground, and then flapped away.

Chapter Thirty.

A Curious Married Couple.

As Ebo reached the tree he turned back to us laughing and pointing with his spear, and then signed to us to come, though even when we were close up to him I could see nothing but a tiny hole in the trunk of the great tree.

"It can't be a nest, uncle," I said, "because it is not big enough. Perhaps it is a wild bees' hive."

"I don't know yet," said my uncle. "I'm like you, Nat, a little bit puzzled. If it were not so small I should say it was a nest from the way that great hornbill keeps flapping about and screeching."

"Shall I shoot it, uncle?" I said eagerly.

"Well, no, Nat, I hardly like to do that. If it is as I think, it would be too cruel, for we should be starving the young, and it will be easy to get a specimen of a hornbill if we want one, though really it is such a common bird that it is hardly worth carriage as a skin."

Just then, to show us, Ebo began to poke at the hole with the point of his spear, and we saw the point of a bill suddenly pop out and dart in again, while the great hornbill shrieked and shouted, for I can call it nothing else, so queerly sounded its voice.

"Why, it can't be the hornbill's nest, uncle!" I said. "Look how small it is."

"Yes, it is small, but it is the hornbill's nest after all," said my uncle, as Ebo kept on poking at the hole and bringing down pieces of what seemed to be clay. Then, seeing how interested we were, he took off his basket, lay down his spear, and taking a hatchet from his waistband cut a few nicks for his toes, and began to climb up, the big hornbill screeching horribly the while, till Ebo was level with the hole, from out of which the end of a bill kept on peeping.

Then the hornbill flew off and Ebo began to chop away a large quantity of dry clay till quite a large hole was opened, showing the original way into the hollow tree; and now, after a great deal of hoarse shrieking the black got hold of the great bird that was inside, having quite a fight before he could drag it out by the legs, and then dropping with it, flapping its great wings, to the ground.

"Undoubtedly the female hornbill," said my uncle. "How singular! The male bird must have plastered her up there and fed her while she has been sitting. That was what we saw, Nat."

"Then there must be eggs, uncle," I cried, with my old bird-nesting propensities coming to the front.

But Ebo was already up the tree again as soon as he had rid himself of the great screaming bird, and in place of bringing down any eggs he leaped back to the earth with a young hornbill, as curious a creature as it is possible to imagine.

It was like a clear leather bag or bladder full of something warm and soft, and with the most comical head, legs, and wings, a good-sized soft beak, a few blue stumps of feathers to represent the tail, and nothing else. It was, so to speak, a horribly naked skin of soft jelly with staring eyes, and it kept on gaping helplessly for more food, when it was evidently now as full as could be.

"Are there more birds?" said Uncle Dick pointing to the hole; but Ebo shook his head, running up, thrusting in his hand, and coming down again.

"Very curious, Nat," said my uncle. "The male bird evidently shuts his wife up after she has laid an egg, to protect her from other birds and perhaps monkeys till she has hatched, and then he goes on feeding her and her young one."

"And well too, uncle; he is as fat as butter."

"Feeding both well till the young one is fit to fly."

"Which won't be yet, uncle, for he hasn't a feather."

"No, my boy. Well, what shall we do with them?" said my uncle, still holding the screeching mother, while I nursed the soft warm bird baby, her daughter or son.

"Let's put the little—no, I mean the big one back, uncle," I said, laughing.

"Just what I was thinking. Climb up and do it."

I easily climbed to the nest and was glad to get the young bird in again without cracking its skin, which seemed so tender; and no sooner had I rolled it softly in and climbed down than my uncle let the mother go, and so strong was her love of her young that she immediately flew to the hole and crept in, croaking and screaming in an uneasy, angry way, as if she was scolding us for interfering with her little one, while from a distance amongst the trees the cock bird kept on answering her with the noisiest and most discordant cries.

Every now and then it came into sight, flying heavily across the openings between the trees, its great cream-coloured, clumsy-looking bill shining and looking bright in the sun, while the cries it uttered tempted one to put one's fingers into one's ears.

And all the time the hen bird inside the tree kept answering it peevishly, as much as to say, Look here: what a shame it is! Why don't you come and drive these people away?

"This is one of the most singular facts in natural history that I have met with," said Uncle Dick, who was still gazing curiously up at the tree and watching the female hornbill's head as she kept shuffling herself about uneasily, and seemed to object to so much light.

"I think I know what it is, uncle," I said, laughing.

"Do you, Nat," he replied. "Well, you are cleverer than I am if you do know. Well, why is it?"

"The hen hornbill must be like Uncle Joe's little bantam, who never would sit till she was shut up in the dark, and that's why Mr Hornbill fastened up his wife."

My uncle laughed, and then, to Ebo's great delight, for he had been fidgeting about and wondering why it was that we stopped so long, we continued our journey in search of the birds of paradise, whose cries could be heard at a distance every now and then.

But though we kept on following the sounds we seemed to get no nearer, and to make matters worse, so as not to scare them uncle said it would be better not to fire, with the consequence that we missed shooting some very beautiful birds that flitted from tree to tree.

"We must give up the birds of paradise to-day, Nat," said my uncle at last. "I see it is of no use to follow them; they are too shy."

"Then how are we to get any?" I said in a disappointed tone; for we had been walking for some hours now and I was tired.

"Lie in wait for them, Nat," he replied smiling. "But come, we'll try and shoot a few birds for food now and have a good dinner. You will feel all the more ready then for a fresh walk."

By means of a little pantomime we made Ebo understand what we wanted, and in a very little while he had taken us to where the great pigeons thronged the trees, many being below feeding on a kind of nut which had fallen in great profusion from a lofty kind of palm.

If we had wanted a hundred times as many of the big pigeons we could easily have shot them, they were so little used to attack; but we only brought down a sufficiency for our present wants, and as soon as Ebo understood that these birds were not to be skinned but plucked for eating, he quickly had a good fire blazing and worked away stripping the feathers off so that they dropped on the fire and were consumed.

The plumage was so beautiful that it seemed to be like so much wanton destruction to throw it away, and I could not help thinking what delight it would have given me before I had seen Uncle Dick's collection, to have been the possessor of one of these noble birds. But as my uncle very reasonably said, we should have required a little army of porters to carry our chests, and then a whole vessel to take them home, if we were to preserve every specimen we shot. We could only save the finest specimens; the rest must go for food; and of course we would only, after we had obtained a sufficiency of a particular kind, shoot those that we required for the table.

Ebo was invaluable in preparing fires and food for cooking, and upon this occasion, as he placed the birds on sticks close to the hot blaze, I watched him with no little interest, longing as I did to begin the feast.

But birds take time to cook, and instead of watching impatiently for them to be ready, I saw that Uncle Dick had taken his gun down a narrow little glade between two rows of trees growing so regularly that they seemed to have been planted by a gardener.

But no gardener had ever worked here, and as I overtook my uncle he began to talk of how singular it was that so beautiful a place should be without inhabitants.

"The soil must be rich, Nat, to produce such glorious trees and shrubs. Look at the beauty of what flowers there are, and the herbage, Nat. The place is a perfect paradise."

"And do you feel sure, uncle, that there are no savages here?"

"None but ourselves, Nat," said my uncle, laughing.

"Well, but we are not savages, uncle," I said.

"That is a matter of opinion, my boy. I'm afraid the birds here, if they can think about such things, would be very much disposed to look upon us as savages for intruding upon their beautiful domain to shoot one here and one there for our own selfish purposes."

"Oh! but birds can't think, uncle," I said.

"How do you know?"

Well, of course I did not know, and could produce no argument in support of my case. So I looked up at him at last in a puzzled way and saw that he was smiling.

"You can't answer that question, Nat," he said. "It is one of the matters that science sees no way of compassing. Still, I feel certain that birds have a good deal of sense."

"But you don't think they can talk to one another, do you, uncle?"

"No, it cannot be called talking; but they have certain ways of communicating one with the other, as anyone who has taken notice of domestic fowls can see. What is more familiar than the old hen's cry to her chickens when she has found something eatable? and then there is the curious call uttered by all fowls when any large bird that they think is a bird of prey flies over them."

"Oh! yes, I've heard that, uncle," I said.

"I remember an old hen uttering that peculiar warning note one day in a field, Nat, and immediately every chicken feeding near hurried off under the hedges and trees, or thrust their heads into tufts of grass to hide themselves from the hawk."

"That seems to show, uncle, that they do understand."

"Yes, they certainly comprehend a certain number of cries, and it is a sort of natural language that they have learned for their preservation."

"I know too about the chickens, uncle," I said. "Sometimes they go about uttering a little soft twittering noise as if they were happy and contented; but if they lose sight of their mother they pipe and cry and stand on their toes, staring about them as if they were in the greatest of trouble."

"I think I can tell you another curious little thing about fowls too, and their way of communicating one with the other. Many years ago, Nat, I had a fancy for keeping some very large fine Dorking fowls, and very interesting I found it letting the hens sit and then taking care of their chickens."

"But how is it, uncle," I said, interrupting him, "that a tiny, tender chicken can so easily chip a hole in an egg-shell, as they do when they are nearly ready to come out?"

"Because, for one reason, the egg-shell has become very brittle, and all the glutinous, adhesive matter has dried away from the lime; the other reason is, that the pressure of the bird's beak alone is sufficient to do it, because the pressure comes from within. There is a wonderful strength in an egg, Nat, if the pressure is from without; it will bear enormous weight from without, for one particle supports another, and in reason the pressure adds to the strength. The slightest touch, however, is sufficient to break a way out from within. I'll be bound to say you have often hammered an egg with a spoon and been surprised to find how hard it is."

"Yes, uncle, often," I said.

"Well, but to go on with my story, Nat. One day a favourite hen had eleven beautiful little yellow downy chickens, and for the fun of the thing I took one soft little thing out of the nest and carried it into the yard, where the great cock was strutting about with his sickle-feathered green tail glistening in the sun, and, putting down the tiny yellow ball of down, I drew back, calling the old cock the while.

"He ran up, thinking it was something to eat; but as soon as he reached the helpless little chick he stopped short, bent his head down, looked at it first with one eye, then with the other, and seemed lost in meditation.

"'Come, papa,' I said, 'what do you think of your little one?'

"Still he kept on staring intently at the little thing till it began to cry *'Peek, peek, peek'* in a most dismal tone, for it was very cold, and then the old cock, who had been looking very important and big, suddenly began to cry *'Took, took, took'*, just like a hen, and softly crouched down, spreading his wings a little for the chick to creep under him and get warm, and no doubt he would have taken care of that chicken and brought it up if I had not taken it back to the hen.

"But look! we are talking about barn-door fowls and losing chances to get lovely specimens of foreign birds and—what's that?"

For just then a shrill wild call rang down the lovely glade, and I thought that Uncle Dick was wrong, and savages were near.

Chapter Thirty One.

Lost in the Forest.

There was no occasion for alarm, the cry only coming from Ebo, who, as soon as he saw us, began making frantic signs to us to come.

"That means the pigeons are cooked, Nat," said my uncle, laughing; and this was the case, for, as soon as he saw us, the black came running up gesticulating and pointing behind him in the direction of the fire, where the delicious birds were waiting for us to eat.

Those were delightful meals that we had out in the shade of some grand wide-spreading tree, in whose branches every now and then a parrot would come shrieking, to be followed by others; and as we ate our dinner so would they busily find and eat theirs, hanging by their legs, perhaps head downwards, or perching on one leg and using the other with its soft clasping yoke toes like a hand to convey the food towards its beak.

I never felt tired of watching the parrots and paroquets, for besides their beauty of plumage of all kinds of soft tints of green, brightened with orange and scarlet and blue, they always looked such plump and delicately feathered birds. I have seen hundreds of them stuffed, and have admired the bird-mounters' skill, but they never get anywhere near nature and the soft and downy beauty of a bird in its native state.

The wonder to me was that they could keep themselves so prim, and with every feather in such perfect order. The paroquets, for instance, had the central feathers of their tail so long and thin and delicate, that it seemed that, flitting and climbing about the trees so much, they must get them broken, but they apparently never did, except when they were damaged by our shot.

It was the same with the lovely racket-tailed kingfishers and the fly-catchers, some of which had tails double the length of their own bodies, and of a delicacy that was beautiful in the extreme.

But I must go back to the rest of our adventures that day, for as soon as we had dined and had a rest, Uncle Dick signed to Ebo that he should make a rough hut beneath this tree, ready for our sleeping that night, and leaving him industriously at work, we started off together to try and explore a little more of the island.

Going as straight as we could, we were not very long before, from a bit of a hill, we could see the blue waters of the ocean spreading far and wide, and soon after we made out the great rollers falling over upon the sands, which spread right and left, of a dazzling whiteness, being composed entirely of powdered-up coral and madrepore.

There was no need, my uncle said, to go farther that day, for we had found out that it was no great distance across the island; the thing now was to discover its length.

"It seems a foolish thing to do, perhaps, Nat," said my uncle, "but I should very much like to try a little more exploration to-day. I don't think we will shoot any more birds, but examine the land instead, so as to be a little at home with its shape, ready for making a trip here and there in the future. We shall be able to mark down good spots, too, for finding specimens in the future."

"But shall you stay here long, uncle?" I asked.

"That I cannot answer, Nat," he replied, as we shouldered our guns and trudged on. "It all depends upon the number of specimens we find, and so far it seems to me that we might travel far before we hit again upon such a wild paradise."

"I wonder how Uncle Joe would like to live here!" I said laughing. "What a garden he might have, and how things would grow! Oh, how I should like to help him build the house and get the garden in order!"

"Your Uncle Joe would be happy anywhere, Nat," said my uncle. "He is one of those contented amiable men who are always at rest; but I'm afraid your Aunt Sophia would soon find it dull, and be grumbling because there was no gas, no pavement, no waterworks, no omnibuses, no cabs, no railroads. No, Nat, my boy, your Aunt Sophia would be miserable here."

"And yet it is such a lovely place," I cried enthusiastically. "Everything is so beautiful. Oh! uncle, I could stay here forever."

"No, Nat, you could not," he replied laughing; "but it is very beautiful all the same. I have travelled a great deal, and have seen some wonderful scenery, but I have never met with so much beauty condensed in so small a space."

We kept on walking, but it was only to stop every now and then before some fresh find—sometimes it would be a curiously-shaped orchid, or a pitcher-plant half full of dead insects. Then some great forest tree full of sweet-scented blossoms, and alive with birds and insects, would arrest our attention; or down in some moist hollow, where a tiny stream trickled from the rocks, there would be enormous tree-ferns springing up twelve or fifteen feet above us, and spreading their beautiful fronds like so much glorious green lace against the sky. A fern is always a beautiful object, but these tree-ferns were more than beautiful—they were grand.

The farther we went the more beauties we found, and we kept on noting down places to visit again where there were palm and other trees full of fruit, which evidently formed the larder of various kinds of beautiful birds. We could have shot enough in that walk to have kept us busy making skins for days, but we kept to the determination my uncle had made, not to shoot any more that day, except once, when the curious hoarse cry of some bird of paradise, answered by others at a distance, tempted us away.

"Birds of paradise are exceptions, Nat," said my uncle, smiling. "We must get them when we can."

I immediately seemed to see the beautiful bird flying amongst the trees, with its lovely buff plumes trailing behind like so much live sunshine, and glancing once at my gun to see that the cartridges were in all right, I crept cautiously on amongst the trees on one side as Uncle Dick made a bit of a curve round in another, so that we had a good many great forest trees between us, whose foliage we carefully watched as we went cautiously on.

Every now and then, after a silence that made us think that our labour was all in vain, and we were about to give up, the loud harsh cry would come echoing from amongst the trees, and always seeming so near that I thought I must get a shot at the bird in a moment or two, and I bent down and crept on as quietly as I could, till the tree from which the sound seemed to come was reached.

Then I would stand ready to fire, watching carefully for a shot, peering amongst the boughs, and fancying a dozen times over that I could catch glimpses of the bird amongst the leaves, when, as if laughing at me for my pains, the cry would come again from a couple of hundred yards away, and the chase went on.

I did not shout to Uncle Dick, for by stopping to listen now and then I could hear the rustling of the leaves and twigs as he went on, besides every now and then catching through the dim light a glimpse of his face.

Once or twice, when a beautiful bird sprang up between us, my heart began to beat more quickly, for I thought that if uncle was tempted to shoot at it he might hit me; but by degrees I grew more confident and walked boldly on, feeling that I had nothing to fear.

That bird must have led us for miles. Every time we were ready to give up, the hoarse cry rang out again, and we followed once more, feeling sure that sooner or later we must get a shot at it, or at one of the others which kept answering from a distance; but at last I heard a peculiar whistle from where my uncle would be, and I forced my way through the undergrowth and joined him.

"Nat," he said, wiping the perspiration from his face, "that must have been a wild-goose instead of a bird of paradise. Have you heard it lately?"

"No, uncle; not for quite a quarter of an hour. I think it must have taken a longer flight this time."

"*Yawk, yawk—wok, wok, wok, wok, wok,*" rang out close behind us, and we both fired simultaneously at a faint gleam of what seemed to be yellow light as it flitted through the glade, running forward to get beyond the smoke in the hope that we might have hit it.

But even if we had we should not have been able to find it, for in the eagerness of our pursuit we had come now into one of the densest parts of the forest that we had found, and after wandering on through a faint warm glow caused by the setting sun shining through the tree trunks, a sudden dull greyness had come upon us, followed almost at once by darkness, and we knew that we were lost.

"I ought to have known better, Nat," said my uncle, with an exclamation of impatience. "I have not the most remote idea where our camp is, and Ebo will be expecting us back."

"Oh! never mind, uncle," I said; "let's have a try. I dare say we can find the way back."

"My dear boy, it would be sheer folly," he replied. "How is it possible? We are tired out now, and it would be only exhausting ourselves for nothing, and getting a touch of fever, to go striving on through the night."

"What are we to do then, uncle?"

"Do, my boy? Do as Adam did, make ourselves as comfortable as we can beneath a tree. We can do better, for we can cut some wood and leaves to make ourselves a shelter."

"What, build a hut, uncle?" I said in dismay; for I was now beginning to find out how tired I really was.

"No; we won't take all that trouble; but what we do we must do quickly. Come along."

I followed him up a slope to where the ground seemed to be a trifle more open and the trees larger, and as we forced our way on my uncle drew his great hunting-knife and chopped down a straight young sapling, which, upon being topped and trimmed, made a ten-feet pole about as thick as my arm was then.

This he fixed by resting one end in the fork of a tree and tying the other to a branch about five feet from the ground.

"Now then, Nat," he cried, "get your big sheath-knife to work and clear the ground here. Does it seem dry?"

"Yes, uncle, quite," I said.

"Well, then, you chop off plenty of soft twigs and leaves and lay them thickly for a bed, while I make a roof over it."

We worked with a will, I for my part finding plenty of tree-ferns, whose fronds did capitally, and Uncle Dick soon had laid sloping against the pole a sufficiency of leafy branches to form an ample shelter against the wind and rain should either come.

"So far, so good, Nat," he said; "now are you very hungry?"

"I'm more tired than hungry, uncle," I said.

"Then I think we will light a fire and then have as good a night's rest as we can."

There was no difficulty in getting plenty of dried wood together, and after a few failures this began to blaze merrily, lighting up the leaves of the trees with a rich red glow; and when it was at its height setting a good many birds flitting about in the strange glow, so that we could have procured more specimens here. But after sitting talking by the fire for some time we crept in under our leafy shed, and it seemed to me that no sooner had I stretched myself out than I fell fast asleep.

Chapter Thirty Two.

Another Night Horror.

I had no idea how long I had been asleep when all at once I started into wakefulness, feeling that we were in danger.

I did not know what the danger might be, but that there was something about to happen I was sure.

It was very dark in our narrow shed, and nearly dark out beyond our feet, only that a faint glow from our fire made one or two tree trunks stand out like dark sentinels just on the other side.

My uncle was so near that I could have wakened him by just moving one hand, but remembering that other night I shrank from wakening him without cause.

"I've got another fever fit coming on," I said to myself; but all the same I did not feel so, only startled and timid, and to encourage myself I thought that I must have had a bad dream.

But no; I could remember no dream. It seemed as if I had sunk at once into a profound sleep from which I had just wakened fancying that we were in danger.

Then I lay quite still listening to my uncle's breathing, and thinking how helpless and unprotected we were out in that wild place, not even having Ebo with us now.

But what was there to fear, I asked myself as I recalled my uncle's words, that he was certain there were no wild beasts in such an island as this, and there were no other inhabitants than ourselves.

Yes, I could think of all this, and it ought to have made me more comfortable; but no, there was still that curious feeling of being in danger, and I felt as certain as if I could see it, that something was coming to attack us.

Then as I could neither see nor hear anything I began once more to conclude that I must be suffering from another attack of fever, and I lifted my hand to awaken my uncle, so that he might give me some quinine again.

Then I recollected that the medicine was in one of our boxes right away from where we were, for we were lost in the forest, and it would be impossible to move until the sun was up once more. So there I lay till another change came over me, and I once more felt sure that it was not fever again. I knew it was not, and this time there was no mistake—something was coming through the forest, though what it was I could not tell.

Should I waken my uncle?

I raised my hand again and again, but always lowered it once more, so fearful was I of being ridiculed; and then I lay thinking that although uncle had said with such certainty that there were neither inhabitants nor wild beasts, there was plenty of room for either to hide away in these forests; and besides, should there be no regular inhabitants, some might have come by canoe from one or other of the islands. And, yes, I was sure of it, they must have seen our fire, and were creeping up to kill us where we lay.

This was a very pretty theory; but would not they make some noise as they came, and if so, where was that noise?

I lay perfectly still with the perspiration oozing out of me and my horror increasing, but still there was no noise.

Yes, there was—a low rustling sound as of some one creeping through the bushes towards us. There could be no mistaking that sound, it was just the same as I had been hearing all the afternoon as we crept cautiously on in search of the birds of paradise.

I listened and tried to pierce the darkness with my eyes, but only just about the embers of the fire was anything visible, where the tree trunks stood all like sentries.

Then the noise ceased and I was ready to believe that I had made a mistake. No, there it was again, and certainly much nearer.

Should I wake Uncle Dick, or should I try to be brave enough to deal with the danger myself?

I was horribly frightened and sadly wanted him to give me his help and counsel; but as I was not sure, in spite of my feelings, that there really was danger, I fought hard with my cowardice and determined to act as seemed best.

Cautiously reaching out my hand I took hold of my gun, and by pressing my finger on each trigger in turn, I cocked it silently, and raising myself on one elbow waited for the danger to come.

The sounds stopped several times, but were always resumed, and the more I listened the more certain I felt that some big animal was creeping up with great caution towards the fire, though I felt that that animal might be a man.

I would have given anything to have been able to sit up in an easier position; but I could only have done so by making a noise and perhaps waking Uncle Dick for nothing. So I remained as I was, watching with eyes and ears upon the strain, the barrel of my gun towards the opening in our leafy shed and well covering the fire; and so minute after minute went by, with the sensation more and more strongly upon me of the near presence of some creature, one which I each moment expected to see cross the faint glow of the fire.

Then all was still, and though I listened so intently I could hear nothing but my uncle's breathing. So still did everything become that I began to feel less oppression at my chest, and ready to believe that it was all fancy, when suddenly the embers of the fire seemed to have fallen a little together, for the glow grew stronger and there was a faint flicker which made my heart give one great bound.

For there, between me and the fire, was what appeared to be the monstrous figure of an orang-outang, which had crawled close up to the fire and was looking at it.

The creature was on all-fours and had its back to me, while the darkness of the night prevented me from making it out properly; but it looked to me very large and dark coloured, and I had read that the strength of these creatures was enormous.

It crouched there about five yards from where I lay, and as I wondered whether I had better shoot, I suddenly recollected that both barrels of my gun were loaded with small shot, and that at such a distance, though the shot would well hang together, they were not certain to make a mortal wound; while the result would be that the monster would be more fierce and terrible than it was before.

I don't think I was afraid to fire, but I hesitated, and as I waited I felt that there was a possibility of the animal not being aware of our presence, for it was evidently the fire that had attracted it.

But these hopes came to an end directly, and I raised my gun softly to my shoulder, for the creature seemed about to crawl towards me. This was only for a moment or two though, and then there was a peculiar scratching noise as if the monster was tearing at the bushes, and I could dimly see its great back waving to and fro. Then all at once the scratching ceased, and it seemed to have thrown some twigs and leaves upon the fire, which blazed up, and my gun nearly fell from my hand.

"Ebo!" I shouted; and as my uncle sprang up and we crept out into the ruddy light spread by the burning wood, there was my monster in the shape of our trusty follower, dancing about like mad, and chattering away as he pointed to the fire, then to himself, then to a distance, and seemed to be trying to make us understand that he had seen the fire and tracked us by its light to where we were.

His delight seemed to know no bounds, for whenever he came to a pause in his performance and stood grinning at us, he broke out again, leaping about, running away, coming back, and shouting and laughing as he slapped himself loudly with his hands. I can compare his conduct to nothing but that of a dog who has just found his master.

The question now arose what was to be done, and by a good deal of sign—making we asked Ebo to lead us back to the camp; but he shook his head and stamped and frowned, and to cut the matter short threw some more wood on the fire, pushed us both into our leaf tent, lay down across the front, and went to sleep.

Chapter Thirty Three.

My Earthquake.

I said very little to my uncle about my alarm, feeling sure that he would laugh very heartily at my mistake, but I lay awake for some little while thinking that it was time I grew to be more manly and brave, and not so ready to be frightened at everything I could not directly understand. It seemed so shocking, too, for I might in my cowardly fear have shot poor Ebo, who was one of the best and truest of fellows, and seemed never so happy as when able to do something for me.

My last thoughts before I went to sleep were that I hoped I might grow into a brave and true man, and I determined to try hard not to be such a weak coward.

I have often thought since, though, that if any ordinary man had been placed in the same situation he would have been as nervous as I; for to awake out of a deep sleep in a dark forest in a wild land, where dangerous beasts might be lurking, to hear a peculiar rustling noise, and through the faint light to make out the figure of the black, looking big and indistinct as he crept on all-fours, was, to put it as you may, very startling.

I was ready enough to laugh at all the dread when I awoke in the morning to find the sun just up, and sending his rays through the long vistas of trees, where the birds were whistling, twittering, and screaming loudly, while every now and then from a distance came the hoarse cry of the birds of paradise.

"It is terribly tempting, Nat," said my uncle, "but I think we had better make straight for camp and get a good breakfast before we do anything else. Hallo! what is Ebo doing?"

"Making up the fire," I said; and directly the black had thrown on a great armful of dead wood he came to us laughing and rubbing the front of his person, squeezing himself in to show how empty he was, after which he picked up a stick, took aim at a bird, said *"Bop!"* and ran to pick it up; coming back laughing for us to applaud his performance.

"Well, Nat, that's a piece of dumb-show that says very plainly we are to shoot some birds for breakfast before we do anything else, and it would perhaps be wise, so come along; there are some of our old friends in that great palm-tree."

I followed my uncle closely, and we had no difficulty in shooting three of the great pigeons, which Ebo pounced upon and carried off in triumph, and in a few minutes they were roasting upon sticks, while our black cook busied himself in climbing a cocoa-tree, from which he detached half a dozen nuts, each of which came down with a tremendous thud.

I was terribly hungry, but Uncle Dick said we should be worse if we stopped there smelling the roasting pigeons. So we took our guns and went across an opening to where there was tree after tree, rising some thirty or forty feet high, all covered with beautiful white sweet-scented starry flowers, each with a tube running up from it like that of a jasmine.

All about this beautiful little birds were flitting, and as we watched them for some time I could see their feathers flash and glitter in the sunshine, as if some wore tiny helmets of burnished gold and breastplates of purple glittering scales. No colours could paint the beauty of these lovely little creatures, which seemed to be of several different kinds, for some had patches of scarlet, of orange, blue, and white to add to the brilliancy of their feathering; and so little used were they to the sight of man that they seemed to pay no attention to us, but allowed us to go very close, so that we could see them flit and hover and balance themselves before the sweet-scented starry bell-flowers, into whose depths they thrust their long thin beaks after the honey and insects that made them their home.

I soon learned from my uncle that they were the sun-birds, the tiny little fellows that were in the Old World what the humming-birds were in the New, for there are no humming-birds in the East.

Following Uncle Dick's example, I took the shot out of my gun, for he said that the concussion and the wad would be sufficient to bring them down. But, somehow, we were so interested in what we saw that neither of us thought of firing, and there we stood watching the glittering feathers, the graceful motions, and the rapidity with which these tiny birds seemed to flash from blossom to blossom, till a loud yell from Ebo summoned us to breakfast.

"Yes, Nat," said my uncle, who seemed to read my thoughts, "that is the way to see the beauty of the sun-birds. No stuffed specimens of ours will ever reproduce a hundredth part of their beauty; but people cannot always come from England to see these things. Take care! What's that?"

We were going through rather a dense patch of undergrowth, where the ground beneath was very soft and full of water, evidently from some boggy springs. There was a great deal of cane and tall grass, with water weeds of a most luxuriant growth, and the place felt hot and steamy as we forced our way through, till, as I was going first and parting the waving canes right and left with my gun barrel, I stepped upon what seemed to be a big branch of a rotten tree that had fallen there, when suddenly I felt myself lifted up a few inches and jerked back, while at the same moment the canes and grass crashed and swayed, and something seemed to be in violent motion.

"Is it an earthquake, uncle?" I said, looking aghast at the spot from whence had been jerked.

"Yes, Nat, and there it goes. Fire, boy, fire!"

He took rapid aim a little to the left, where the canes and broad-leaved plants were swaying to and fro in a curious way, just as if, it seemed then, a little pig was rushing through, and following his example I fired in the same direction.

But our shots seemed to have no effect, and whatever it was dashed off into a thicker part, where it was too swampy to follow even if we had been so disposed.

"Your earthquake has got away for the present, Nat," said my uncle. "Did you see it?"

"No, uncle," I said.

"But you must have trodden upon it, and it threw you back."

"No, uncle; I trod upon the trunk of a small tree, that was all."

"You trod upon a large serpent, Nat, my boy," he exclaimed.

"Ugh!" I ejaculated; and I made a jump back on to more solid ground.

"The danger has passed now, Nat," he said, smiling at my dread; "but really I could not have believed such a creature existed in so small an island."

"Oh, uncle!" I cried, "I shall never like to go about again for fear of treading upon another."

"You will soon get over that, Nat, and perhaps we may have the luck to shoot the brute. I don't think we did it much mischief this time, though I got a good sight of it as it glided amongst the canes."

"Why, we had no shot in our guns, uncle," I cried; "we took them out so as not to knock the sun-birds about too much."

"Of course!" cried my uncle. "How foolish of me not to remember this!"

We had both reloaded now, and then, without heeding a shout from Ebo, we stood looking in the direction taken by the reptile, though now all the luxuriant canes and grasses were quite still.

"What do you say, Nat?" said my uncle. "Shall we follow the monster and try and shoot it?"

"It must be forty or fifty feet long, uncle," I said, feeling a curious creeping sensation run through me.

"Forty or fifty nonsenses, my boy!" he said, laughing. "Such serpents as that only exist in books. They rarely exceed twenty feet where they are largest. That fellow would not be fifteen. What do you say — will you come?"

"Ye–es, uncle," I said hesitatingly, feeling hot and cold by turns.

"Why, Nat," he said quietly, "you are afraid!" I did not speak for a moment or two, but felt the hot blood flush into my face as I stood there looking him full in the eyes, and unable to withdraw my gaze.

"Yes, uncle," I said at last. "I did not want to be, but a serpent is such a horrible thing, and I am afraid."

"Yes, it is a horrible monster, Nat," he said quietly. "I don't like them myself, but if we could kill it—"

"I can't help feeling afraid, uncle," I said, "but I'm ready to go on now."

"What! to attack it, Nat?"

"Yes, uncle."

"It will be rather dangerous, my boy."

"Yes, uncle," I said. "I suppose so; but I want to get over being so afraid of things. I'm quite ready now."

I looked to him to come on at once, but he did not move, and stood looking at me for some minutes without speaking.

"Then we will go and attack the brute, Nat," he said; "but it will not go away from that bit of a swamp, so we will try and put a little more nerve into our hearts with a good breakfast, and then have Ebo to help us, unless he proves to be a worse coward than you."

"He could not be, uncle," I said pitifully; and I felt very, very miserable.

"Oh! yes, he could be, Nat, my boy," said my uncle, smiling, and grasping me affectionately by the arm. "You are a coward, Nat, but you fought with your natural dread, mastered it, and are ready to go and attack that beast. Master Ebo may be a coward and not fight with and master his dread. So you see the difference, my boy."

Another shout from the black made us hasten our steps to where he was dancing about and pointing to the crisp brown pigeons, big as chickens, with great green leaves for plates, and the new ripe cocoa-nuts divested of their husks; but for a few moments I could not eat for thinking of the serpent. My fresh young appetite asserted itself though soon after, and, forgetting the danger to come, I made one of the most delicious of meals.

Chapter Thirty Four.

Many Feet of Unpleasantry.

It was only while I was scraping out the last of the delicate cream from the inside of a huge cocoa-nut that I recalled the task we had to come, and a curious shiver ran through me as I glanced in the direction of the swamp where, nearly a mile away, the reptile lay.

Ebo knew nothing about it as yet, and I hardly conceived how he would be made to understand what we had seen.

"Do you think he will be ready to help kill the serpent, uncle?" I said, after waiting for some time to see if he would say anything about the attack.

"I hardly know, Nat," he replied cheerily; "but we'll soon try him. By the way, use the cartridges with the largest kind of shot, for we must make up for this morning's mistakes. Here, Ebo, we've seen a snake," he said.

"Ung-kul, Nat-mi-boi. Hal-lo, hal-lo hal-lo!" replied Ebo, laughing merrily, and showing his white teeth.

"We shall not get at his understanding like that," said my uncle quietly; and he sat thinking for a moment.

"Shall I try and draw a snake, uncle?" I said.

"To be sure, Nat," he replied, laughing; "but where are paper, pencil, or chalk? Stop a minute—I have it."

We generally carried a stout piece of cord with us, ready for any emergency, and this cord, about ten yards long and a little thicker than clothes-line, my uncle now untwisted from his waist, where he had worn it like a belt, and calling Ebo's attention to it he laid it out upon the ground. Then holding one end he made it wave about and crawl and curve and twine, ending by knotting it up in a heap and laying the end carefully down as if it were a serpent asleep.

Ebo watched the process attentively, at first seriously and then as if delighted, clapping his hands, dancing, and chattering away as if telling my uncle how clever he was.

"But that does not show him what we want, uncle," I said.

"Well, then, you try."

I took up the rope, made it undulate a little, and then as Ebo looked on I gave it a quick twist and wound it round him, pretending to make the end bite.

He took to it directly, pretending that the reptile was crushing him, fighting his way free of the folds, picking up his club and attacking it in turn, beating the make-believe head with his club, and finally indulging in a war-dance as he jumped round, dragging the imaginary serpent after him, pretending all the while that it was very heavy, before stooping down to smell it, making a grimace, and then throwing down the rope, which he pretended to bury in the sand.

"It's all right, Nat. He understands, and has evidently encountered big snakes. Now, then, to show him our enemy, for he will fight."

My uncle was right, for it was evident that Ebo quite understood us and meant fighting, for, sticking his spear in the ground, he made signs to me that I should lend him my hunting-knife, which I at once did, and laughing and chattering away he looked about him a little, and then proceeded to cut down a sapling tree about as thick as his arm, from whose trunk he selected a piece a couple of feet in length and carefully trimmed it into a formidable club with a smooth, small handle, while he left the thick end jagged with the ugly places from which he had cut the branches.

He was not long in getting it into shape, and no sooner had he satisfied himself with his work than he returned my hunting-knife, making believe that he was horribly afraid lest it should cut off his head, and then proceeded to attack an imaginary serpent that was trying to escape through the bushes. Now he was trying to strike it, now retreating, now making blows at it upon the ground, now in the air, ending by dropping his club and seizing the neck of the creature, which he pretended had coiled round him; now he was down upon one knee, now overthrown and rolling over and over in a fierce struggle; but at last his acting came to a conclusion by his striking the reptile's head against a tree, kicking off an imaginary coil from his leg, and strutting about proudly to show how he had conquered.

The most surprising part of the affair was that he did not seem to be in the slightest degree exhausted by his efforts, but picked up his club and began chattering to us, and pointing to the marsh as if asking us to come on.

"Well, Nat," said my uncle, "if he will only fight half as well as that when we encounter the serpent, there ought to be nothing to fear. We ought to master the brute easily."

"Would such a serpent be very strong, uncle?" I asked.

"Wonderfully strong," he replied. "Their muscles are tremendously powerful. See what strength anything of similar form possesses; an eel, for instance."

"Yes, uncle," I said thoughtfully, as I recalled how difficult I had once found it to hold a large one that I had caught. "Eels are very strong."

"Look here, Nat," said my uncle kindly, "I don't think we should run any risks in following up this serpent, for one good shot would disable it; but still it may be a little perilous, and it is not just to expect a boy of your age to face such a danger. You stop back at a distance, and I will send Ebo into the marsh to drive it out, while I try to get a shot at it."

"Oh, no, uncle!" I said quickly.

"Come now, my boy," he cried, clapping me on the shoulder. "You are going because you think I shall consider you cowardly if you stay behind. I tell you truly, Nat, I shall not."

"I did feel something of that kind, uncle," I said warmly; "but that is not all. I want to try and be brave and to master all my cowardly feelings, and this seems such a chance."

He stood looking at me for a few minutes, and then said quietly:

"Very well then, Nat, you shall come. But be careful with your gun, and do not fire unless you have a clear shot. Don't hurry, and mind that Ebo is not near. As to the danger," he said, "there is very little. The worst thing that could happen would be that the serpent might seize you."

I could not help a shudder.

"Coil round you."

The shudder felt now was the serpent wrapping me round.

"And giving you a severe squeeze," continued my uncle. "It is a hundred to one against its teeth catching you in the face, and it is doubtful whether they would penetrate your clothes, and even if they did you would suffer no worse than from a few thorns, for these constricting reptiles are not poisonous."

"It don't sound very nice, uncle," I said, feeling as if my face was showing white through the brown of the sunburns.

"No, Nat, it does not," he said; "but now I have told you the worst I may as well say something on the other side. Now the chances are that the brute will try its best to escape, and be shot in the act; and even supposing that it did seize you, which is no more likely than that it should seize Ebo or me, we should immediately get hold of it by the neck and have its head off before it knew where it was."

"Yes, uncle, I know you would," I said with more confidence and a strange thrill of excitement running through me. "Let me come, please."

"You shall, Nat," he replied; "and now I'll confess to you, my boy, that I should have felt disappointed if you had held back. Come along, my lad, and I think we shall soon slay this modern dragon."

All this time Ebo had been looking at us wonderingly; but no sooner did we examine our guns and start forward, than he shouldered his club and went before us towards the piece of marshy ground.

I walked on by uncle's side with my gun ready, and all the time I kept on wondering what he would have said to me if he had known how nervous I felt.

The thoughts of what we were approaching seemed to take all the brightness and beauty out of the scene, which was as lovely as could be. Strange birds flew by us, glorious trees were on every side, some of them covered with flowers, while the brilliant greens of various shades made up for the want of colour in others. Where we were the land seemed to slope down into a little valley, while farther back there was a ridge clothed to its summit with beautiful vegetation.

But just then, as the poetical writer said, the trail of the serpent was over it all, and I kept on seeing imaginary reptiles' heads reared above the beautiful waving canes and grasses, and fancied I detected the rustling noise made by the creature's scales as they glided through the dry stems.

"Now," said my uncle, as we stood at last on the edge of the moist depression, "we must contrive some plan of attack, Nat. We must not let the enemy escape, or he will be scaring us all the time we stay."

I thought it very kind of him to say *us* when I know he meant *you*, but I did not say anything, only eagerly searched the thickly-spread canes and broad-leaved plants as far as I could see with my eyes, and then I could not help thinking what a beautiful spot that marsh was in spite of the serpent, as two or three of the lovely pitta thrushes flitted amidst the bamboos, and half a dozen sun-birds darted about a convolvulus-like plant, and kept flashing in the sunshine, which every now and then seemed to make their feathers blaze.

"Now, Nat," said my uncle, "I think this will be a good place for you, by this trickling rill; you see the place is roughly in the shape of a ham, so you shall have the place of honour, my boy, by the knuckle-bone, while I and Ebo go round the fat sides and see if we can find the enemy there."

"Do you think it will come this way, uncle?" I said.

"Yes, Nat, just below you there, so be cool, and give it both your barrels as it goes by. You may depend upon one thing, and that is that the reptile, if it comes down here, will be trying hard to escape. It will not attack you."

I hoped Uncle Dick was right, but could not feel sure, as I remained on the side of the steep slope, at the bottom of which a tiny stream trickled amongst a long patch of luxuriant canes through which I expected the serpent would try to escape to another part of the island.

The next minute I was quite alone, for in obedience to my uncle's signs, and eagerly falling into his plans, Ebo ran off to get to the back of the little marsh, my uncle also disappearing quietly on my own side, but of course higher up.

"Perhaps the serpent won't be here after all," I thought to myself as I stood there in the midst of the profound silence; and I could not keep back the hope within me that this might be the case.

Everything was now very still, only that once from a distance came the hoarse cry of a bird of paradise and the scream of a parrot, but directly after I seemed to detect the peculiar noise made by a hornbill, one of which birds flapped across the little valley towards a clump of trees.

Not a sound came from beyond the cane swamp, and the slightest grasses hardly moved, but stood there with their feathery plumes bathed in sunshine, while with strained eyes I counted the knots on every light-brown and cream-coloured cane.

I was watching for a wavy, undulating movement, which I felt sure must follow if the serpent was there and creeping about; but all was perfectly still.

"It must be farther up to the top of the marsh than he thinks," I said to myself; and then I heard a cry which made my blood bound through my veins. But there was nothing the matter; it was only Ebo on the move, and I heard my uncle answer him. Then there was a beating noise as if the black was thrashing the canes with his club.

Then my heart seemed to leap to my mouth, for there was a rustling in the tall grasses, something seemed to be forcing its way through, and with my gun at my shoulder I was ready to fire at the first glimpse of the scaly skin, but feathers appeared instead, and a couple of large wading-birds flew out.

The beating went on, and bird after bird took flight from its lurking-place, some being very beautiful; but no serpent appeared, and I began to feel more bold.

Still the beating went on, with Ebo shouting from time to time and my uncle answering, till they could not have been more than fifty yards above me, when suddenly the black seemed to change his tone, shouting excitedly to my uncle.

"They've found it," I said to myself; and in my excitement I forgot all about my fears, and stood there with my eyes sweeping the cane growth and my ears strained to their utmost.

All at once, and so close that the noise made me jump, I heard a shot, followed by a shout from Ebo, and a loud crashing noise, as if the canes were being thrashed together with a big stick.

Bang once more, and then perfect silence, but directly after the thrashing, beating noise began once more, and as I gazed excitedly in that direction I heard my uncle's voice.

"Look out, Nat," he cried. "It's coming your way."

"Yolly-to, yolly-to!" cried Ebo; but I hardly heard him, for, rushing down amongst the reeds and canes, writhing and bounding in the most extraordinary way, beating, whipping the tall leaves, tying itself up in knots and then throwing itself out nearly straight, came what to me seemed to be a most monstrous serpent.

I ought to have fired, but as the reptile came towards me I felt as if I must run, and I turned and fled for a dozen yards before shame stopped me, and I faced about.

The creature was close at hand, writhing horribly, and leaving behind it a beaten track, as in a fit of desperation I raised my gun, took quick aim, and fired, leaped aside to get away from the smoke, and fired again at something close to me.

The next moment I was knocked down, my gun flying out of my hand, and when I struggled up the serpent was gone.

"Hurt, Nat?" cried my uncle, who came running up with Ebo, who began to feel me all over.

"I don't think I am, uncle," I said angrily; "but the thing gave me a horrible bang."

"Pick up your gun then and come along, lad. You hit the brute with both barrels, and I know I did once. Come along; load as you run."

Ebo had already gone on in the serpent's track, for after I had been sent over by a blow as the reptile writhed so fiercely, it had straightened itself out, and gone straight down the little valley towards more open ground.

"Obe-ally-yolly!" shouted Ebo, and running after him I found that the serpent was gliding about in a rapid way amongst some tall trees, with the black darting at it and hitting it with his club from time to time, but apparently without making any impression.

"Stand back, Ebo," cried my uncle, waving the black away, and then, as Ebo leaped back, preparing to fire. But he lowered his gun as I came up. "No," he said, "you shall give him the *coup de grace*, Nat;" and feeling no fear now I finished the loading of my gun and went in among the trees.

"Fire at its head, Nat," cried my uncle; but it was not easy to see it, for the creature kept on twining about in a wonderfully rapid way; but at last I caught it as the head came from behind a tree trunk, fired, and the monster leaped from the ground and fell back in a long straight line, perfectly motionless, till Ebo darted in to give it a final thump with his club, when, to my astonishment, the blow seemed to electrify the creature, which drew itself up into a series of waves, and kept on throbbing as it were from end to end.

"Shall I fire again, uncle?" I said excitedly.

"No, Nat," he replied; "it would only be slaying the slain. Bravo, my boy! you did capitally."

"But I ran away at first, uncle," I said sorrowfully. "I did not stop when the serpent first came out."

"It was enough to make a Saint George run away from such a dragon, Nat," he said laughing. "I could not have believed such a serpent existed in these isles. Let's see how long he is."

"Thirty feet, uncle," I cried excitedly.

AT CLOSE QUARTERS WITH A SERPENT

"Your eyes magnify this morning, Nat," he said merrily. "No, my boy," he continued, after pacing along by the writhing creature's side; "that serpent is barely fourteen feet long, but it is wonderfully thick for its size, and it proves that there must be animals here such as would form its prey."

"Shall you have it skinned, uncle?" I asked.

"Yes," he replied, handing his knife to Ebo, who readily understood what was wanted, and leaving him to his very nasty job, my uncle and I went in search of birds of paradise.

Chapter Thirty Five.

Another Fishing Trip.

We had a long tramp after the birds of paradise that day, but did not get one. We shot some lovely sun-birds though, and a couple of thrushes such as we had not seen before. Our walk took us well in sight of the sea once more, and we began to have a pretty good idea of the form of the island. But the more we went about the more my uncle was satisfied that it was only a matter of time to make here a glorious collection of the birds of the eastern islands. We saw four different kinds of birds of paradise in our walk, though we did not get one on account of their shyness, but we did not despair of getting over that; and at last, well tired out, we returned to Ebo, who had hung up the serpent's skin to dry, and following his guidance till nightfall we got back to our hut by the sea-shore, where the boat lay perfectly safe, and being too tired to make a fire and cook, we lay down and fell asleep at once.

It was still dark when I was awakened by a hand shaking my arm, and, starting up, there was the black face of Ebo bent over me.

"Ikan-ikan," he kept on repeating.

"Ikan—fish," said my uncle, starting up. "Yes, we may as well get some for a change, Nat;" and in a few minutes we were all down on the sand launching the boat, which rode out lightly over the rollers.

We had plenty of fishing-lines, so fine that Ebo shook his head at them, and proceeded to show us how easily they would break; but after trying over and over again without success, and only cutting his hands, he grinned and jumped up to dance, but evidently thinking there was no room he settled down again and began to examine some hooks and glittering tin baits which we had in a box.

These he scanned most carefully as the boat skimmed along, my uncle steering, and after trying the sharpness of the hooks he performed what always seemed to me a conjuring trick, in bringing a couple of mother-of-pearl baits out of his waist-cloth, with a roll of twine.

The savages of the East, in fact most of the eastern people, wear a cord round the waist made of a material in accordance with their station. The poorer people will have it of cotton or twisted grass, the wealthier and chiefs of silk, while some have it threaded with gold. This thin cord is used as a support for their waist-cloth, and is rarely taken off, but is fastened so tightly that I have seen it appear completely buried in the flesh, just as if the wearers had an idea that they ought to make themselves look as much like an insect as possible.

Ebo wore a very tight *lingouti*—as it is called—round and over which he tucked the coarse cotton cloth which formed his only article of attire, and it was by means of this cotton cloth that he performed what I have spoken of as being like conjuring tricks, for somehow or another, although he had the appearance of carrying nothing about with him, he had always a collection of useful articles stored away in the folds of that waist-cloth.

Upon the present occasion he brought out two mother-of-pearl baits such as would be used to attract the fish when no real bait could be obtained.

It was a sight to see Ebo comparing his pearl baits with our specimens of tin and tinned copper, and for a time he seemed as if he could hardly make up his mind which was the better. Then he laid his coil of line made of roughly twisted grass beside ours, and inspected the two carefully, after which he uttered a sigh and put his own away, evidently quite satisfied that the civilised article was by far the better.

We sailed out about a mile and then anchored at the edge of a reef of coral, which acted as a shelter against the great rollers which broke far away upon its edge, seeming to make a ridge of surf, while where we lay all was undulating and calm, but with the tide running strongly over the reef, where the water was not a fathom deep and growing shallower moment by moment.

Ebo laid his short club ready to his hand, signing to me to draw my big hunting-knife and place it beside me.

"That looks as if we were to catch some large and dangerous fish, Nat," said my uncle; and he drew his own knife before passing to each of us a line with the artificial baits affixed.

"Won't you fish, uncle?" I asked.

"No, my boy. You two can fish, and as soon as you catch one we will cut him up for bait. I don't believe in artificial bait when you can get real."

By this time Ebo had thrown out his line and I followed his example, seeing the swift current seize upon the bait and carry it rapidly out over the reef, twinkling and sparkling in the water as I jerked it by paying out more line.

All at once, when it was some fifteen yards away. I felt a jerk and a snatch.

"I've got one," I said; but the tugging ceased directly, and I felt that the fish had gone.

Either the same, though, or another seized it directly, for there was a fierce tug which cut my hand, and I had to give line for a few moments while the fish I had hooked darted here and there like lightning, but I had it up to the side soon after, and gazed at it with delight, for it was, as it lay panting in the boat, like a magnificent goldfish, five or six pounds weight, with bars across its side of the most dazzling blue.

"Poo—chah—chah!" Ebo cried with a face full of disgust as he twisted his own line round a peg in the boat, and seizing his club battered the fish to death after unhooking it, and threw it over the side, where, as it was carried away, I could see that dozens of fish were darting at it, tearing it to pieces as fast as they could.

"What did you do that for?" I cried angrily, for it seemed wasting a splendid fish.

Ebo chatted away in reply, almost as angrily, after which, evidently satisfied that I did not understand, he behaved very nastily, though his dumb-show was so comic that it made us roar with laughter.

For he pretended to eat, as we supposed, some of the fish. Then he jumped up, sat down, jumped up again, rubbed his front, kicked out his legs and shouted, making hideous grimaces as if he were in pain, ending by leaning over the side of the boat, pretending to be horribly sick, and finishing his performance by lying down, turning up his eyes, and moaning.

"We must take what he shows us for granted, Nat," said my uncle, as Ebo jumped up smiling, as much as to say, "Wasn't I clever?" "These people know which are the wholesome and which are the unwholesome fish; but I was going to use some of that fellow for bait."

Just then Ebo hooked and brought in a fine fish that was all blue, but even this one would not do, for he killed it and tossed it overboard, chattering at it the while as if he were abusing it for being so bad.

We saw scores of fish dart at it as it was thrown in, and now they bit so freely at the artificial baits that there was no occasion to change.

I had hold of what seemed a nice fish directly, and after letting it run a little I began hauling in, watching its progress through the shallow clear water and thinking how bright and beautiful it looked against the brilliant corals, the softly waving weeds of every shade of brown and scarlet, while now and then some other fish darted at it.

All at once I uttered a cry of astonishment, for a long line of undulating creamy white seemed to dart at my fish, seize it with a jerk, and twist itself round it, till fish and the eel-like creature that attacked it resembled a knot.

I kept on hauling in, but only slowly now, for fear the hook should break out, the weight being double what it was and the water lashed into glittering foam.

"What is it, uncle?" I cried excitedly.

"Don't hurry, Nat," he replied; and just then Ebo, who had been too busy pulling in a fish to notice my line, threw out again, and then fastening his cord came over to my side to see.

No sooner did he make out what I had at the end of the line than he seized his club, gesticulated furiously, and began beating the side of the boat, chattering aloud, and signing to me to give him the line.

"Let him have it, Nat," said my uncle. "He has had experience with these things."

I gave up my hold of the fishing-line most unwillingly, for the little adventure was intensely exciting, and every jerk and drag made by the creature that had seized my fish sent a thrill through my arms to my very heart.

"It is some kind of sea-snake that has taken your fish, Nat, and is regularly constricting it. As I told you before, there are some of them dangerously poisonous, and not like our great friend out in the swamp."

Meanwhile Ebo was jerking and shaking the line furiously, as if endeavouring to get rid of the snake, but without avail, for it held on tightly, having evidently got one fold twisted round the line, and I must confess, after hearing about the poisonous nature of these creatures, to feeling rather nervous as to its behaviour if it were brought on board.

But Ebo did not mean to bring it on board. He wanted to shake it off, and what with the struggles of the fish and the writhing and twisting of the snake, it seemed every moment as if the line must break.

The black brought it close in, then let it go almost to the full length of the line, jerked it, made fierce snatches, but all in vain; and at last getting the unwelcome visitor close in, he signed to my uncle to take his knife while he raised his club for a blow, when there was a sudden cessation of the rush, and foam in the water, and fish and snake had gone.

Ebo grinned with triumph, and after examining the bait threw it out again, returning to the other side directly to draw in a satisfactory fish for our breakfast, while my uncle chatted to me about my last captive.

"This is new to me, Nat," he said. "I never could have thought that these snakes or eels, for they seem to partake of the character of the latter, would have wound themselves round the prey they seized. The elongated fish in our part of the world, congers, dog-fish, guard-fish, and similar creatures, fasten their teeth into their prey, then setting their bodies in rapid motion like a screw, they regularly cut great pieces out of their victim. This was precisely the same as a serpent with its prey, and it is a natural history fact worth recording. But look!"

I had already felt a fish snap at my bait, checked it, and knew that I was fast into a monster. For a few moments he let me feel something heavy and inert at the end of my line, then there was a plunge and a rush, the line went hissing out, and try as I would to check it, the fish ran straight off till I dragged with all my might, and felt that either the line must break or my hands would be terribly cut.

"Give and take, Nat," cried my uncle.

"It's all give, uncle, and I can't take a bit."

I had hardly said the words when I was at liberty to take in as much as I liked, for the fish was gone, and upon drawing in my line in a terribly disappointed way, it was to find that the fish had completely bitten through the very strong wire gimp, not broken it, but bitten it as cleanly as if it had been done with a knife.

"That must have been a monster," said Uncle Dick. "But never mind, my boy. Here, hold still and I'll loop on another bait."

He was in the act of doing this when Ebo began to dance about in the boat, striving hard to drag in the fish he had hooked. His plan was to haul in as quickly as he could, never giving the fish a moment's rest, and any form of playing the swift, darting creature did not seem to enter his head.

He seemed to have found his match this time, for the fish refused to be dragged on board, but after a fierce struggle the black's arms were too much for it, and a dozen rapid hand-over-hand hauls resulted in its being hauled over the side, a sharp-nosed glittering silver-fish about four feet long, and I was about to fling myself upon it to hold it down and stop its frantic leaps amongst our tackle, when Ebo uttered a cry of alarm, darted before me, and attacked the fish with his club, dealing it the most furious blow upon the head, but apparently without any effect, for as one of the blows fell, the great fish seemed to make a side dart with its head, and its jaws closed upon the club, holding on so fiercely and with such power that it was not until Uncle Dick had cut off its head that the club could be wrenched away, when Ebo showed me the creature's jaws full of teeth like lancets and pretty well as sharp.

"No wonder your wire was bitten through," said my uncle. "Hallo! is he not good to eat?"

Ebo evidently seemed to consider that it was not, for the fish was thrown over, and the fierce monster, that must have been a perfect tyrant of the waters, had not floated a dozen feet before it was furiously attacked and literally hacked to pieces.

There was no difficulty in getting fish that morning, the only thing was to avoid hooking monsters that would break or bite through our tackle, and those which were not good for food.

The reef literally swarmed with fish, some large, some small, and every now and then we could see the rapid dash of one of the snake-eels as I called them. I saw them regularly leap out of the water sometimes and come down in a knot, twisting and twining about in the most extraordinary way, and at last, so interesting was the clear, shallow water, that we laid aside our lines and leaned over the side gazing down at the fish that flashed about, till the reef was dry, and leaving Ebo in the boat we landed to walk about over the shining weeds and coral, picking our way amongst shell-fish of endless variety, some with great heavy shells a couple of feet long, and some so small and delicate that I had to handle them with the greatest delicacy to keep from crushing their tissue-papery shells.

I could have stayed there for hours and filled the boat with wonders. There was scarlet and orange coral, so beautiful that I was for bringing away specimens; but Uncle Dick showed me that it was only the gelatinous covering that was of so lovely a tint, and this, he told me, would soon decay.

Then there were the brilliantly tinted weeds. There were sea-slugs too, delicacies amongst the Chinese under the name of *trepang*, and so many other wonders of the sea that I should have gone on searching amongst the crevices of the sharp coral, if I had not had a sharp warning given to me to make for the boat by the parts that had only been an inch or two deep rapidly increasing to a foot, and my uncle shouting to me to come aboard.

It was quite time, for I was some distance from the boat, with the tide flowing in so rapidly that in a few minutes I should have had to swim, and a swim in water swarming with such furious kinds of the finny tribe was anything but tempting.

As it was I had to swim a few strokes, and was of course soaked, but my uncle hauled me uninjured into the boat and I little minded the wetting, but laughed at my adventure as we sat over our breakfast and feasted upon frizzled fish to our hearts' content.

Chapter Thirty Six.

Ebo satisfies our Wants.

It would be tedious if I were to go on describing the almost endless varieties of birds we shot, glowing though they were with rainbow colours, and to keep repeating how we skinned and preserved this sun-bird, that pitta, or trogon, or lovely rose-tinted dove. Parrots and cockatoos we found without number, and as we selected only the finest specimens, our collection rapidly increased, so fast, indeed, by steady work, that I began to understand how my uncle had brought so great a number from the West.

But still one of the great objects of our visit to this part of the world had not been achieved; we had shot no birds of paradise; and these were scarce things in England at the time of which I write.

There were plenty of rough specimens of their plumage worn in ladies' bonnets; but a fair, well-preserved skin was hardly known, those brought to England being roughly dried by the natives; so at last my uncle declared that no more birds should be shot and skinned until we had obtained specimens of some at least of the lovely creatures whose cries we often heard about us, but which tantalisingly kept out of shot.

It was a difficult task, but we at last made Ebo understand that we must shoot some of these birds, when by his way he seemed to indicate that if we had only told him sooner we might have had as many as we liked.

That very day he obtained a good little store of provisions, shouldered his spear, and went off by himself, and we saw no more of him for forty-eight hours, when he came back in the most unconcerned way, just as if he had never been out of sight, and sat down and ate all that we put before him.

After that he lay down and went to sleep for some hours, waking up ready to dance around us, chattering vehemently until we had finished the skins we were preserving, when he signed to us to take our guns and to follow him.

We obeyed him, but he did not seem satisfied until we had collected some provision as well, when once more he set off, taking us through a part of the island we had not visited before, and, if anything, more beautiful than that we had.

It was a long journey he took us, and we could have secured hundreds of brilliantly coloured birds, but we only shot a few large ones, such as we knew to be good food, ready for our halt by the camp fire, for it seemed that we were not to return to our hut that night.

Over hillsides, down in valleys where tree-ferns sprang up, of the most beautifully laced fronds, great groves of palms and clumps of cocoa-nut trees, some of whose fruit Ebo climbed and got for us, and still we went on, avoiding the marshy-looking spots which experience had taught us to be the home of the serpents, which, in very small numbers, inhabited the isle.

Several times over we looked inquiringly at Ebo, but he only smiled and pointed forward, and we followed him till he stopped suddenly and showed us some wood ready for making a fire.

Here we had a welcome rest and a hearty meal, but he did not let us stay long, hurrying us forward, till, just before sundown, he brought us to a dense patch of forest, with huge trees towering upward and spreading their branches, making an impenetrable shade.

"It will be too dark to travel far here to-night, Nat," said my uncle. "Where does he mean to go? But this ought to be the place for the birds of paradise, Nat, if we are to get any."

Just then Ebo stopped, and we found a rough hut of leaves with a bed of fern already waiting for us, this having been part of his work during his prolonged absence.

His delight knew no bounds as he saw that we were pleased, and as usual he indulged in a dance, after which he caught us in turn by the arm and tried very hard to explain that the birds of paradise were plentiful here.

We were too tired to think about anything much besides sleep, and very gladly crept into our hut, to sleep so soundly without a single thought of serpents or huge apes, that I seemed hardly to have closed my eyes, and felt exceedingly grumpy and indisposed to move when Ebo began shaking me to get me up.

"All right!" I said, and then, as I lay still with my eyes closed, Ebo kept on:

"Hawk, hawk, hawk; kwok, kwok, kwok;" and it seemed so stupid of him, but there it was again; "Hawk, hawk, hawk; kwok, kwok, kwok."

"Come, Nat," cried my uncle; "unbutton those eyelids, boy, and get up. Don't you hear the birds calling?"

"I thought it was Ebo, uncle," I said. "Oh! I am so sleepy."

"Never mind the sleepiness, Nat. Come along and let's see if we cannot get some good specimens."

Just then I saw Ebo's face in the opening, and cutting a yawn right in half I followed my uncle out into the darkness, for though the birds of paradise were calling, there was no sign of day.

But if we wished for success I felt that we must get beneath the trees unseen, and, examining my gun, I followed my uncle, who in turn kept close behind Ebo.

The black went forward very cautiously, and looking very strange and misty in the darkness; but he evidently knew what he was about, going along amongst the great tree trunks without a sound, while we followed as lightly as we could.

On all sides we could hear the hoarse cries of the birds, which we felt must be in good numbers, and I felt less sleepiness now in the fresh morning air, and a curious feeling of excitement came over me as I thought of the lovely amber plumes of these birds, and wondered whether I should be fortunate enough to bring one down.

All at once Ebo stopped beneath an enormous tree, and as we crept up close to its mighty trunk we gazed up into the darkness and could here and there catch a glimpse of a star; in fact, so black was it, that but for the cries of the various birds we heard, it might have been taken for the middle of the night.

There was nothing to see but an almost opaque blackness, though now and then I fancied I could make out a great branch crossing above my head. It seemed nonsense to have come, but the loud cry of one of the birds we sought, sounded loudly just then and silenced my doubts. I raised my gun ready for a shot, but could see nothing.

Just then my uncle whispered with his lips to my ear: "Don't make a sound, and don't fire till you have a good chance. Look out."

The loud quok, quok, quok, was answered from a distance, repeated above our heads, and then there was the whistle of wings plainly heard in the solemn silence of the forest, and all this repeated again overhead till it seemed as if we were just beneath a tree where the birds of paradise met for discussion, like the rooks at home in the elms. But no matter how I strained my eyes I could not distinguish a single bird.

The minutes went by, and I longed for the light, for though I knew it would betray our presence, still I might catch sight of one bird and bring it down. But the light did not come, and as my arms ached with holding up my gun I lowered it, and patiently waited with my heart beating heavily, as I listened to the cries that were on the increase.

All at once I felt an arm glide over my shoulder, and I could just make out that Ebo was pointing upward with his black finger steadily in one direction.

I tried to follow it but could see nothing, and I was thinking how much better a savage's sight was than ours, when from out of the darkness there came the hoarse "*Hawk, hawk, hawk; quok, quok, quok,*" and as the cry seemed to direct my eye, I fancied that I could see something moving slightly at a very great height, bowing and strutting like a pigeon. I looked and looked again and could not see it; then a star that was peeping through the leaves seemed to be suddenly hidden, and there was the movement again.

I forgot all about my uncle's orders about not firing until I had a good chance, and taking a steady aim at the dimly seen spot just as the hoarse cry arose once more, I drew the trigger.

The flash from my gun seemed to cut the blackness, and the report went echoing away amongst the trees; then there was a sharp rustling noise, and a dull, quick thud, and I was about to spring forward and seek for what I had shot, but Ebo's arms closed round me and held me fast.

I understood what he meant, and contented myself with reloading my gun, the click of the lock sounding very loud in the silence that had ensued, for the report of my gun had caused a complete cessation of all cries, and I felt that we should get no more shots for some time; but all the same I had heard no rush of wings as of a flock of birds taking flight, and I wondered whether any of them were still in the dense top of the tree.

Five or ten minutes must have elapsed, and then once more Ebo's arm glided over my shoulder and rested there, while I laid my cheek against it, and gazed in quite another direction now till I fancied I saw what he was pointing at, but which looked like nothing but a dark spot high up amongst the twigs; in fact, when I did make it out I felt sure that it was a nest.

But I recalled how accurate Ebo had been before, and once more taking aim, making it the more careful by leaning my gun barrel against the trunk of the tree, I fired; there was a quick rustle of leaves and twigs, and another dull thud, but no one moved.

After a few minutes' waiting Ebo pointed out another, whatever it was, for I was still in doubt as to whether these were birds of paradise that I had shot, for the silence had not been broken since I fired first.

I took a quicker aim this time and drew the trigger, and once more there was a heavy fall through the branches, and then as if by magic it seemed to be daylight, and I saw several big birds dotted about the tree.

Uncle Dick and I fired together, and then came a rush of wings as another bird fell, the loud cries being repeated from a distance; while Ebo, evidently considering that it was of no more use to wait, ran out to pick up the birds.

Only one bird had fallen when my uncle and I fired together, for I believe I missed; but as Ebo and I picked up the result of our expedition here the sun rose, and in the bright light that came between the trees we stood gazing in ecstasy at the lovely creatures.

"Oh, uncle!"

That was all I could say for some time.

"I think it ought to be 'Oh, Nat!'" he replied laughing. "Why, you young dog, what eyes you have! you got all the luck."

"Oh no, uncle," I said laughing; "I shot with Ebo's eyes."

"Then next time I'll do the same," he said.

"But let's go and shoot some more," I said excitedly.

"No, Nat, we shall get no more of these to-day. I suppose it will only be by hiding in the darkness beneath the trees they frequent that we shall have any success. They are wonderfully shy, and no wonder when they have such plumage to protect."

I suppose most people have seen specimens of the great bird of paradise, but they can have no conception of the beauty of a freshly shot specimen such as were two of those which I brought down. I felt as if I could never tire of gazing at the wonderful tinting of the bird, here of a pale straw yellow with the feathers short and stiff like velvet, there of a rich chocolate with the neck covered with scales of metallic green. Their tails seemed to have, in place of centre feathers, a couple of long beautiful curving wires nearly a yard long; but the chief beauty of the birds was the great tuft of plumage which seemed to come out from beneath the wings, light and soft, quite two feet long, and all of a rich golden orange.

It seems to me impossible to conceive a more lovely bird, and we took them in triumph to our hut, where we breakfasted, my uncle afterwards carefully making skins of all four.

The other two were evidently younger birds, and had not their full plumage, but they were very beautiful and formed a splendid addition to the collection.

Chapter Thirty Seven.

Beauties in Plume.

Our work done, my uncle decided that we should stay here for a couple of days at least, even if we did not afterwards come round to this side of the island, for our good fortune was not yet at an end. In taking a look round, towards mid-day we heard a harsh cry, and by means of a little stalking Uncle Dick got within shot and brought down a bird that was almost as beautiful as those we shot before daylight.

This had shorter plumes of a rich red, but it had two long double curved wires in its tail, and its upper plumage was more plush-like and richer in its colours. The metallic green was more vivid, the golden yellow a colour which was most bright upon its neck and shoulders.

Almost directly after I shot a big dull brown bird which gave me no satisfaction at all; but Uncle Dick was delighted, saying that it was the female bird of the kind we had shot, and we decided that it was the red bird of paradise.

Even then we had not come to the end of our good fortune, for after passing over hundreds of sun-birds, pittas, and trogons, such as we should have been only too glad to meet a short time back, my uncle suddenly raised his gun and fired at what seemed to be, from where I stood, a couple of sturdy-looking starlings.

One fell, and Uncle Dick shouted to me as the second bird came in my direction.

I made a quick shot at it just as it was darting among some bushes, and brought it down, and on running to pick it up I found that I had shot something entirely fresh to me.

"Well done, Nat!" cried my uncle. "Mine is only the hen bird. What a lovely little creature, to be sure! It is a gem."

"What is it, uncle?" I said.

"Evidently a paradise bird, my boy."

It was a curious little short-tailed fellow, but wonderful in its colours; while from the centre of the dumpy tail sprang two wires of about six inches long, which formed two flat spiral curls at the end, and of a most intense green. Instead of the long plumes of the birds we shot before—birds three times the size of this—it had under each wing a little tuft of grey, tipped with green, which the bird could set up like tiny tans. The whole of the upper surface was of a rich red, and the under part of a glistening floss-silky or glass-thready white, but relieved here and there with bands and patches of metallic green. There were shades of orange crimson here, and when I add that the bird's legs were of a delicious blue, and its beak of orange yellow like a blackbird's, you can realise how beautiful a creature I had shot.

"There, Nat," said my uncle, "we will do no more, only carefully preserve the treasures we have got."

But hardly had he spoken before he fired again and brought down another bird, which was again a wonder. It seemed about the size of the last, but was entirely different, though sufficiently similar to mark it as a paradise bird. It had nearly as short a tail, with the two central wires crossed, but instead of forming the beautiful curves of the other with the flat disc at the end, these wires ended in a point and curled round so as to form a circle. The prevailing colours were orange, buff, and yellow, but its great peculiarity was a couple of ruffs or capes of feathers hanging from the back of its neck, the upper one of a pale yellow, the lower of a reddish-brown.

Uncle Dick was in as great a state of delight as I, and our pleasure seemed to be reflected upon Ebo, who showed his satisfaction at having brought us to the place, by shouldering his spear and striding up and down with one hand upon his hip, as if proud of his position as companion of the white man.

The time glided by very fast during our stay at the island, where we found plenty of fruit, as many fish as we liked to catch, and abundance of large pigeons and other birds to help our larder. The climate was hot, but the breezes that came from the sea always seemed to modify the heat and make it bearable. Several storms occurred, during which the trees bent before the fury of the blast, and the waves piled the sands high with weeds and shells. The lightning was terrific and the thunder deafening. At times it was awful, and a curious scared feeling used at first to come over me. But I soon grew used to the storms, and as they were soon over, took but little notice of them, except to enjoy the delicious freshness of the air that seemed afterwards to make everything ten times more beautiful than it was before.

It would become wearisome if I kept on writing of the beauty of the different varieties of the birds of paradise we found, and the lovely tinting and arrangement of their plumes; let it be sufficient when I tell you that scarcely a day passed without Ebo finding some fresh specimen for us to shoot, and then dancing round with the delight of a boy as we skinned and preserved the new treasure. Sometimes we had a beetle day, sometimes a butterfly day, collecting the loveliest specimens; but birds formed our principal pursuit, and our cases began to present a goodly aspect as we packed in carefully the well-dried aromatic skins.

I had had one or two more slight touches of fever, and my uncle was poorly once, but he so skilfully treated us both that the disease was soon mastered, and the trouble passed over. Taken altogether, though, we found the island, in spite of the heat, a most delightful place of residence, and it was with feelings of real regret that I sat in our swift boat one day with the big sail set, skimming over the smooth sea, all our stores on board, and Uncle Dick at the helm steering due north, for we had bidden the beautiful island farewell, and its shores were beginning to grow distant to our eyes.

Chapter Thirty Eight.

Ebo does not approve of New Guinea for Reasons that appear.

It did not seem to matter to Ebo where we went so long as he was with us. He must have been a man of five-and-thirty, and he was brave as a lion—as the lion is said to be in the story, for in reality he is a great sneak—but Ebo seemed to have the heart of a boy. He was ready to laugh when I did, and sit by me when I was ill or tired, his face full of sympathy, and no sooner was I better than it was the signal for a triumphal dance.

Ebo was as happy now as could be. It did not matter to him where we were going, and he laughed and chattered and pointed out the fish to me as we skimmed over the shallow water of the coral reefs, sometimes approaching islands whose names we did not know, and which were apparently too small to be down in the chart; but whatever temptations they might hold out my uncle steered right on due north, and on the evening of the second day there was land stretching east and west as far as we could see.

"Now, Nat," he cried, "where is your geography? what place is that?"

"I should say it must be New Guinea, uncle," I said.

"Quite right, my boy. Hallo! what's the matter with Ebo?"

That gentleman had been lying down in the bottom of the boat fast asleep for the past three hours, as he was to sit up and bear me company through a part of the night; but having woke up and caught sight of the land he seemed to have become furious.

Having been with us now so long, he had picked up a good many words, just as we had picked up a good many of his, so that by their help and signs we got along pretty well. But now it was quite startling to see his excitement. He seemed so agitated that he could only recollect the word *no*, and this he kept on repeating as he dashed at me and then left me, to run to my uncle, seizing the tiller and trying to drag it round so as to alter the direction of the boat.

"No, no, no, no, no!" he cried. Then pointing to the land he came at me, caught up his spear, and I thought he was going to kill me, for he made a savage thrust at me which went right past my arm; dropped the spear, caught up his club, forced back my head over the gunwale of the boat, raised his club and made believe to beat me to death, hammering the boat side with all his might. After this he made a sham attack upon my uncle, who, however, took it coolly, and only laughed after seeing the attack upon me, though I had noticed one hand go to his gun when Ebo made at me with the spear.

After the black had worked himself up into a perspiration, instead of, as I expected, bursting out laughing, he kept on pointing to the land, crying, "No, no, no!" and then, "Kill bird, kill man, Nat, mi boy, kill Ung-kul Dit; kill Ebo. No, no, no!"

"You mean that the savages will kill us if we land?" I said.

"Kill, kill," he cried, nodding his head excitedly, and banging the side of the boat with his club; "kill, kill, kill. Kill Ebo, kill Nat, mi boy, kill Ung-kul Dit, kill boat, kill, kill. No, no, no!"

"Well done, Ebo!" cried my uncle laughing. "Your English is splendid. Good boy."

"Ebo, good boy," cried the black. "No, no, no. Kill, kill."

"They sha'n't kill us, Ebo," said my uncle, taking up his gun and pointing it at the shore; while, to make his meaning clearer, I did the same. "Shoot—kill man."

"Shoot! kill!" cried Ebo, who evidently understood, for he picked up his spear, and thrust with it fiercely towards the shore. "Yes, shoot; kill man," he continued, nodding his head; but he seemed very much dissatisfied and gazed intently towards the distant land.

"He seems to know the character of the New Guinea savages, Nat," said Uncle Dick. "I have always heard that they are a fierce and cruel set, but we shall soon see whether it is safe to land."

We sailed gently on, for it turned out a glorious moonlight night, and altering our course a little we were at sunrise within a couple of miles of what seemed to be a very beautiful country, wooded to the shore, and rising up inland to towering mountains. Great trees seemed to prevail everywhere, but we saw no sign of human being.

"The place looks very tempting, Nat," said uncle, "and if we can hit upon an uninhabited part I expect that we should find some capital specimens for our cases. Let us see what the place is like."

Ebo tried in his fashion to dissuade us from going farther, and it was evident that the poor fellow was terrible uneasy as the boat was run in close to the shore, when all at once about a dozen nude black savages came running down to the water's edge, making signs to us to land, and holding up bunches of bright feathers and rough skins of birds.

"They look friendly, Nat," said my uncle.

"Look here; I will land and take them a few presents in beads and brass wire; we shall soon see if they mean mischief."

"I'll come with you, uncle," I said.

"No; you stop with the boat and keep her afloat. Here are the guns all ready loaded. I don't suppose there will be any danger; but if there is, you must pepper the enemy with small shot to keep them back—that is, of course, if you see them attack me."

"Hadn't I better come, uncle?"

"No; I shall take Ebo. They may be as simple-hearted and friendly as the others we have met, and this country must be so grand a collecting ground that I cannot afford to be scared away by what may be false reports raised by people who have behaved ill to the natives."

He took out a few strings of brightly coloured beads and a little roll of brass wire, and waved them in the air, when the savages shouted and kept on making signs to us to land.

We were only about twenty yards from the sandy shore now, and we could see every expression of face of the New Guinea men, as my uncle threw one leg over the side and then stood up to his knees in the clear water.

"Kill Ung-kul Dit," said Ebo, clinging to his arm.

"No, no! Come," replied my uncle.

Ebo's club was already in his *lingouti*, and picking up his spear he too leaped into the water, while I sat down in the boat with the barrel of my gun resting on the gunwale as the sail flapped and the boat rocked softly to and fro.

The people seemed to be delighted as my uncle waded in; but I noted that they carefully avoided wetting their own feet, keeping on the dry sand talking eagerly among themselves; and though I looked attentively I could see no sign of arms.

So peaceful and good-tempered did they all look that I was completely thrown off my guard, and wondered how Ebo could be so cowardly as to keep about a yard behind my uncle, who walked up to them fearlessly, and held out his hand with a string of beads.

The New Guinea men chattered and seemed delighted, holding out their hands and catching eagerly at the beads, snatching them from the giver's hands, and asking apparently for more.

I saw Uncle Dick sign to them that he wanted some of their birds in exchange.

They understood him, for they held out two or three skins, and he advanced a step to take them; but they were snatched back directly, and, as if by magic, the savages thrust their hands behind them, and in an instant each man was flourishing a war-club.

It all seemed to happen in a moment, and my heart seemed to stand still as I saw one treacherous savage, over six feet high, strike my uncle over the head with his club, my poor uncle falling as if he had been killed.

It was now that I saw why Ebo had held back behind my uncle, and it was fortunate that the faithful fellow had followed the guidance of his own reason. For as, in the midst of a tremendous shouting and yelling, the tall savage bent forward to again strike my uncle I saw Ebo's lance point strike him in the throat, and he went down.

This checked the savages for an instant, long enough to enable the black to stoop down and get a good grip of Uncle Dick's collar with his left hand, while with his right he kept making darts with his spear at the yelling savages who kept striking at him with their clubs.

So tremendous and so true were Ebo's thrusts that I saw another great black go down, and a couple more run yelling back towards the dense cover from which they had come; but Ebo was in a very critical position. My uncle was heavy, and the black had hard work to drag him over the sand towards the boat, and keep his enemies at bay.

It was now that I saw what a brave warrior and chief our follower must be; but I also saw how his enemies had formed a half circle and were trying to get behind him and cut him off from the boat.

For the first few moments I had felt helpless; then I had determined to leap over and go to their help; then I saw that I was best where I was, and took aim, ready to fire at the first chance, for I could do nothing at first for fear of injuring my friends. And besides, a horrible feeling of compunction had come upon me at the thought of having to fire at men—fellow creatures—and I shrank from drawing trigger.

At last, though, I saw that further hesitation would be fatal. Ebo was making a brave defence, and had wounded several of his assailants as he dragged my uncle to the water's edge. Another step and he could have waded, easily dragging my uncle over the water, but his enemies had made a savage dash, and one of the boldest had got hold of his spear.

Another moment and he would have been struck down, when, hesitating no longer, I took quick aim and fired right into the thick of the black group as far on one side of my uncle as I could.

As the report rang out, and the stinging shot hissed and scattered, injuring several, they uttered fierce yells and separated for a moment, giving me a better chance to fire again, and I did with such effect that the savage who was dragging at Ebo's spear loosed his hold, turned, and ran for his life.

It was a golden moment for our black friend, who made a couple of darts with his freed weapon, and then backing rapidly drew my uncle through the water towards the boat.

The savages were staggered by the shot from my gun. Many were wounded, but they were trifling small shot-wounds, which only infuriated them as they saw their prey escaping, and with a rush they came tearing through the water, whirling their clubs above their heads and yelling furiously.

My blood was up now, and in those brief moments I saw our fate, that of being massacred by these treacherous ruthless wretches, to whom we had made offerings of peace and good-will. I seemed to see our battered boat, and then friends at home waiting for news of those who had sailed out here on a peaceful expedition, news that would never come; and a curious pang came over me as I felt that I must save Uncle Dick and his brave defender if I could.

I had already picked up my uncle's loaded double gun, and there were two rifles also loaded ready to my hand, so, taking careful aim now at the foremost of the savage crew just as they were pressing Ebo hard, I fired.

I could not see for a moment for the smoke, but as it parted I saw that the men were close enough now for the shot to have much more serious effect. Two had fallen, but after a moment's hesitation the others made a fresh rush, which I met with another shot, which checked them again; but though another man fell, and half a dozen more were streaming with blood, they only seemed the more infuriate and again came on.

I did not even then like to use the fatal rifles, but found time to cram in a couple more cartridges, and by this time Ebo had dragged my uncle to the boat, stooped, lifted him in, and then with one hand upon the gunwale kept shoving her off, backing and wading, and thrusting with his spear at the fierce wretches who came on more savagely than ever.

The boat moved slowly, but I was hot with excitement now, and I fired once at a savage who was striking at Ebo, then at a group, and then there was a dull heavy thud as a war-club that had been thrown with clever aim struck me full in the forehead, and I fell senseless in the bottom of the boat.

Chapter Thirty Nine.

Ebo's Song of Triumph.

When I came to, it was with a terrible pain in my head, and a misty feeling of having been taken by the savages, who had laid me down and were having a war-dance of triumph around me.

"Hi, yi, yi—Hi, yi, yi—Hi, yi, yi!"

Then it kept on in a shrill tone till it seemed, as my head ached so badly, almost maddening.

At last I raised my heavy eyelids and saw that instead of lying on the sand surrounded by savages, I was some distance from the shore and in the boat. I could dimly see, as through a mist, the savages on the beach, and they were shouting, yelling, and threatening us with their war-clubs; but it was Ebo who was apparently about to dance the bottom out of the boat, and keeping up that abominable "Hi, yi, yi!" his song of triumph for the victory he had won.

"Hi, yi, yi—Hi, yi, yi—Hi, yi, yi! *hey!*"

The *Hey!* was accompanied by a tremendous jump, and a flourish of the spear at the savages on shore, whom the defiance seemed to madden as they rushed about furiously waving their clubs and yelling with all their might. Sometimes they dashed into the water right to their chests, some swam out with their war-clubs in their teeth, and some went through a pantomime in which we were all supposed to be beaten down and being pounded into jelly upon the shore.

All this delighted Ebo, who varied his war-song by making derisive gestures, showing his utter contempt for his cowardly enemies, all of which seemed to sting them to fury, and I began to wonder how we should get on if they had canoes.

For our boat was floating gently along about sixty yards from the shore with the sail flapping about, the current driving her away, but the rollers carrying her in.

At first I could do nothing but sit there and gaze, sometimes at Ebo, and sometimes at the savages. Then in a sleepy stupid way I looked at my uncle, who was lying in the bottom of the boat with his eyes closed and perfectly motionless.

Somehow my state then did not trouble me much, only that I wished my head would not ache quite so badly. I was quite aware that we were in danger, but that seemed to be quite natural; and at last I began to wonder why I did not begin doing something, and why my uncle did not get up.

At last it seemed to occur to Ebo that it was time for him to finish shouting, and he laid his spear down, came to me, and lifted me, so that my head was over the side of the boat, and he then scooped up the cool water and bathed my face, with such satisfactory effect that I was able to think clearly; and thanking him, I was about to perform a similar duty for my uncle, when, to my horror, I saw a crowd of savages running a couple of canoes over the sands, evidently to launch them, and finish the treacherous work that they had begun.

For a few moments I felt paralysed, but recovering myself I made a sign to Ebo, hoisted the great sail to its fullest height, and as the boat careened over I hurried aft to the tiller and the sail began slowly to fill, and our boat to move gently through the water.

But never had it moved so slowly before, for the breeze was very light, and it seemed as if the savages must get their canoes launched, and have paddled out to us before we could get up any speed.

They saw this, and kept on shouting and working with all their might, moving first one canoe and then the other to the edge of the water, launching them, springing in, and the next moment the air was black with paddles.

Again an instant and the sea was foaming with their vigorous strokes.

But for the fact that the canoes were very large and heavy and took time to get well in motion, we must have been overtaken, for the wind seemed to be playing with our sail, one moment filling it out, the next letting it flap idly as the boat rose and fell upon the waves.

Seeing that I could do no more I fastened the tiller with a piece of cord and rapidly reloaded the guns, Ebo picking up his spear, and, to my horror, beginning to shout at and deride the savages.

It would have made little difference, I suppose, for the blacks would have killed us without mercy had they overhauled us, and that they seemed certain to do, for they were paddling steadily and well, their blades being plunged into the water with the greatest regularity, making it foam and sparkle as they swept along.

So fast did they seem to come, uttering in chorus a sort of war-cry at each plunge of the paddles, that I wondered why they did not overhaul us, so slowly did we seem to move, and at last, as they got their canoes in full swing, they came on hand over hand, getting so near that the men in the bows made ready their spears to hurl, and I raised my gun, meaning to make as brave an end as I could.

I was too much excited to feel frightened now. I suppose there was not time, all my thoughts being turned upon the acts of the savages, one of whom now threw a spear, which fell short.

I took aim at him, but did not fire, thinking that I would reserve the shot till we were in greater danger, and hoping that a couple of well-directed charges might have the effect of deterring them from further pursuit. But still on they came just abreast, and it was evident that they meant to attack on each side of our poor little boat, which looked so small beside the long war-canoes, each of which contained about forty men.

They uttered a loud yell now, for the boat seemed to stand still and the sail began to flap, and, somehow, just then, as I felt what dreadful danger we were in, I began thinking about Clapham Common, and running there in the sunshine, while Uncle Joe looked blandly on, evidently enjoying my pursuits.

Just then half a dozen spears were thrown, and I nearly fell overboard, only saving myself by making a snatch at one of the stays.

It was not that I was struck by a spear, but that the boat had given a leap and bent down till it seemed as if she would capsize. In fact she would have gone down with her sail flat upon the water if I had not eased off the sheet as she went slipping through the waves at a tremendous rate.

It was a work of moments, and then when I turned my head it was to see that the canoes were double the distance behind, with the savages paddling furiously; but I saw that if the wind held, their case was like that of a pet spaniel running after a greyhound, for our boat kept careening over and literally racing through the sea.

In five minutes I found that the canoes were so far behind that we had no more cause for fear, and, altering our course so as to sail gently on about a mile from the shore, I gave Ebo the sheet to hold, knelt down, bathed Uncle Dick's face, and bound up a great cut that had laid open his head.

My work had its reward, for, partly from the freshness of the water, partly from the pain I must have caused him, my uncle revived, stared wildly about him for a few minutes, and then, as he realised our position, he muttered a little to himself, and ended by shaking hands with me and Ebo, holding the black palm of the latter in his own for some moments, as he looked our follower in the face.

"I was much to blame, Nat," he said at last.

"I ought to have been more guarded; but I could not think that these people were so treacherous."

Chapter Forty.

We secure Fresh Treasures.

Our injuries soon grew better, but though we kept on sailing for days and days past the most tempting-looking spots, we never dared to land, for always as soon as we neared some gloriously-wooded track, all hill, dale, and mountain, and amidst whose trees the glasses showed us plenty of birds, the inhabitants began to cluster on the shore, and when once or twice my uncle said that we would go in nearer and see, the same custom was invariably observed: the people came shouting and dancing about the beach holding out birds and bunches of feathers and shells, making signs for us to land.

There was no need for Ebo to grow excited and cry, "No—no! man-kill! man-kill!" for my uncle laughed and shook his head.

"They must try another way of baiting their traps, Nat," he would cry laughing. "My head is too sore with blows and memories to be caught again."

It was always the same. No sooner did the treacherous savages find that we would not land than they rushed to their canoes, and began to pursue us howling and yelling; but the swift-sailed boat was always ready to leave them far behind, and we were only too glad to find that the pleasant brisk breezes stood our friends.

"I would not loiter here, Nat," he said, "amidst such a treacherous, bloodthirsty set, but the great island is so tempting that I long for a ramble amongst its forests. I know that there are plenty of wonderful specimens to be obtained here. New kinds of paradise birds, butterflies, and beetles, and other attractions that it would be a sin not to obtain."

"Perhaps we shall find a place by and bye where there are no inhabitants, uncle," I said.

"That is what I have been hoping for days," he replied; and not long after we sailed round a headland into a beautiful bay with the whitest of sand, trees clustering amidst the lovely yellow stone cliffs, and a bright stream of water flowing through a gorge and tumbling over two or three little barriers of rocks before losing itself in the calm waters of the bay.

Some six or seven miles back was a high ridge of mountains, which seemed to touch the sea to east and west, cutting off as it were a narrow strip from the mainland, and this strip, some fifteen miles long and six wide at its greatest, was fertile in the extreme.

"Why, Nat," cried my uncle, "this should be as grand a place as our island. If it is free of savages it is the beau idéal of a naturalist's station. Look! what's that?"

"A deer come out of the wood to drink in the stream," I said.

"Poor deer," laughed my uncle, "I'm afraid it will have to come into our larder, for a bit of venison is the very thing we want."

As he spoke he cautiously took up a rifle, rested it upon the edge of the boat, waited a few moments, and then fired at fully five hundred yards' distance, and I saw the deer make one great bound and fall dead.

"Good! Eatum," said Ebo approvingly; but instead of indulging in a frantic dance he shaded his eyes and gazed about in every direction, carefully sweeping the shore, and paying no heed to us as the boat was sailed close in.

As the keel was checked by the sand Ebo leaped out, and I thought he was about to rush at the deer to skin it for food, but he ran off rapidly in one direction right along the shore, coming back at the end of a quarter of an hour, during which, after dragging our prize on board, we remained, gun in hand, upon the watch.

Ebo started again and went in the other direction, being away longer this time, but returning triumphant to indulge in a dance, and help drag the boat into a place of safety before proceeding to light a fire.

Venison steaks followed, and after another exploration we found that we were in so thoroughly uninhabited a part of the island that we built a hut and slept ashore perfectly undisturbed.

The next morning we had another exploration, to find that, as my uncle had supposed, the ridge of mountains cut us off from the rest of the island, and finding nothing to fear we once more set to work.

Parrots were in profusion, and so were the great crowned pigeons; these latter becoming our poultry for the table. There was an abundance, though, of birds of large size, whose skins we did not care to preserve, but which, being fruit-eaters, were delicious roasted. Then we had another deer or two; caught fish in the bay; and literally revelled in the bounteous supply of fruit.

Meanwhile we were working industriously over our specimens, finding paroquets that were quite new to us, splendid cockatoos, and some that were as ugly as they were curious.

Sun-birds, pittas, lovely starlings, kingfishers, and beautifully-tinted pigeons were in abundance. Bright little manakins of a vivid green were there, so feathered that they put me in mind of the rich orange cock-of-the-rocks that Uncle Dick had brought over from Central America.

Sometimes we were shooting beside the lovely trickling stream where it gathered itself into pools to form tiny waterfalls, places where some birds seemed to love to come. At others, beneath some great flower-draped tree, where the sun-birds hovered and darted. But the great objects of our search, the birds of paradise, haunted the nut and berry bearing trees. Some were always to be found by a kind of palm that attracted the pigeons as well, these latter swallowing fruit that looked as big as their heads.

Here, to our intense delight, we shot the paradise oriole, a magnificent orange, yellow, and black bird, its head looking as if it was covered with a lovely orange plush.

One day we had made a longer excursion than usual, and had been so successful that we were about to turn back, having a long afternoon's work before us to preserve our specimens. We had penetrated right to the mountainous ridge, and finding the ground rise very rapidly we came to a standstill, when a peculiar cry up amongst the tree-shadowed rocks above us made us forget our fatigue, especially as Ebo was making signs.

The cry was so different to any that we had before heard that we felt that it must be some new bird, and full of eagerness set to work to stalk it.

All at once what seemed a flash of dark blue darted from a tree, and before gun could reach shoulder it was gone.

But Ebo had been on the watch, and away he crept amongst the rocks and trees, following what we now took to be a prize, till we saw him a quarter of a mile away holding up his spear as a signal.

We followed cautiously, and with a look of intelligence in his eyes he signed to my uncle to go one way towards a clump of tall palms, and to me to go in the other direction.

"Fire upwards," whispered my uncle, and we parted.

I knew from Ebo's ways that the bird must be in one of these trees, and with my eyes sweeping the great leaves in all directions I tried to make out the bird, but in vain, and I had advanced so near that I gave up all hope of seeing it, when suddenly from the other side there was a shot, then another, and feeling satisfied that my uncle had secured the prize I was completely taken off my guard, and stared with astonishment as a large bird, with tail quite a couple of feet long, swept by me towards the dense undergrowth of the lower ground, where it would have been in vain to hunt for it.

Just, however, as the bird was darting between the trees I raised my gun and made a quick snapshot at quite sixty yards' distance, and then called myself a stupid for not being more ready and for wasting a charge of powder and shot.

My uncle hailed me now.

"Any luck, Nat?" he cried, as he came up.

"No, uncle," I replied. "I made a flying shot, but it was too far-off."

"So were mine, Nat, but I fired on the chance of getting the bird. It was a bird of paradise different to any I have seen. We must come again. I never had a chance at it."

"But I did, uncle," I said dolefully, "and missed it."

"Where was it when you fired?"

"Down among those trees, uncle. I let it go too far."

"Why, you hit it, Nat! There's Ebo."

I looked, and to my intense delight there was our black companion holding up the bird in triumph. He had seen it fall when I shot, marked it down, and found it amongst the dense undergrowth, placing it before us with hardly a feather disarranged.

It was a splendid bird, the last we shot in New Guinea, and over three feet long, its tail being two and of a lovely bluish tint. If looked at from one side it was bronze, from the other green, just as the light fell, while from its sides sprung magnificent plumes of rich blue and green. They were not long, filmy plumes like those of the great bird of paradise, but short, each widening towards the end, and standing up like a couple of fans above the wings.

It was a feast to gaze upon so lovely an object of creation, and I felt more proud of having secured that specimen than of any bird I had shot before.

"Well, Nat the Naturalist," cried my uncle, when he had carefully hung the bird by its beak from a stick, "I think I did right in bringing you with me."

"I am glad you think so, uncle," I said.

"I mean it, my boy, for you have been invaluable to me. It was worth all the risk of coming to this savage place to get such a bird as that."

"There must be plenty more wonderful birds here, uncle," I said, "if we could stop in safety."

"I am sure there are, Nat, and there is nothing I should like better than to stay here. It is a regular naturalist's hunting-ground and full of treasures, if we dared thoroughly explore it."

"Just now, uncle," I said, "I feel as if I want to do nothing else but sit down and rest by a good dinner. Oh! I am so fagged!"

"Come along, then," he said smiling, "and we will make straight for camp, and I dare say we can manage a good repast for your lordship. Home, Ebo. Eat—drink—sleep."

"Eat—drink—sleep," said Ebo nodding, for he knew what those three words meant, and carefully carrying the treasures we had shot, tied at regular distances along a stick, he trudged on in advance towards our hut upon the shore.

Chapter Forty One.

Our Terrible Losses.

We had only about three miles to go if we could have flown like birds; but the way lay in and out of rocks, with quite a little precipice to descend at times, so that the journey must have been double that length. The hope of a good meal, however, made us trudge on, and after a few stops to rest I saw that we must now be nearing the shore, for the ground was much more level.

So different did it appear, though, that I hardly recognised some of it, and had it not been for Ebo I am sure we should have gone astray; but, savage like, he seemed to have an unerring instinct for finding his way back over ground he had been over before, and we had only to look back at him if we were in front for him to point out the way with the greatest of confidence.

We were trudging on in front, talking in a low tone about making another expedition into the mountainous part, in the hope of finding it, the higher we climbed, more free from risk of meeting natives, and we were now getting so near the shore that we could hear the beat of the waves upon a reef that lay off our hut, and sheltered the boat from being washed about, when all of a sudden, as we were traversing some low, scrubby bushes which were more thorny than was pleasant, Ebo suddenly struck us both on the shoulder, forcing us down amongst the leaves and twigs, and on looking sharply round we saw that he had dropped our splendid specimens, and, wild-eyed and excited, he was crouching too.

"Why, Ebo," began my uncle; but the black clapped his hand upon his mouth, and then pointed to the shore in front.

I felt my blood turn cold; for there, not fifty yards away, and dimly seen through the shade of leaves, was a party of about fifty New Guinea men, with a couple of dozen more in three canoes that were lying just outside the reef. They were a fierce-looking lot, armed with spears, axes, and clubs, and they were gesticulating and chattering fiercely about our boat.

I heard my uncle utter a groan, for it seemed as if the labours of all these months upon months of collecting were wasted, and that specimens, stores, arms, everything of value, would fall into the hands of these savages. He was perfectly calm directly after, and crouched there with his gun ready for a chance, should there be any necessity for its use; but he knew that it was useless to attempt to fight, all we could do was to save our lives.

After about half an hour's talk the savages embarked, taking our boat in tow behind one of their canoes, and we saw the bright water flash as the paddles beat regularly, and the men sent their craft along till they swept round the headland west of the bay and were gone.

"Oh, uncle!" I cried, as soon as we were safe.

"It is very hard, Nat, my boy," he said sadly; "but it might have been worse. We have our lives and a little ammunition; but the scoundrels have wrecked my expedition."

"And we have no boat, uncle."

"Nor anything else, Nat," he said cheerfully. "But we have plenty of pluck, my boy, and Ebo will help us to make a canoe to take us to the Moluccas, where I dare say I can get some merchant to fit us out again. Well, Ebo," he cried, "all gone!"

"Man—kill—gone," repeated Ebo, shaking his spear angrily, and then he kept repeating the word Owé—boat, as we went down to the shore.

"Let's see if they have left anything in the hut, Nat," said my uncle. "We must have food even if we are stripped."

We turned through the bushes and made our way into the little arbour-like spot beside the stream where Ebo had built our hut beneath a splendid tree, when, to our utter astonishment, we found that the savages had not seen our little home, but had caught sight of the boat, landed and carried it off, without attempting to look for its owners. No one had been there since we left, that was evident; and pleased as we were, our delight was more than equalled by Ebo's, for laying down our specimens, this time more carefully, he refreshed himself with a dance before lighting a fire, where a capital meal was prepared, which we thankfully enjoyed as we thought of the benefits we received by having the forethought to carry everything out of the boat and placing it under cover for fear of rain.

The savages then had taken nothing but our boat, and the next thing was to set to work to construct another, for my uncle said he should not feel satisfied to stay where we were longer, without some means of retreat being ready for an emergency.

Before lying down we managed to ask Ebo what he thought of our being able to build a canoe that would carry us and our luxuries. For reply he laughed, pointed to our axes and to the trees, as if to say, What a foolish question when we have all the material here!

I was so wearied, and slept so heavily, that I had to be awakened by my uncle long after the sun was up.

"Come, Nat," he said, "I want you to make a fire. Ebo has gone off somewhere."

I made the fire, after which we had a hasty breakfast, and then worked hard at skin making—preserving all our specimens.

The day glided by, but Ebo did not come, and feeling no disposition to collect more, in fact not caring now to fire, we had a look round to see which would be the most likely place to cut down a tree and begin building a boat.

"It is lucky for us, Nat," said my uncle, "that Ebo belongs to a nation of boat-builders. Perhaps he has gone to search for a suitable place and the kind of wood he thinks best; but I wish he would come."

Night fell and no Ebo. The next morning he was not there; and as day after day glided by we set ourselves to work to search for him, feeling sure that the poor fellow must have fallen from some precipice and be lying helpless in the forest. But we had no success, and began to think then of wild beasts, though we had seen nothing large enough to be dangerous, except that worst wild beast of all, savage man.

Still we searched until we were beginning to conclude that he must have been seen by a passing canoe whose occupants had landed and carried him off.

"I don't think they would, uncle," I said, though; "he is too sharp and cunning. Why, it would be like seeking to catch a wild bird to try and get hold of Ebo, if he was out in the woods."

"Perhaps you are right, Nat," said my uncle. "There is one way, though, that we have never tried, I mean over the mountain beyond where you shot that last bird. To-morrow we will go across there and see if there are any signs of the poor fellow. If we see none then we must set to work ourselves to build a canoe or hollow one out of a tree, and I tremble, Nat, for the result."

"Shall we be able to make one big enough to carry our chests, uncle?"

"No, Nat, I don't expect it. If we can contrive one that will carry us to some port we must be satisfied. There I can buy a boat, and we must come back for our stores."

We devoted the next two days to a long expedition, merely using our guns to procure food, and reluctantly allowing several splendid birds to escape.

But our expedition only produced weariness; and footsore and worn out we returned to our hut, fully determined to spend our time in trying what we could contrive in the shape of a boat, falling fast asleep, sad at heart indeed, for in Ebo we felt that we had lost a faithful friend.

Chapter Forty Two.

An Experiment in Boat-Building.

"It is of no use to be down-hearted, Nat," said my uncle the next morning. "Cheer up, my lad, and let's look our difficulties in the face. That's the way to overcome them, I think."

"I feel better this morning, uncle," I said.

"Nothing like a good night's rest, Nat, for raising the spirits. This loss of the boat and then of our follower, if he is lost, are two great misfortunes, but we must bear in mind that before all this hardly anything but success attended us."

"Except with the savages, uncle," I said.

"Right, Nat: except with the savages. Now let's go down to the shore and have a good look out to sea."

We walked down close to the water, and having satisfied ourselves that no canoes were in sight, we made a fire, at which our coffee was soon getting hot, while I roasted a big pigeon, of which food we never seemed to tire, the supply being so abundant that it seemed a matter of course to shoot two or three when we wanted meat.

"I'd give something, Nat," said my uncle, as we sat there in the soft, delicious sea air, with the sunshine coming down like silver rays through the glorious foliage above our heads—"I'd give something, Nat, if boat-building had formed part of my education."

"Or you had gone and learned it, like Peter the Great, uncle."

"Exactly, my boy. But it did not, so we must set to work at once and see what we can do. Now what do you say? How are we to make a boat?"

"I've been thinking about it a great deal, uncle," I said, "and I was wondering whether we could not make a bark canoe like the Indians."

"A bark canoe, eh, Nat?"

"Yes, uncle. I've seen a model of one, and it looks so easy."

"Yes, my boy, these things do look easy; but the men who make them, savages though they be, work on the experience of many generations. It took hundreds of years to make a good bark canoe, Nat, and I'm afraid the first manufacturers of that useful little vessel were drowned. No, Nat, we could not make a canoe of that kind."

"Then we must cut down a big tree and hollow it out, uncle, only it will take a long time."

"Yes, Nat, but suppose we try the medium way. I propose that we cut down a moderately-sized tree, and hollow it out for the lower part of our boat, drive pegs all along the edge for a support, and weave in that a basket-work of cane for the sides as high as we want it."

"But how could we make the sides watertight, uncle?" I said; "there seem to be no pine-trees here to get pitch or turpentine."

"No, Nat, but there is a gum to be found in large quantities in the earth, if we can discover any. The Malays called it *dammar*, and use it largely for torches. It strikes me that we could turn it into a splendid varnish, seeing what a hard resinous substance it is. Ebo would have found some very soon, I have no doubt."

"Then I must find some without him, uncle," I said. "I shall go hunting for it whenever I am not busy boat-building."

He smiled at my enthusiasm, and after examining the skins to see that they were all dry and free from attacks of ants, we each took a hatchet and our guns, and proceeded along by the side of the shore in search of a stout straight tree that should combine the qualities of being light, strong, easy to work, and growing near the sea.

We quite came to the conclusion that we should have a great deal of labour, and only learn by experience which kind of tree would be suitable, perhaps having to cut down several before we found one that would do.

"And that will be bad, uncle," I said.

"It will cause us a great deal of labour, Nat," he replied smiling; "but it will make us handy with our hatchets."

"I did not mean that, uncle," I replied; "I was thinking of savages coming in this direction and seeing the chips and cut-down trees."

"To be sure, Nat, you are right. That will be bad; but as we are cut off so from the rest of the island, we must be hopeful that we may get our work done before they come."

We spent four days hunting about before we found a tree that possessed all the qualities we required. We found dozens that would have done, only they were far away from the shore, where it would have been very difficult to move our boat afterwards to the water's edge.

But the tree we selected offered us a thick straight stem twenty feet long, and it was so placed that the land sloped easily towards the sea, and it was sufficiently removed from the beach for us to go on with our work unseen.

We set to at once to cut it down, finding to our great delight as soon as we were through the bark that the wood was firm and fibrous, and yet easy to cut, so that after six hours' steady chopping we had made a big gap in the side, when we were obliged to leave off because it was dark.

We worked the next day and the next, and then my uncle leaned against it while I gave a few more cuts, and down it went with a crash amongst the other trees, to be ready for working up into the shape we required.

Next morning as soon as it was light we began again to cut off the top at the length we intended to have our boat, a task this which saved the labour of chopping off the branches. I worked hard, and the labour was made lighter by Uncle Dick's pleasant conversation. For he chatted about savage and civilised man, and laughingly pointed out how the latter had gone on improving.

"You see what slow laborious work this chipping with our axes is, Nat," he said one day, as we kept industriously on, "when by means of cross-cut saws and a circular saw worked by steam this tree could be soon reduced to thin boards ready for building our boat."

Birds came and perched near us, and some were very rare in kind, but we felt that we must leave them alone so as to secure those we had obtained, and we worked patiently on till at the end of a week the tree began to wear outside somewhat the shape of a boat, and it was just about the length we required.

It was terribly hard work, but we did not shrink, and at last, after congratulating ourselves upon having got so far without being interfered with by the savages, we had shouldered our guns and were walking back to the hut one evening when we caught sight of a black figure running across an opening, and we knew that our time of safety was at an end.

"It is what I have always feared, Nat," said my uncle quickly. "Quick; put big-shot cartridges in your gun. We will not spill blood if we can help it, but it is their lives or ours, and we must get safely back home."

"What shall we do now?" I said huskily.

"Wait and see what the enemy mean to do, and—"

"Hi, yi, yi—Hi, yi, yi—Hi, yi, yi. Hey. Nat, mi boy. Ung-kul!" came shrilly through the trees.

"Hooray!" I shrieked, leaping out of my hiding-place. "Ebo! Ebo! Hi, yi, yi—Hi, yi, yi. Hooray!"

We ran to meet him, and he bounded towards us, leaping, dancing, rolling on the ground, hugging us, and seeming half mad with delight as he dragged us down to the sea-side, where a new surprise awaited us.

For there upon shore, with her anchor fixed in the sands, lay our boat apparently quite uninjured.

As Ebo danced about and patted the boat and then himself, it was plain enough to read the cause of his disappearance. He had gone off along the shore following the savages to their village, and then watched his opportunity to sail off. And this he had of course done, placing the boat safely in its old moorings.

He made signs for something to eat, and then I noticed that he looked very thin; and it was evident that the poor fellow had suffered terrible privations in getting back our treasure, and proving himself so good a friend.

RE-APPEARANCE OF MR. EBONY

Chapter Forty Three.

Farewell to a Friend.

"Don't you feel disappointed, Nat?" said my uncle smiling. "We shall not be able to finish our boat."

"I shall get over it, uncle," I said. "Hallo! what's the matter with Ebo?"

For before he had half finished eating he jumped up and made signs to us which we did not understand, and then began to drag one of the chests down towards the boat.

"I see, Nat; he means it is not safe to stay," said my uncle; and setting to work we got all our treasures safely on board, with such food and fruit as we had ready, filled the water barrel, and then paused.

But Ebo was not satisfied; he chattered excitedly and signed to us to launch the boat.

"I'll take his advice," said my uncle. "He means that the savages may be in pursuit."

So, pushing off, the sail was hoisted, and in the bright starlight of the glorious night we sailed away, carefully avoiding the reef, where the rollers were breaking heavily, and before we were half a mile from the shore Ebo pressed my arm and pointed.

"Only just in time, Nat," said my uncle.

"What an escape!"

For there, stealing cautiously along between us and the white sandy shore, we counted five large canoes, whose occupants were paddling softly so as to make no noise, and but for Ebo's sharp eyes they would have passed us unseen.

We had no doubt that they were going after our boat, and had they been half an hour sooner our fate would have been sealed. As it was they did not see the tall sail that swept us swiftly along, and by the time the sun rose brightly over the sea we were far enough away from danger to look upon it as another trouble passed.

We ran in two or three times where we found that there were no inhabitants and obtained a few birds and some fruit; but this was so dangerous a task that we afterwards contented ourselves with fish, which we cooked upon some sandy spot or reef where the coast was clear, and we could have seen the savages at a great distance, so as to leave plenty of time for escape.

My uncle turned the boat's head south very reluctantly at last, for there was a mystery and temptation about the vast isle of New Guinea that was very attractive. The birds and insects we had collected there were, some of them, quite new to science, and he used to say that if he could have stayed there long enough our specimens would have been invaluable.

Still it was impossible, for the danger was too great, and besides, as he said, we should have been nearly three years away from home by the time we reached England, and it would be our wisest course to make sure of what we had obtained.

In due time we sailed to Ebo's island, where we found that the captain of the prahu on board which we had come, had been, and sailed once more, so that it would be months before we could see him again.

Under these circumstances, and to Ebo's great delight, we left our chests of specimens sealed up in a hut, where we felt that they would be quite safe, and then, with Ebo for guide, we sailed to Ceram, a large island, where we were able to purchase stores, and from there to the Moluccas, where we did better.

At both of these places we made many expeditions, collecting both birds and insects, some of them being very lovely; but there was a want of novelty about them, my uncle said, the ground having been so often visited before. And at last we sailed south again to Ebo's island, finding all our stores and specimens quite safe and sound, and spending a few days in sunning and repacking them.

By that time the captain of the prahu had arrived, ready to welcome us warmly, for he had been afraid that ill had befallen us.

He could not stay long, so our chests were placed on board, and at last there was nothing to do but to take farewell of Ebo, the true-hearted fellow, whose dejected look went to my heart.

He cheered up a little as my uncle gave him four new axes, as many pocket-knives, the residue of our beads and brass wire, and the remaining odds and ends that we had bought to barter; but above all, the gift that sent him off into a fit of dancing was that of the boat, all complete as it was.

At first he seemed to think that he was to give us something in exchange, and consequently he began to fetch all sorts of treasures, as he considered them. When at last, though, he knew it was a present, his delight knew no bounds, and he danced and sang for joy.

The next morning we said good-bye, and the last I saw of poor Ebo was as he stood in his boat watching us and waving his spear, and I'm not ashamed to say that the tears stood in my eyes as I wondered whether I should ever see that true, generous fellow again.

Chapter Forty Four.

Home Again.

It was on a bright sunny day in July that my uncle and I jumped into a cab and bade the man drive us to the old house, where I had passed so many happy as well as unhappy days.

"We will not stop to go and see barbers or to dress, Nat, but go and take them by surprise," said my uncle; and for the first time I began to wonder whether I had altered.

"Am I very much more sunburnt than I used to be?" I said suddenly, as we drew near the door.

"Well, you are not quite black," he said laughing, "but you have altered, Nat, since they saw you last."

How my heart beat as we walked up to the front door, where the maid, a stranger, stared at us, and said that her mistress was out, and looked suspiciously at us, evidently, as she afterwards owned, taking us for sailor fellows with parrots and silk things for sale.

"Where's Uncle Joseph?" I said sharply.

"Oh, please, sir, are you Master Nathaniel, who's far away at sea?" she cried.

"I am Nathaniel," I said laughing, "but I'm not far away at sea. Where's Uncle Joe?"

"He's down the garden, sir, smoking his pipe in the tool-house," said the girl smiling; and I dashed through the drawing-room, jumped down the steps, and ran to the well-remembered spot, to find dear old Uncle Joe sitting there with all my treasures carefully dusted but otherwise untouched; and as I stood behind him and clapped my hands over his eyes, there was he with poor old Humpty Dumpty before him.

"Who—who's that?" he cried.

"Guess!" I shouted.

"I—I can't guess," he said. "I don't know you. Let go or I shall call for help."

"Why, Uncle Joe!" I cried, taking away my hands and clasping his.

He stared at me from top to toe, and at last said in a trembling voice:

"You're not my boy Nat?"

"But indeed I am, uncle," I cried.

"My boy Nat *was a boy*," he said nervously, "not a big six-foot fellow with a gruff voice, and—my dear Dick. Why, then, it is Nat after all."

The old man hugged me in his arms, and was ready to shed weak tears, for Uncle Dick had followed me and was looking on.

"Why, why, why—what have you been doing to him, Dick?" cried Uncle Joe excitedly. "Here, he can't be our Nat, and he has got a man's voice, and he is bigger than me, and he is nearly black. Why, here's Sophy—Sophy, dear, who's this?"

I caught her in my arms and kissed her, and she too stared at me in surprise, for I suppose I had altered wonderfully, though in my busy life of travel I had taken little note of the change.

It was very pleasant to settle down once more in quiet and sort our specimens, or tell Uncle Joe of all our dangers by land and sea; but after a time, although Aunt Sophia was now very kind and different to what she had been of old, there came a strong feeling upon me at times that I should once more like to be wandering amidst the beautiful islands of the Eastern Seas, watching the wondrous beauties of the world beneath the shallow waters, or the glorious greens of the trees upon the tropic shores. The boy who loves nature goes on loving nature to the end, for I may say that Uncle Dick spoke the truth when he said that I ought to be called Nat the Naturalist, for I feel that I am Nat the Naturalist still.

"Uncle Dick," I said one day, "shall we ever have another trip together collecting birds?"

"Time proves all things, my boy," he said; "wait and see."

Lightning Source UK Ltd.
Milton Keynes UK
UKHW010631230921
391069UK00001B/42